Crazy on the Waltzer

Austin Burke

Copyright © 2024 Austin Burke

All rights reserved.

www.sawnoffbooks.co.uk

ISBN: 978-1-0369-0172-1

DEDICATION

For Nikki, the catalyst for writing this story in the first place, and for supporting and believing in me throughout.

And for Tucka, (RIP)

CONTENTS

Prologue: Any Two Can Play

Chapter 1: The Life That I Choose

Chapter 2: Money for Muscle

Chapter 3: Bandit Fever

Chapter 4: Rockaway

Chapter 5: Crazy On the Waltzer

Chapter 6: A Torture Tattoo

Chapter 7: Tunnel of Love

Chapter 8: Sing About the Six Blade

Chapter 9: Ticket for the Races

Chapter 10: The Roar of Dust and Diesel

Chapter 11: Scream and Slam

Chapter 12: Danger, Danger

Chapter 13: My Heart and My Soul

Chapter 14: The Big Wheel Keeps On Turning

His days of burgling and ram-raiding were nearly over; that was for the younger lads now and he wasn't one of them anymore, although he did partake in the odd ram raid and robbery now and then, half for the money and half for the buzz. Selling drugs was money for nothing as far as he was concerned; just pay someone to do all the donkey work and take all the risk, then sit back and collect the money. His fearsome reputation meant that all he had to do was put the word around town that someone was working for him or that he was looking after someone, and they had virtually no chance of being taxed. It still happened on the odd occasion though, either through ignorance or bravado. The culprits would be weeded out and brought to street justice which normally involved a visit from Carl and relieving them of their worldly possessions, along with a few punches and a fine. Sometimes he let them keep their stuff, provided they agreed to do his bidding.

He moved with purpose like he always did, past the free weights and the other gym patrons to the locker room, sweat dripping from his massive, shaved head and body. He silently nodded his hairless head to Paul Docherty and his mate as he went. Carl didn't shave his head because he was going prematurely bald like some people his age; he did it because it got in the way while fighting, and to stop the other guy getting a handful of hair and controlling the fight.

Showering quickly, he dressed into a shirt and fresh jeans for his date that afternoon, a date that he had to keep quiet. He admired himself in the mirror as he squirted a generous amount of Kouros onto his thick tanned neck and

and bats, unlike half the lads around who didn't have real fight in them, but if that was the way it was going to go then he certainly wouldn't back down. He'd do what he needed to and had come out on top with his fists a few times when fighting a tooled-up wannabe.

He'd only been beaten once, when he was eighteen years old and by a doorman twice his age and size outside Puzzles nightclub in Tynemouth. He was sucker punched and knocked out after being refused entry and left with a sore jaw. The bouncer had known who he was and been aware of his up-and-coming reputation, so he thought he'd make an example of Carl and a name for himself. For six months afterwards, all Carl saw each time he slammed his oversized fist into the heavy leather punch bag was the doorman's face, imagining the satisfaction when he returned the beating. It finally came on a dark October evening and there would be no cheap shots this time. He went to Puzzles' door and offered the guy out for a straight go in the back lane – and deliberately in front of the other two doorman because he knew he couldn't lose face and back down. As they walked into the alleyway, Carl knew he'd won before the first punch was thrown. The doorman only had half a fight in him, and Carl finished it quickly with a few punches and a boot to the ribs as repayment for the cheap shot. His reputation was in the ascendant, and things only went up from there. Since then, he'd never lost a fight, not to a doorman nor to any other villains during the ins and outs of daily life, a life that revolved around protection rackets, selling drugs and the occasional bit of thievery if the pay day was worth it.

1993

1: THE LIFE THAT I CHOOSE

Carl Liddle counted in his head as he threw heavy combinations into the bag: *3, 4, 5, 4, 1* – left hook – right hook – uppercut – right hook – jab . . . The gym patrons looked over when they heard the crack of a shiny new Everlast glove smashing into the age-old leather. *1, 2, 6, 9, 3, 2* – jab - straight - right – uppercut – left body hook – left head hook – straight right. The worn silver tape only just held the stitching together as each crashing impact struck home. He glanced into the floor length mirrors that lined the gym wall as he admired his muscular, thirty-two-year-old frame. He was aware that his rugged jawline, steely, narrowed eyes and thin-lipped sneer made the women go wild for him.

A local legend on the streets of North Shields, and not for the right reasons. He was a born fighter, it was what he was infamous for. Never one to run with a crowd, he was equally respected and feared around the coast, a well built and powerful man who very few messed with. Growing up he'd fought many of the local hard men with his fists and, when it was called for, the odd weapon. Not one for knives the safe and grabbed a loose wad of notes that the taller robber had missed. He looked down at the old pub landlord and felt a genuine pang of remorse.

That's life, he concluded; sometimes you were up and sometimes you were down. And, at this point their victim was permanently down. Turning to leave, he caught sight of a shape on the floor resting in the blood that seeped slowly from the old man's head. The warm sticky liquid oozed onto the edge of a Sand's Night Club membership card showing the name and address of his partner in crime. He gasped in horror and then exhaled with relief. Had he not returned for the forgotten cosh, the game would have been well and truly up and they'd each be looking at twenty years inside at least. He picked up the card, stuck it in the front pocket of his jeans and then left again through the pub's kitchen window.

He would never enter The Spring Gardens again.

"Leave the coins!" the stocky robber barked. "We need to get out of here. Now."

The taller robber packed the notes into a Woolworth's carrier bag and stuffed it inside his black bomber jacket. Then, without a word, they exited back up the passageway and into the kitchen whose entrance faced the sitting room door. Climbing back through the window they'd climbed in only ten minutes earlier; they made their way along the wall and onto the garage roof, where they would shimmy down the lamp post, whose light they'd smashed out a few days earlier, and away to freedom.

"Shit!" the taller robber blurted out.

"What?" said the stocky robber.

"The cosh . . . I left it in there."

"For fuck's sake! Why did I bring you along? I'll get it. You piss off and stash the cash. I'll find you tomorrow." The stocky robber turned and retraced his steps to the kitchen window. "And don't run," he added from the window's edge. He made his way briskly back to the room with the safe. He stared at the sight of his own balaclava-clad face in the mirrored fitted wardrobes that lined the right-hand wall. Well, if he couldn't recognise himself then neither could anybody else.

He needed to be in and out in a minute – no hanging around and looking for further treasure. Already, his mate would have crossed the pitched garage roof, slid down the lamppost into the dark alley and would be off. No looking back.

Surveying the scene for the second time that night, the stocky robber picked up the cosh. He took a last look into

The old bloke hadn't had a chance to even see what was coming before the heavy metal bar crashed down with a dull and heavy thud onto his skull. He was now sprawled on his back, eyes open and blood pouring from a three-inch wound between his forehead and temple. Both masked men stared at him, his eyes and mouth open in the silence of the pub, eyes that would haunt the dreams of one of them for the rest of his life, and maybe for eternity. But all that was in the future. For now, time seemed to stand still as they watched the life drain out of the frail old man.

"I think I've fucking killed him." The panic in the taller man's voice was unmistakable.

"What the fuck did you hit him that hard for?"

"I dunno know, man, I–"

"Just get the cash, empty the fucking safe and let's go, there's fuck all we can do about it now" the short squat robber replied.

If truth be known, he was just as scared, but after being a thief for all of his short adult life and a good portion of his childhood he was better placed to keep calm in a situation like this. He pulled the prostrate old landlord across the room, glancing at his face and thinking how much he looked at peace – apart from the blood and the gaping wound on his forehead.

The taller robber switched out the light and knelt, laying the bloodstained cosh on the floor. The streetlight from outside illuminated their plunder as he reached inside the darkness of the safe and pulled out piles of purple, brown and blue bank notes, a full week's takings as Jimmy always banked on a Monday.

few quid in the retirement fund and a little bit closer to his Benidorm dream.

After two glasses, he made his way down the half-lit corridor and past his bedroom to the office adjacent to Paul's bedroom. Not that Paul stayed over very often. Like most lads his age, he was out with his mates doing God knows what with God knows who and God knows where. Jimmy hoped that he wouldn't end up in Low Newton Remand Centre like half his friends for nicking cars, joy riding or in some cases far worse. He'd heard the stories, the whispers in the bar, the names of Paul's mates and what they'd been up to. He also knew a few people around town and wasn't shy to make some discreet enquiries about the latest goings on, desperately hoping that Paul's name wasn't mentioned in the neighbourhood highlights.

Jimmy made his way to the office and knelt in front of the Whitfield's Birmingham safe that must have been the same age as the pub itself and slid the old brass key into the age-worn hole in the centre. The handle turned with ease and the door swung open with a satisfying heaviness, and a small squeak, which caused him every night to resolve to oil the hinges the next morning. He shoveled the coins onto the bottom shelf and the notes onto the top with the ledger. His head turned as he heard a sound, and he looked up to the right, sweeping his hair back out of his eyes. He turned halfway – and no further. The blinding light and searing pain was the last thing he would ever know.

* * *

after all the years in hospitality he still couldn't stand the smell of a dirty ashtray when he came down in the morning. He walked along the dimly lit corridor behind the bar that was the main artery of the pub. The cellar was down to the left and the kitchen was up a small flight of stairs. He switched off the lights and the pub plunged into darkness. All he could hear was the sound of the traffic outside and the distant wail of a siren.

The day had been a busy one; the long summer Sundays always were, plenty of alcohol and drugs resulting in a busy night for the North Shields police. It always had and always would.

Picking up the till trays, he headed upstairs, habitually avoiding the creaking third step as he climbed to the flat above. It was sparsely furnished and plainly decorated, which was just the way he liked it. No clutter, no mess and no fuss, just like the way he lived his life. He turned left into the front room, placed the takings on the table and then reached over to pour himself his "Horlicks" – not real Horlicks, but a generous glass of Lambs Navy Rum over ice. He struggled to sleep without it. He'd acquired a liking for the sweet, spiced molasses as a teenager, working as a deck boy on the Cunard liners in the Caribbean. Three glasses before bed helped him forget the loneliness he felt night after night, lying in his bed alone and thinking how his life would have been if Sheena hadn't left him. As he counted out the takings he glanced at the day's newspaper, amazed that Liverpool had just broken the British transfer record and paid £2.7 million to bring Ian Rush back from Juventus. It hadn't been a bad day. Another along with a reduced bank account and pension pot.

Paul was seventeen and a man of the world – or that was what he thought. Jimmy only saw him once a week or so unless he wanted a few quid, which he would normally ask for in a half-stoned state. Jimmy didn't mind Paul smoking hash, or pot as Jimmy called it, but he wouldn't have it smoked in the bar anymore, not since the last time North Shields's finest stormed the pub and searched the customers. He didn't complain too much if the odd spliff was smoked in the pool room when he had a lock in, just providing it was kept out of the bar area and away from the non-dope-smoking punters. Jimmy knew that a few shady deals went down in that back room, but a blind eye was beneficial to the till receipts and barring the culprits wasn't worth his windows being put out – or worse. His clientele were mainly harmless, good people most of them, but a few who Jimmy wouldn't like to get on the wrong side of, even though his age and natural charm would get him out of most situations.

As he moved through the pub to the pool room, he ran a hand through his slightly greasy hair and caught his reflection in the McEwan's Best Scotch mirror. He saw what he was: a slim and tired old man, grey haired and walking with a slight stoop, hollowed out by the relentless grind of a lifetime in the pub trade. Picking up the last of the empties, the smell of stale beer and dirty ashtrays permeated the air and reinforced his thinking that retiring was the best thing to do. He didn't have the energy to finish cleaning the pint pots and put them on the draining board with the rest of the empties. The ashtrays were always emptied, though; even

PROLOGUE: ANY TWO CAN PLAY

Jimmy Docherty locked the big red pub door, his mind consumed with worry about his wayward son Paul. He'd fallen in with a bad crowd, and at seventeen he wasn't young enough to be treated as a child but wasn't man enough to be unimpressed by the colourful villains, thieves and drug dealers who frequented the streets of North Shields. The noise of the heavy bolts slamming into place reminded him of a police cell door locking. Paul wasn't far away from hearing that for the first time, that is, if he hadn't heard it already.

Pub days were long days and Jimmy felt tired. He'd had his name over the door of The Spring Gardens for seven years and now he was feeling his age. At fifty-nine he was thinking of retiring from the pub game and was counting down the years. He was torn between buying a small flat in his native North Shields and close to his mates, or an apartment in Benidorm to relax in the sun for his twilight years. He had happy memories of Benidorm. He'd been there with Sheena and Paul as a family almost yearly. But that was before Sheena left him and took Paul with her. They didn't move far, just three Metro stops to Whitley Bay. Paul still visited but not as much, as he was older now. Jimmy thought daily that he should have listened to his pals and not married a woman fifteen years his junior. Everyone said she was just after his money and an easy life. And maybe she was. But at least he had Paul to show for it, onto the large portion of his chest that was visible above his three-quarter buttoned, Thomas Burberry shirt. The door to the locker room swung open and in came Mark Taylor and his younger brother, Liam. There was no real love between the Taylor brothers and Carl but there was no great dislike either. The brothers had ambitions in the underworld. They had the brawn but not the brains to be somebodies, although that wasn't how they saw themselves. Their pale-skinned, shaved heads were adorned by matching sets of ears that stuck out slightly further than they should. Their faces bore scars and pock-marked cheeks, both a remnant of their teenage years and their burly bodies swelled from twice-daily gym sessions, pumped up further by the steroids they injected. They were duo of short tempered, violent, water boys who most people avoided like the plague.

Carl lifted his head in their direction. "Alright lads?"

"Alright Carl, how's it going?" Liam unzipped his Sergio Tacchini tracksuit top and laid it down on a bench. "Good workout?"

"Yeah, not bad, I heard you had a little trouble on the door last week. Turn out alright, did it?"

"Aye it was a good un," said Mark. "A bunch of stags from fuck knows where. Normal shite . . . went to kick one of them out for being too pissed and they kicked off. I knocked two out, Liam knocked one out and then the bizzies turned up. The other doorman took a canny hiding, but we rescued him in the end."

Carl had heard a different version. The lads were young – nineteen, twenty at the most – and there was no asking them to leave. In typical Taylor brothers fashion, they'd told one of the lads he was leaving and when he asked why Mark knocked him unconscious and dragged him towards the back exit. His mates put up what could be classed as a loud protest at worst and then the brothers waded in, fists flying, before the police turned up and rescued the lads from a night in A and E.

Mark and Liam looked like the thugs that they were, paid muscle and enforcers who lacked the finesse and intelligence to rise to the top in their criminal world. Most people feared them, and few would stand up to their bullying ways, but they weren't big enough to front up to Carl and never would be.

"Yeah, you've got to watch them foreigners," said Liam.

"So, what youse on today? Weights or boxing?" asked Carl, not that he cared; he was just making conversation.

"Just a bit of sparring and a few rounds on the bag," replied Mark.

"Canny. Enjoy then, lads. Have a good one." Carl shoved his wet towel and sweaty training gear into his blue Reebok duffle bag before heading out the door to his secret rendezvous at the Copthorne Hotel.

As he squeezed his pumped-up frame into the driver's seat of his black, Escort RS Turbo, he had a little smile to himself, thinking of the afternoon of champagne, cocaine and sex that awaited him with his beautiful princess. The sleek black car took off onto Whitley Road emitting a low whistle from the engine as the turbo kicked in.

*   *   *

From the first-floor window of Proflex gym, Mark watched Carl drive away, jealous of the respect, street power and the life that Carl had. A life he wanted for himself but hadn't worked out how to get.

*   *   *

As Paul Docherty got off the Metro at Whitley Bay, there were three things on his mind: food, hash and Lindsey Gray. He'd smoked half the spliff he had left over from the night before and it had given him the munchies, so he decided that his first port of call would be the Chinese outside the station for a takeaway curry, fried rice and chips. He turned left onto Whitley Road, practically inhaling the food as he went, then walked along the high street with its closed-up shops. The neon lights of Kebab King illuminated his way past Boots the Chemist on his left.

His thoughts turned to his dad, Jimmy, who'd been dead for five years, and as usual he felt a mixture of anger and sadness. Sometimes he blamed himself for not being there but mostly he blamed the murderer or murderers who killed the defenseless old man and were still at large. How could they be so cold and devoid of humanity to leave him bludgeoned to death in the small office of that lonely little flat? Other times he saw it as bad luck, both on the robber's part and his dad's, and he was certain that they didn't mean to kill him. It just got out of hand and, like any criminal, they left him because they didn't want to face the music. This part he could understand as a thief himself, but he wasn't at the pub tie-up level of criminality yet – just stealing cars, shoplifting, burgling and nicking anything that wasn't tied down.

He walked with a purpose on the cool late September evening, zipping up his Diesel jacket and hunching down his shoulders with his hands thrust deeply into his pockets as he looked down at his slightly worn British Knights Hi-Top trainers. He decided he needed a pair of Fila boots – the coolest footwear around.

The stench of stale urine assaulted his nose as he cut through the alley between the closed-down fire station and the Victoria pub. This wasn't surprising considering where he was: halfway between the top of South Parade and Sands nightclub it was often used as a public urinal for men – and occasionally women – heading to Sands for a night of drinking, dancing and sometimes drugs after the lively bars. Taking and especially dealing drugs in Sands was a risky business; most of Whitley Bay's doormen didn't mind dishing out a punch or three and, for good measure, those at Sands would often throw the offender down the fire escape and into the empty bus station below. They'd let them back in the following week so they could do the same again – it was their idea of fun.

As he walked, he thought of his mam, Sheena, and her despair at the path he was taking. She'd tried shouting at him and guilt-tripping him over his father's death but she just didn't understand. He would have prefered to have a job but almost everyone he knew was a thief or drug dealer and even most of the straight people he knew had a side hustle. Apart from his mam and Lindsey, he didn't associate with a single straight-goer on a daily basis. People with jobs were weird, knob-heads who took shit from some arsehole who spoke to people in a way that they had no right to.

Turning left and then right down the back lane before the hardware shop, he fulfilled the second part of his journey. He quietly pressed down the latch on the tall blue gate and entered the back yard of the downstairs flat that belonged to Emily and Tracey Fisher, Whitley Bay's favourite dope-dealing couple. He threw the almost empty take away carton into their metal bin, tapped lightly on the front room window and the white net curtain moved back an inch or two. A big blue eye belonging to Tracey stared at him for a second before the curtain returned to its original position. The sound of two deadbolts slowly sliding back and the key turning in the door signaled that they had hash in the house and it was for sale. Had there been nothing, then the door wouldn't have been unlocked and a shaking head at the window would mean come back another time.

Emily opened the door and raised a finger to lips adorned with bright red lipstick and motioned for him to enter quietly. Considering the couple spent most of their day smoking hash, it always surprised Paul that the house always smelled so fresh, the kitchen was always spotless and there was never a cushion out of place. She replaced the bolts and re-locked the door. "What you after? she asked, in a stoned and raspy voice.

"Just an eighth, and I owe you a fiver from last time."

He handed her a crumpled twenty-pound note, which she in turn handed to Tracy, who looked at it with slight disgust, straightened it, folded it in half and slid it into the back pocket of her tight Pepe jeans. Not for the first time, Paul pondered the waste of a good arse. But then it probably didn't get wasted; Emily would make sure of that.

"You stopping for joint?" asked Tracey. She flicked a clipper lighter and burned a small piece of dark brown soap bar before crumbling it into open Rizlas and the contents of a broken cigarette.

"Yeah, why not? Been a while since I've seen you both." He kicked off his trainers.

Walking on their white, patterned carpet would get you a sharp word at best. He sat down in the corner chair and Emily handed him the cling-film-wrapped brown package he'd paid for. He opened it and did what hash smokers the world over do as soon as they score: he raised it to his nostrils, inhaled slowly and deeply, testing it for quality. After smoking since he was fifteen, he could generally tell if it was good or bad before he burned it. If in doubt, smelling the burning brown substance after touching it with a flame would be the next test, but he knew immediately that it was top notch gear and tucked it into his ticket pocket with his thumb.

Tracey pushed the roach into the open end of the spliff, tore off the twist on the other and put it between her small sexy lips. Paul looked at her, imagining what she would be like in bed. If only she wasn't in love and in a relationship with Emily he might have had a chance – she'd been into men before. It was a good job she couldn't hear his thoughts.

"So, what you been up to Paul?" asked Emily from the settee where she had sat herself close to Tracey. "You still hanging around in Shields?" She laid her hand deliberately on Tracey's thigh to tease him, something she did to most men who came in and had one eye on Tracey and her slim little arse.

"Aye, I have. Been doing a bit with a few lads over there – you know how it is. You two been up too much?"

"Apart from coping with the CID kicking the door in last month?" said Emily. "Nah, not much apart from the usual." She pointed to the small pile of hash deals on the table.

"We had nowt in the house," said Tracey, "so they left empty handed and left us with a broken front door. It could have been worse. And hopefully it'll be the same when they come back next time." She handed the joint to Emily, who took a large lungful and exhaled purposely through both nostrils. The room filled with another cloud of grey-blue smoke.

Emily passed him the joint and he took a few tokes, feeling the heat rise in the back of his throat as he inhaled the thick, strong smoke. There was definitely no front-loading in that one.

"Are you out this weekend?" asked Tracey. "World's End's having K-Klass on, we've got tickets and the Es are sorted already. You can take that lass of yours."

"My lass? Who's that, like?" Paul put a pretend look on his face and tried to come across all innocent.

"You know . . ." said Emily. "What's she called again?

The blonde one . . . Lindsey."

"She's not my lass, man. We're just . . .friends." He was slightly embarrassed to be getting into a conversation about a girl with two gay women and he felt heat rise to his cheeks.

"Aye whatever . . . she'd be mine." Tracey giggled. "If I wasn't taken, of course," she added, before a sharp look from Emily came her way.

There was a short uncomfortable silence for a few seconds while they looked at each other: Paul to Emily and then to Tracey and the girls to each other until Paul said, "Right, I'll be off then. Cheers for the joint and the hash." He stood up and made his way to the back door, bending down and slipping on his untied trainers.

"No bother," said Tracey. "any time. Where you off to? Round to Lindsey's, is it?" She continued to tease as she unlocked the door.

"Aye, haven't seen her for a while. – thought I'd pop in," Paul half lied.

"Well, have a good night then," Emily said. "Tell her we said hello and tell her to pop round for a smoke sometime." She stretched out on the black leather settee where she would lie and wait for Tracey to return after she'd secured the back door.

"And don't do anything I wouldn't do." Tracey winked cheekily as Paul made his way out of the door and onto the next part of his night.

"That doesn't leave much!" Emily called from the settee, before bursting into a loud cackle.

Crazy on the Waltzer

* * *

He made his way up the lane, passed the closed hardware shop then crossed the road, which was busy with the evening's traffic. The 326 bus was pulling in as he dodged between the cars because he was too inpatient to wait for the traffic lights to turn red. He didn't have to go far to get to Lindsey's flat. It was his little sanctuary, somewhere he could escape to for some peace and to offload his problems. They had an unusual relationship: somewhere between friendship and something more. She was the person he trusted most apart from his mam and, if truth be told, he was in love with her. But he couldn't tell her that because, deep down, he couldn't handle the rejection if he did.

He passed Ivy Court Gym and looked into the brightly lit room where thirty or so women were doing the evenings aerobics class, red faced, panting and sweating, jumping to the beat of the house music and following the instructor as best they could. Paul went to Ivy Court a few times a week. It was a change from the muscle gyms like Proflex and the YM in Shields that most of his friends trained at and were generally full of meatheads, doormen and gangster wannabes. He had no time for hearing them brag to anyone who would listen about how hard they were and who they'd chinned lately, the majority of which was lies or a massive exaggeration of the truth. They were pumped up with steroids, which gave them nothing but a short temper and a pair of bitch tits as their bodies produced estrogen to counteract the inflated levels of testosterone they regularly injected into their backsides.

Steroids weren't for Paul. He smoked hash most days, ate reasonably well and kept himself fit running and lifting weights. He would never be one of the local hard men but at the same time he didn't want to be; there always was some drama or other going on if that was the life that you chose.

He turned right, crossed the road and then left onto Alnwick Avenue and knocked on the door of Number 29, Lindsey's downstairs flat. He saw the net curtain twitch out of the corner of his eye, but he turned his head too late and missed the face in the window. A few seconds later, the door was opened by Lindsey, barefoot and dressed in black leggings and a plain white Nike t-shirt, her shoulder length blonde hair tied back in a simple ponytail.

"Hiya," she smiled. Her step back was his invitation to enter.

"Hiya, yourself." He smiled a big smile before bending down and pecking a kiss on her milky, smooth cheek.

"Keep your voice down," she said, "I've only just got the bairn down,"

"OK," he whispered. He slipped off his trainers and coat and entered the front room in silence. He wondered if any other women were going to tell him to keep quiet that night.

She followed him in, closed the front room door and busied around tidying up kid's toys, storing them in the wooden box that was decorated with boats of various colours. He sat down on the worn and ageing, green velour settee in the seat closest to the bay window, and when she was finished, she joined him at the other end.

"I've just got him to sleep ten minutes ago," Linsey said. "Quarter past bloody nine and he's only three. He ought to sleep right though." She shook her head.

"That's late." He tried to cheer her up. "It'll get better when he gets older, though. It won't be like this forever."

"Knock up a joint, would you? I could do with one. It's been a long day. You want a cuppa?"

"Yeah, please. One sugar and milk."

"I know," she laughed. "You've been coming here for long enough."

He slid the tray from under the settee which held the joint making paraphernalia and made the spliff that the secret love of his life had requested.

*   *   *

Lindsey was a year younger than Paul and they'd been at Monkseaton High School together. At eighteen she'd fallen in love with a guy a few years older than her who she'd met at a house party after an illegal rave in Newcastle. She'd been high on life and Ecstasy. He was from Elswick and wasn't like the boys she knew from down the coast; he was older, cockier and more streetwise. He'd told her she was the one and that he loved her and that they'd be together forever. And she believed him, until she fell pregnant with Jason. She only saw him once after that, and when she wouldn't have an abortion, he walked away. He told her that if she was going to keep the baby she would have to look after it herself and that he wasn't ready to be a father.

He turned his back that day and she never saw him again.

Her parents were good people, but they wouldn't have a baby in the house at their age. They'd brought up three kids and married young and, as far as they were concerned, she had to move out and find a place. They gave her the deposit and helped her out with babysitting and kids clothes when they could, but she still had to find the rent and the bill money. Packing tea at the Twinings factory down the Royal Quays was just enough to pay the bills. She wasn't left with much at the end of the month, but she still managed the odd night out down Whitley Bay. She was in love with him too and just like him she wouldn't say it, but unlike him she wasn't scared of rejection because she knew in the way that only a woman could that he was in love with her. The issue was his lifestyle. He was a criminal, albeit a petty one, and she wouldn't let herself get involved with someone who could be out of her life tomorrow if he got arrested. And, more than that, she couldn't let her son get attached to a man and then have to explain why he suddenly wasn't there anymore.

Returning with the tea and to a half-smoked joint, she sat back down and stretched her long slim legs across the settee and rested her naked feet over his thighs. He looked at her and she gave him a smile while the THC started flowing to her brain, relaxing her after a long day. Even though they weren't a couple, they quite often acted like one, and he knew exactly what she wanted and started to gently massage her feet. She closed her eyes and tilted her head back and then told him to put on some music.

"Wear FM?" he asked.

"No, none of that rave shit. I want to relax not start jumping about." She kept her eyes closed as she spoke.

He lifted her feet, dropped to his knees and slid across to the Pioneer Hi-fi. It wasn't the best Hi-fi out there, but it was good enough for them.

"Dire Straits?" He was opening the CD case before he received an answer.

"That'll do," she said.

"You get a shiver in the dark, it's raining in the park but meantime . . ." Mark Knopfler sang out.

* * *

They smoked and chatted for a couple of hours, mostly about nothing, in the way people can when they know each other as well as they did. Knowing they could be candid and honest with each other and knowing that whatever was discussed that night would never leave those four walls. It was past midnight and he thought she'd fallen asleep; she'd turned around and was lying in the fetal position with her head resting on his thighs. He looked at his watch and then down at her and thought her flawless, smooth, face was the most beautiful he'd ever seen. He wanted to reach down and kiss her heart shaped lips, a kiss that he'd thought of a thousand times but wasn't brave enough to plant. If she rejected him, it would kill him inside, it was a risk he didn't dare to take.

"Paul, can I ask you something?'" she said.

He'd thought she'd nodded off and was surprised when she spoke. "What's that?"

"When are you going to grow up and stop hanging around with a bunch of clowns?"

"What do you mean?" he shot back defensively.

She sat up and looked at him through half closed eyes. "You know. You need to get out of this shit – stealing and hanging around with arseholes. It's not going to do your life any good. You're only going to end up in jail like the rest of them."

"I dunno, I'll sort it out one day, I know what you mean but, what else can I do?"

"Get a job . . . find a lass . . . live a normal life."

"I will . . . one day," he promised, not knowing if he really meant it or not.

"Anyway, it's late and I'm off to bed. God knows what time Jason'll have me up in the morning." She stood up and stretched out.

They headed to the front door and Paul zipped up his coat to the collar before stepping into the cool dark night, checking his pockets for the hash, cigarettes, Rizlas and Clipper lighter he would need for his night cap spliff when he got home. "You going to see K-Klass at World's End next week?" he asked.

"Chance would be a fine thing. I'm skint."

"Shame. There's still tickets available,"

"Maybe next time." Paul sensed the disappointment in her voice?

They kissed the same kiss they had kissed on his arrival and said goodnight to each other. As they parted, he wondered if it could be possible that they had the same dream: of love and a life together; of a happy place they could share forever.

*   *   *

As Paul walked along the deserted Park View towards home at 1a.m, he was still turning over again and again what Lindsey had said before he left. Was she saying she'd have him if he sorted his life out and got a job or was she just looking out for him as a friend? Unless he went straight, he would never find out. His biggest issue was his dad's death. He knew in his bones that whoever killed him was local and he believed that if he stayed in the world of drugs and crime it would eventually all come out. He had no real evidence of this and neither did the police, but something deep inside told him that this was the truth. Somebody would definitely slip up one day. It was a thought he had daily. Pick up a titbit here, a hint there, a carless whisper, or a slip of the tongue was all it would take.

The wind had picked up slightly and he felt cold after the warmth of Lindsey's flat, their shared body heat as she lay with her head resting in his lap. A good job he hadn't got a hard on he thought; how embarrassing would that have been? He almost giggled out loud as he walked on.

In his half-stoned stupor, he was barely aware of the Sierra Cosworth passing him from behind and travelling towards the centre of Whitley, nor did he did pay that much notice when it pulled up outside Pickard's newsagents – not until three black-clad figures with ski masks on emerged from it, the first of whom removed a large plastic bin from the boot of the car. Then the calm of the night was disturbed by the sound of splintering wood and the crash of breaking glass as the trio caved in the newsagent's door. The alarm wailed and the strobe light flashed and pulsated down the street. It had taken Paul a second or two to grasp what was happening, but he continued to walk towards the car, partly out of curiosity and partly because he hadn't done anything wrong himself. As he got closer, he slowed, and the blaggers ran out of the shop. The first raider carried the bin, which he emptied into the boot before throwing it into the street. The second threw two large boxes into the boot before slamming it shut. They both opened the back doors of the car and dived in. The third passed two boxes into the back seat then opened the front passenger door. Then he stopped and looked straight at Paul with a pair of deep-set dark eyes.

"Get yourself in there!" he shouted, before flinging himself into the getaway vehicle.

Then they were off. No screeching getaway but a fast one nonetheless, turning right out of Whitley towards Shields and away from the scene of the crime. They hadn't been in the shop for more than a minute and now they were gone. Paul saw the prize that night: cigarettes and lots of them – and he didn't need to be told twice.

He pulled up his coat as high as he could so his eyes were barely visible and entered the shop. Glass crunched underfoot as he moved gingerly across the floor. It was only eight metres to the back and, like most newsagents, it was set out plainly. The walls were adorned with magazines and card displays, with a double-sided console running the full length of the shop and the counter facing him at the back. He moved rapidly and was at the counter in seconds, looking for loot that the robbers had left behind. The cigarette locker had been ripped open; its grey steel roller shutter hung on from one side. The cigarettes had gone and the excess packets were strewn around the floor. The wail of the alarm was almost deafening. He had his thieving head on now and his mind had gone from zero to a hundred, like it always did when there was a sniff of an opportunistic payday.

Bypassing the counter, he headed straight to the storeroom and saw in the darkness what he was looking for. The cigarette storage cage had already been ransacked and opened with a set of bolt cutters, the broken, silver lock glimmered in the low light that permeated through the small room's high barred window above. He grabbed a six thousand pack of Mayfair from the floor, excess goods for the robbers who would target the high-end brands like B&H, Embassy, Marlboro and Silk Cut first. He grabbed the box with two hands, turned and ran back through the store over the broken shards and back through the splintered doorway. Then he was off into the night, to the churchyard across the road and away from the police station on Laburnum Avenue, which would be receiving a call from the residents and the alarm company about now.

The trees and the old stone church covered his escape as he moved from shadow to shadow to the back corner of the graveyard. Placing his swag on the high garden wall he pulled himself up slowly, his jacket sleeves down over his hands while he watched for lights from the house. He saw the flash of blue lights and heard the wail of the siren as the boys in blue arrived on the scene while he lowered himself quietly down into the pitch-dark garden below. Picking up the box, he tiptoed down the side of the house to the wooden gate, which he hoped wasn't locked – and tonight his luck was in. Covering his hand with his right sleeve he slid back the bolt and opened it, creeping slowly out into the street and checking it in both directions. There was no sound of cars and no blue lights flashing. All he could hear was the faint sound of the newsagent's alarm and his own heart pounding. He ran on, across the road and over the fence and onto the Metro lines, adrenaline coursing through his veins. Crossing the dirty tracks, he stashed the cigarettes in the bushes behind the advertising hoardings on Hillheads road, camouflaging them the best he could with branches and rubbish. He would return the following night to retrieve his ill-gotten gains.

Slipping back onto the deserted metro lines, he went off into the night and then home, mentally spending the £300 or so his haul would net him.

As he closed his front door behind him, he breathed a sigh of relief, and looked down at his filthy jeans and even filthier British Knights trainers. It looked like new Fila boots time after all, he thought, and slipped off upstairs to bed.

2: MONEY FOR MUSCLE

The queue to the door was a long one, even for a Saturday night. It snaked three deep around the corner at the top of South Parade and almost to the top of Oxford Street. The bass from the club upstairs could be heard from the street below and the members of the clientele who had already dropped their Love Doves or snorted away their speed were bouncing to the beat, jaws gurning from left to right as the MDMA took hold. There was no dress code here and no real fashion to follow. Anything went just as long as you were comfortable in yourself. Tight Destroy tops or baggy jeans and bucket hats? Nobody cared. It was all about the music – and the drugs: Speckled Doves, Brown Biscuits or some speed to keep the party faithful going all night long, and what a night it was going to be if you managed to get yourself a ticket! K-Klass in Whitley Bay, who'd have thought it? Everyone who bought a ticket had been delighted when they parted with their eight quid. As they got to the door where Mark and Liam Taylor were standing guard, the club's manager and promoter apologised to each of the punters as he returned them £3 of the ticket fee. He uttered the phrase that he would repeat a hundred times.
"Sorry, K-Klass cancelled at the last minute. They've been in a bus crash leaving Sheffield."
It was as big a lie as anyone would tell that night. K-Klass were never making an appearance; they weren't even booked. It was all just a ruse to ensure a full house and maximise ticket sales.

"You're fucking joking – this is bullshit!" complained a freshly-shaven-headed lad to the manager as he held out his hand for his paltry refund. He decided not to complain further as the death stare from Liam's eyes burned a hole into his own.

"I'll be a good night anyway lads," Mark said. "Enjoy."

The lads weren't happy but there was nothing they could do as they strode off up the winding staircase, brightly decorated with coloured flyers from different raves. They went through the double doors and into the club, still complaining to each other about missing their favourite act. They were still grumbling when they got to the bar.

Paul and Lindsey were in the queue outside, sheltering from the drizzle and pushing closely into each other to keep the cold breeze at bay. He'd surprised her with a ticket from the money he'd made off the cigarettes, but he hadn't let on where it came from. He presumed that she knew it was from something dodgy, but she didn't protest too much when he gave her the ticket, a Love Dove and £20 for a few drinks. In fact she seemed delighted. Half of Whitley, which included most of her friends, would be there and she hadn't been out in ages. Her mam had agreed to keep Jason until Sunday night and she obviously intended to make the most of it.

They were nearing the front of the queue and about to pass the entrance when the unmistakable figures of George Bolton and Kenny Reid by-passed them and went to the front. Generally referred to as "the Boltons", George and

Kenny were the unofficial board of directors to Whitley Bay's criminal fraternity.

They moved with purpose and walked straight in, only stopping to shake hands and exchange small talk with the Taylor brothers and the manager. No need for tickets, and no need for a £3 refund for them, they would be taking their cut later in the week, the same as they did every week from there and from most of the bars on South Parade.

The Bolton's weren't brothers, although the resemblance was such that people thought they were. Their tall, thickset build and identical strawberry blond haircuts made them almost indistinguishable from behind. Years of street fighting and boxing bouts had left them both with flattened noses and beaten skin from the contusions and abrasions that violent lives had left behind on their faces. They were cousins on their mother's side and people joked behind their backs that George's father had knocked up both sisters. Maybe that was true as Kenny never knew who his father was, but nobody was brave enough to ask. They were in their late thirties, powerful, dangerous and ruthless men. Like two peas in a pod, neither of them took drugs, smoked or drank that much, but when they did almost everyone gave them a wide berth.

A sober Bolton was more than enough for most people to contend with and a drunken one was even worse. They had a reputation for ordering people about when they were drunk and a reputation that few would stand up to, even if it meant humiliation in a bar full of people. They'd started out working the doors together at the Avenue Pub when they were teenagers and had managed to keep violence out of the bar once they'd battered and barred the troublemakers. Not long after, the owners of Parkes and Spencers across the road enlisted their services and then they were off. In short time they'd given up working the doors themselves but continued to take in £50 a week from most of them on South parade and beyond. The police called it a protection racket, but they called it insurance. Insurance against trouble from the locals or your bar getting raided because someone had set up a drugs shop in it. That wouldn't be tolerated unless it was their drugs, of course. Like Carl in Shields, they didn't touch a thing.

The Taylor's had worked the doors for the Bolton's for a year or two. George and Kenny put up with their level of violence and would continue to do so as long as there wasn't too much interest from the police to affect their door and drugs rackets. They all understood that violence was only good for business if it didn't involve the regular punters, the straight-goers who would generally involve the police if they were on the receiving end of a kicking from the door staff. Violence between the criminals and the drug taking fraternity was rarely reported so effectively didn't matter nor interfere with anything too much. Even so, George had found the need to have a quiet word with the Taylor's on more than one occasion for overstepping the mark and attracting unwanted police attention.

"Move your body . . . move your body to the rhythm of love . . ." the speakers blasted out as Paul and Lindsey entered the inner sanctum of the club.

"They're taking the piss," said Paul loudly to Lindsey. "Playing K-Klass after they've filled us full of shit about them being here? I knew it was a fucking wind up to sell tickets!"

"Don't worry about it!" she shouted back over the music. "We're here now!" She took his hand and led him through the heaving crowd to the bar.

The club was packed full of a few hundred ravers, dancing and sweating, swinging their arms and moving their bodies to the beat of the house music. The dance floor was full, along with the podiums, and the crowd faced the DJ who was the star of the night, a drug fueled congregation merging like a single organism and praying to their electronic god. He lifted them up with the music and carried them away on a wave of euphoria as the strobes and the lasers flashed and lit up the dance floor, mixing with the smoke that pumped out from each side of the DJ booth.

Paul and Lindsey made their way, hand in hand, stopping to hug and kiss a few friends on the way. But, on a night like this, everyone was a friend; the Es just made it that way.

Reaching the bar, Paul ordered two cans of Red Stripe and after receiving his change he slipped the small white pill from the ticket pocket of his jeans and quickly checked for the bouncers before slipping it into his mouth. Wincing slightly as his tongue tasted the bitterness, he swallowed what was generally regarded as the best pill on the market. They might not last as long as the Brown Biscuits, but they were a much better buzz. Lindsey followed suit and they made their way to the chill out area with the oversized cushions to wait for the Es to kick in. And half an hour later that was it: a wave of bliss rode through their bodies as the MDMA took hold and the rushes came on, intensifying the colours and sounds of the club and making the pair come alive. They headed for the dance floor and for the next two hours that's where they stayed. Dancing. Together but not with each other. In paradise, on top of the world and in a place where the straight people, the beer monsters of Whitley Bay, would never go and would never understand. Later, they made their way back to the chill out area, hand in hand, hair matted with sweat and soaked to the skin. Paul sat against the wall with Lindsey between his open knees, hands massaging her shoulders to intensify the rushes as they moved to the baseline of the music. She lit a cigarette, and he winced as the smoke furled upwards and into his eyes, neither of them talking as the rushes continued.

"These Es are amazing," he said eventually into her ear as his jaw chattered.

"I know," she said. "And thank you so much for tonight. I really needed this."

"It's OK. Any time. You know I think the world of you . . . you deserve a night out. Don't worry about it . . . it's on me . . . I just want to see you happy . . ." he rambled on. What he really wanted to say was *I love you and I want you as my girlfriend* but, even in his ecstasy filled state of mind he still couldn't muster up the courage.

"Are you coming to Amy's after this," she asked. "She's having a few people back to hers and wants to know if we'll go."

"Course I will," he said with a smile. "I'm not going to leave you, am I?"

Half an hour later he'd peaked and the E was wearing off. He knew he'd be coming down soon and either wanting another pill to pick him back up or a smoke to get him to sleep. A come-down session at Amy's place sounded perfect to him.

The good vibes of the night were interrupted by the sound of someone being thrown through the fire exit door as a shaven headed body was dragged through it by Mark Taylor, closely followed by his brother. Half the chill out area stared at the door until it quickly closed and the club went back to normal. The noise of the music took over again like it had never happened. Most of the punters were either too off their heads to comprehend what had occurred or knew better than to get involved.

*   *   *

On the other side of the door, it was a different story. The lad was on his back, eyes wide open in terror as Mark strangled him with his left hand while raining blows down on him with his right.

"I'm sorry man, I'm sorry!" the lad squealed, as if unable to comprehend what was happening to him and why.

What he'd done was to have the audacity to complain about the cancelling of K-Klass again to the manager who'd told the Mark and his brother to remove him. A simple telling might have been enough, but that was no fun.

"Sorry? sorry?" yelled Mark. "Who the fuck do you think you are, causing trouble in here?"

"I wasn't, I just . . ."

Crack! Mark landed another blow on the lad's already blood-covered face.

"Pull his fucking eye out!" snarled Liam, his steroid rage kicking in. "He fucking deserves it!"

"Noooooo, pleeeese . . . I'm sorry!" the lad pleaded again.

Mark pushed his right thumb into his eye socket. "Aye, I fucking will." He applied more and more pressure.

The lad curled up, pulling his legs up to his chest in a vain attempt to protect himself while unsuccessfully trying to push Mark's much stronger arms away. He was powerless to do anything except shout and cry and pray that the attack would stop as he tasted his own salty blood on his tongue from his smashed-up lips.

The fire door flew open and in came George Bolton. Meanwhile, the manager hovered around outside. It was just like him – always whining about how he and Liam did their job – as if the soft shite had any idea about how to handle a crowd of pissed-up punters. He'd probably complain to the Boltons about them again. Well, fuck him, and fuck the Boltons too.

"Mark!" George snapped, as he grabbed a hold of Mark's right bicep.

Mark looked around, taking his thumb from the lad's eye. "What?" He grinned, doing his best to look all innocent-like.

"What the fuck are you doing, man?" said George

Bolton. "He's just a kid. You seen the fucking state of him?"

"What's the matter?" said Mark. "He kicked off when we tried to get him out."

"You're fucking joking?" said George. "Him? What the fuck was he going to do? We can't have this shit in here. The manager's going fucking off it. Take him down the fire exit and out the back... and don't fucking do owt else to him."

"It's alright, man, It's just a few slaps." Mark couldn't see what all the fuss was about.

George ground his teeth and exhaled through his nose. He stared at Mark and Liam in turn and looked like he was about to explode.

Mark was determined to keep face, putting on his best and-what-the-fuck-are-you-going-to-do-about-it-like look.

"Get rid of him now!" snarled George. "Get him out!" He turned away and pushed his way back through the fire exit door and into the club.

"What's the crack?" Mark heard Kenny say on the other side of the door.

"Those fucking arseholes!" said George. "They've took a liberty on some young kid and smashed him up. I'm fucking sick of this."

Mark and Liam dragged the whining punter down the fire exit. Mark handed him a twenty-pound note and told him to go home and keep his mouth shut if he knew what was good for him.

* * *

As the door swung open onto the back lane the sodium lighting from the glow of the orange streetlights streamed into the beaten lad's face, mixing with the cold evening wind and making his already sore eye even worse. The tears flowed harder down his cheeks. He zipped up his hoodie to hide the blood-soaked t-shirt that the bouncer had made him use to wipe his face clean. He was too terrified to look back. Off he walked, stumbling down the back lane and holding onto his battered face, past the broken bottles and the bar room rubbish, through the stench of stale beer and with the noise of South Parade's revelers ringing distantly in his ears. Just as he'd been told to, and to keep him away from the prying eyes of any passing police cars. He was shaking and prayed that the brothers wouldn't follow him and treat him to Round Two, which thankfully for him they didn't.

*   *   *

The night was over in World's End for Paul and Lindsey. They were coming down, so they decided to head off back to Amy's flat for a few drinks and a smoke which was their usual way to end a Saturday night. Passing the fire escape door, they didn't pay a thought to the ongoings of a few minutes earlier and even if they had they would have ignored them. The breeze that came in through the main entrance chilled them and they shivered as the sweat on their bodies cooled while they collected their coats before making their way into the street outside. They stopped abruptly due to what was obviously trouble brewing between the Bolton's and the Taylor's. Paul wanted to wait and see how things would unfold but Lindsey took him by the arm and led him away which was the sensible option. Having a story to tell was good for the night and for a Sunday afternoon in the pub, but this was gangster business, and something that was best not to be anywhere near for the likes of them.

*   *   *

George was still seething, with Kenny looking as if he was trying to calm him down, as Mark and Liam rounded the corner.

"How many fucking times am I going to have to tell you to stop doing shit like this, Mark? It attracts too much fucking attention." He glowered at the pair of them.

"I've told you," Said Mark, "he was kicking off. What the fuck do you expect us to do? Tickle him?"

"Are you taking the fucking piss? Do you think I'm fucking stupid? He was only a kid! What you going to do if he runs to the bizzies? We can't have it in the bar. You were about to pull his fucking eye out!" George was getting redder by the second.

"Fuck off, man," said Mark "I gave him twenty quid." He glanced at Liam and laughed.

"Don't tell me to fuck off! Who the fuck do you think you're talking to? You fucking work for me, remember? I'm fucking sick of telling you–"

"You don't tell me anything." Mark abandoned all attempts at forcing a smile. He and George stared coldly into each other's eyes as his body tensed up. George hesitated for a split second while the ramifications of what Mark had just said seemed to go through his mind. This was it, there could be no backing down. Face couldn't be lost.

George was the faster man, and he threw a right that connected with Mark's chin, sending him reeling and stumbling backwards. He didn't go down, but he would have if Liam hadn't caught him. Few men down the coast could have taken punch like that from George and still been awake. Kenny reared up into his southpaw boxer's stance, ready to back up his cousin, chin down, preparing to throw his hands at Liam, who sensibly backed off.

"Come on then, cunt!" George growled at Mark. "I'll fucking do you!"

Mark and Liam inched away. For a second or two, Mark considered having a go, and then thought better of it. Maybe one on one, but not with both. Liam was no match for Kenny so it would end up two on one and he knew he couldn't win that fight. Sometimes you had to pick your battles, and this time it was better to walk away. As Mark stared at George all he could think was *I'll get you one day. You'll fucking see.*

Then he turned and left with Liam.

"Aye, go on!" George shouted. Fuck off! And don't come back. You're fired. You're off the fucking firm."

Mark turned to Liam as he skulked off like a beaten wolf retiring to the woods to lick its wounds. The pain in his jaw was rising as he checked over his shoulder for the Boltons coming after them. "I'm gonna do that prick, I'm fucking telling you . . . I will," he said through gritted teeth to his little brother. "Mark my fucking words."

*   *   *

Unbeknown to any of them they'd been watched by North Shields CID from their Vauxhall Cavalier parked up a short way down South Parade. Detective Inspector Sharon Manstone was in the back with her arms outstretched across both front seats and leaning forward so her head was almost in line with her two detective constables in the front. Graham "Cookie" Cook was driving and Lee "Gibbo" Gibson was in the passenger seat. This was because Lee's bodybuilder's bulk struggled to fit comfortably in the driver's side, which made it difficult for him to get out from behind the wheel in a hurry.

Sharon was a copper with ambition, and she was going places. She'd just turned forty, and nothing gave her more satisfaction than locking up crooks, and the higher up the criminal tree they were the more satisfaction she got. She had an average build, light brown hair and kept herself athletically fit. She believed that a good villain was a fit villain and the same could be said for coppers. Her stature and plain looks meant that she could blend into a crowd with ease. She didn't consider herself a bent copper, but she would bend the rules when it suited her and turn a blind eye to her workmates who would pocket a bit of drugs money on a raid or punch a suspect around to get a confession.

Her favourite Detective Constables were with her that

night. She'd taken Cookie under her wing when he first joined the CID and she'd shown him the big local villains, the ones he'd dreamed of nicking when he was in uniform. And then there was Gibbo, a six-foot meathead who wouldn't have looked out of place on the other side of a cell door with his body builder frame, shaved head and tattoos. She'd done the same for Gibbo as he had for Cookie, although it wasn't all selfless. It was good for her to have someone of GIbbo's size and stature at her side, especially when it came to the rough stuff or booting in a door.

Gibbo was an unusual candidate for the police force. He came from a well-to-do and professional family of accountants and doctors who all lived in Gosforth and the surrounding area. They'd expected him to follow in the family footsteps, go to university and get an honourable job once he'd graduated, but that was too boring for him. He yearned for an exciting career. He'd considered joining the army, but his mother forbade it and threatened to cut him out of their will if he did. He settled on the police force. With a private school brain and the brawn to match it didn't take him long to be snapped up by the CID, and his career as a copper looked like a long and eventful one.

His only problem was the pay, which couldn't keep him in his Champagne Charlie lifestyle of partying and chasing women in Julie's or on the *Tuxedo Princess*. His childhood friends had taken the professional route and he struggled to keep up with their salaries, which comfortably paid for their drinking and lady chasing. He supplemented his income trading secondhand cars and flipping property, something that the police weren't allowed to do. Sometimes he flew close the wind, and on more than one occasion he'd borrowed money from his parents just to keep him afloat. He secretly admired the lifestyle the big villains led: the easy money, high end clothes and the good-looking women who gravitated to them.

Gibbo loved the job, but most of all he loved a good raid. Smashing someone's door off its hinges and dragging their half-asleep arses out of bed at 5am was something that he buzzed off. Sometimes they would struggle or try to escape, but once they'd opened their eyes fully and saw the big, tattooed lump that stood before them they'd normally think twice and give up.

They were working overtime, keeping an eye on the drug dealers who plied their trade around the bars of South Parade and looking for a few wanted suspects, and tonight they'd stumbled on what they hoped would be something big.

"Look!" Cookie said abruptly, which immediately caught the others' attention.

"What?" said Gibbo.

"Bit of action here, lads." said Sharon excitedly. "Watch . . ." She lifted her head to see, sticking her neck further out into the front of the car to try and get a better view.

"It's Bolton," said Gibbo. "And... is that, Mark Taylor?" He squinted, then lifted the radio to his lips.

"Don't call it in – not yet, Gibbo," Sharon said. "Let's see what happens here." She reached across and put her right hand on Gibbo's radio and he lowered it from his mouth.

There was no way they would stop anything between the Taylor's and the Bolton's unless weapons were used, and even then, they would let a few injuries get dished out before intervening. Villains hacking lumps out of each other was typically a win-win situation for them: one ending up in hospital and the other in the cells.

"Good punch – he's down!" said Gibbo. "No he's not. Is he going to have go back?" He seemed just as excited as Sharon and was talking like he was a ringside commentator and playfully bobbing, weaving and throwing his hands around like a boxer in the front seat.

"Aw, for fuck's sake," said Sharon, as she watched Mark and Liam skulk away. "I thought we were in for a bit of excitement there. Wonder what that's all about?"

"Fuck knows," said Cookie.

*　　*　　*

Cookie knew fine well that he would find out about what lay behind what they had just observed the next time Mark got in touch.

Mark was Cookie's secret snitch, an off the record informer that even Sharon didn't know about. Six months earlier, Cookie had stopped him with a kilo of hash in his car. There was nobody around and instead of taking the chase like most villains would, Mark pulled over and fronted it out, hoping it wouldn't be found. It was. Always one to exploit an opportunity, and especially with someone who moved in the circles that Mark did, Cookie proposed a gentleman's agreement. Mark walked away with the hash and escaped a few years in Acklington jail and Cookie walked away with three hundred pounds and a reasonably high-level criminal as an off the record informant.

It wasn't just information Cookie wanted. His eight-year-old daughter, Alecia, had Ewing Sarcoma and he needed more money than he could ever make as a Detective Constable to pay for the drugs and the treatment she needed. He had to prolong her life. The NHS had given up on her; they said the treatment was too expensive and the result would be the same. They were happy enough let her die as comfortably as they could, and that tore him apart. He was determined to give her another round of treatment even if he had to pay for it himself. Giving up on her wasn't an option. It was costing him £3000 a month and if Northumbria Police weren't paying him enough then he'd have to find it another way.

Having someone like Mark working for him meant he could pass on the drugs he stole from other dealers to make up the shortfall in his policeman's pay. There wasn't much left once he'd paid the bills each month, certainly not enough to pay for Alecia's medical costs. Maybe he wouldn't have turned out to be such a bad man, but he felt like life was always up against him and no matter what he did he could never catch a break. He had very little compassion and patience for anyone or anything, but most of all he was angry with the burden of having a dying daughter. He loved her like any father would, but he didn't see why he had to struggle through life when it looked to him like everyone else had it easy.

He was being prescribed beta blockers from his GP for

the stress, which was something he didn't declare to the Police. They controlled his bouts of rage and violent behaviour, but caused him to sleep badly and suffer from nightmares, something he counteracted by drinking a half bottle of whisky almost every night. He would quite happily take a young criminal up a back lane and beat him just to see the fear in his eyes, and he genuinely enjoyed it. It was his escape, his way of hitting back at life, the life that gave him a misery that he passed on to others.

Cookie's wife turned a blind eye and never questioned where the money came from. She knew it wasn't legitimate, but as long as her daughter was getting the treatment she needed, she didn't care. She correctly thought that it was being stolen from the bad guys which justified it to her: if it wasn't getting robbed from regular people but rather from the scum of society, then that was okay.

* * *

Paul sat back on Amy's couch, closed his eyes and thought of his dad and how much he missed him. This was a regular thing when he was coming down and quite often when he wasn't. It could vary in its intensity from him being a little bit sad to curling up in a ball and sobbing his heart out. Lindsey was aware of the place he went to in his head and would comfort him when she saw the signs. She came in from the kitchen and put her arm around his shoulder and pulled him in close. Amy knew the score too and busied herself in the kitchen for a few minutes longer than necessary to give them a minute alone. Amy was Lyndsey's best friend and confidant. She'd been in a few rough and failed relationships in the past and prefered living the single life.

"You okay Paul?" said Lindsey. "It's been a belting night. Come on, don't be down." She was clearly trying to get his mind off what she knew was his dad.

"Aye, I'm fine," he said. "Just having a moment."

She hugged him again and kissed him on top of his head. "Thanks again for tonight, it means a lot that I've got you there for me, it really does."

"It's OK. Now, where's the skins?" He gave his head a shake and rubbed his hands through his hair before picking up the green Rizla packet from the table.

Amy came in from the kitchen and handed them each a can of LCL Pills, which Paul opened straight away. Lindsey stood up to get a glass from the kitchen.

"Can't drink from a can me, like," she said to Amy, while looking at it in pretend disgust. "Don't know where it's been. It could have rat's piss on it or anything."

Paul and Amy looked at each other and both shook their heads, then Paul made the first joint of the night.

"I've got a bit of black here," said Amy to Paul.

"Nah keep it. I've got some soaps here. That black's like smoking diesel." Paul spoke as if he was some kind of marijuana expert, which in his mind he was. After the cigarette raid, the first thing he did was go and score a half ounce from Tracey and Emily, which would be enough to keep him going for a week or so.

There was a scream from the kitchen and Amy and

Paul turned in the direction of the noise. Amy jumped up to see what Lindsey was screaming about. She was standing facing the kitchen window with her hand on her chest and smiling at a face in the window that Amy couldn't see. The big grin and broken teeth of Alan Richards beamed back at her with his even bigger nose almost touching the glass.

Alan was a petty criminal and one that was destined to get another sentence before long. He knew that the straight life wasn't for him, and at the age of twenty-one he'd decided that he was going to be a career criminal and acted like he didn't care if he ended up in jail of not. He had plenty of balls in the criminal sense but not much in the way of brains to go with it and would get arrested at least once a month for fighting or thieving. He loved his drugs of whatever variety. He dabbled in heroin when he could get it and shot up speed on regular occasions.

Even though he was a friend, Paul kept him at arm's length these days because more and more he was developing a reputation for pulling sly tricks and ripping people off. There were rumours that he'd burgled his best mate's mam's house, but nobody could prove it and it was something Paul expected him to deny to his dying day.

Amy opened the door and in came Alan followed by his half girlfriend, Jenny Thompson. Most people couldn't understand what Jenny saw in Alan, but he did have a certain charisma and an extremely manipulative manner, he could turn on the charm when needed and was also an exceptional liar. It wasn't that people believed what he said, it was more that they couldn't disprove it, which got him out of a lot of tricky situations.

"Come in," said Amy, "Haven't seen you two in ages. Were you in World's End?"

"Nah," said Alan, "I'm fucking barred. Liam Taylor hates me guts, blamed us for breaking into his mate's shop. It wasn't fucking me."

Everyone looked back at him with the same look that said *yeah, right*.

"It fucking wasn't! I swear on me ma's knife," he joked, pleading his innocence to his audience.

Paul passed him the joint and immediately started making another, while Alan sat down on an armchair with Jenny sitting at his feet. Amy bought them both a can from the kitchen and then stretched out on the floor and put Wear FM on the radio. Every time the MC came on, they would listen for shouts out to their friends who would phone into the pirate radio station.

"You might not have to worry about that anymore," Paul said to Alan.

"Why's that like?" Alan cocked his head and half closed his right eye as the smoke from the spliff curled its way into it.

"Bit of trouble between them and the Bolton's tonight . . ."

"Aye? What happened?"

"Not sure exactly. Didn't hang around to see but they were arguing outside Words End. Looked like it was going to kick off so we nashed. I'm not hanging around when they're smashing lumps out of each other."

"Best way," said Alan. "Find out the crack sooner or later anyway." He took a deep toke of the spliff and passed it on to Jenny.

"So, you been up to much Jenny?" asked Amy.

"Nah not too much. Just the usual,"

Paul took that to mean shagging other people's boyfriends and stirring the shit, which was the reputation that Jenny carried. As good looking as she was, Jenny could fight. Most women wouldn't cross her, and neither would a fair share of men. She wouldn't back down to anyone. She did what she wanted and didn't care what anyone thought of her at all. Part of the reason she was in an on-off relationship with Alan was that he brought unpredictability and excitement into her life. And when he did have a score she was right there with him, drinking, smoking and snorting until the cash ran out. Then she was off, looking for the next man with a few quid in his pocket who would take her along for the ride.

There was another tap on the kitchen window and Paul got up to see who it was. He peered into the dark back yard and saw the imposing mass of Carl Liddle looking back at him.

"Two minutes mate," Paul mouthed to the window, knowing fine well that Carl couldn't hear him through the glass.

"Who is it?" Amy asked from the front room.

"It's Carl Liddle," whispered Paul. "What the fuck's he doing here?"

Lindsey gave Amy a sideways glance, cocked her head slightly, lifted her eyebrows and gave her a cheeky smile.

"We're not here!" Alan blurted out. "Let us out the

front way!" He and Jenny stood up and put their coats on in a hurry. They made their way out of the front room and into the passage while the other three looked at each other confused.

Paul returned to the kitchen window and looked out at Carl. He shrugged his shoulders while moving his right hand back and forth, pretending he was looking for the key. Carl looked back and nodded his head while Amy ushered Alan and Jenny through the front door. Paul had no idea why they had to leave so quickly but Alan was in the habit of pissing off a lot of people, some of whom it was best not to get on the wrong side of.

Amy stopped to look in the mirror and quickly checked her hair and makeup, then gave Lindsey a smile before waltzing into the kitchen and unlocking the back door. "Hiya, come in," she said shyly to Carl.

"Not too late, is it?" Carl asked. He stepped into the house, bending to kiss Amy on her cheek while placing his left-hand half on her hip and half on her bum as he pulled her in gently. He walked into the front room, two shirt buttons open as usual and with his Nokia 1011 phone in his left hand, which looked like a brick with an aerial.

"Carl, this is Lindsey and Paul," Amy announced. "Guys, this is Carl." Both Paul and Lindsey knew exactly who he was.

"I know you," Carl said to Paul. "You train at Proflex don't you? I've seen you in there before," He reached out his hand for Paul to shake.

"Aye," said Paul. "Sometimes. But I get myself to Ivy Court as well."

"Not my kind of place, but I hear it's OK for the cardio."

"Aye, it's not bad. Makes a change from all he meatheads at Proflex and the YM." Paul almost panicked when he realised what he'd said. He hoped Carl didn't think he meant him.

Carl smiled and laughed which put Paul more at ease and he said "Yeah, I suppose it is." He sank down into the warm seat that Alan had just vacated and then pointed at the two half-drunk cans of lager on the floor. "Had a few more people back?"

"Yeah, a couple of friends, but their taxi came early," lied Lindsey.

"So, you been in Whitley tonight?" Amy asked Carl.

"Nah, I've been up the town and then to the casino for a bit."

"Busy?" she enquired.

"Yeah. Youse been at that K-Klass thing?"

"Aye," said Paul. "It was canny apart from no K-Klass. Looked like a bit of trouble at the end, though, with the Boltons and the Taylors squaring up to each other outside. Not sure what was going on, but we fucked off anyway. I'm not getting involved in their shit."

"Aye, wise move." Carl said. Paul got the impression that he hadn't told Carl anything that he didn't already know.

The clock struck four and Amy asked if anyone wanted another drink. The boys took one each and Paul rolled another joint to go with it. Lindsey was falling asleep on the settee, half sitting and half in the fetal position with her mouth slightly open. Amy gave her a nudge and told her that she could crash in the spare room, which Lindsey said sounded like a good offer. "Sorry, I'm knackered. I'm off to bed," she said to everyone. "Nice to meet you, Carl, and thanks for the night, you two. I'll see you all tomorrow, I have a date with DJ quilt and MC pillow." She kissed everyone in turn and gave Amy a big hug before making her way to the spare room.

Carl and Paul swapped seats while Amy went to the toilet. She found it slightly amusing. Not too long afterwards, she fell asleep. The boys continued to talk about mutual friends, training, drugs and money making, both trying to sound each other out, but Carl more than Paul. Carl had to be careful because people would try to befriend him for a variety of reasons which is why he found it difficult to trust people. Some people wanted protection or a had a scam they wanted to get off the ground and needed someone with his stature to make happen. Sometimes they were just plain scared of him and wanted to keep him on side. It could be a lonely life at times. He knew hundreds of people, but he only had a few close friends, and in the life he led there were even fewer he could actually trust. "So, did you get yourself in then?" he asked Paul with half a grin.

"Eh, what?" said Paul.

"Pickards. did you get yourself in or what?"

The penny fully dropped for Paul. "Was that you? Aye, I fucking did. I got a six thousand pack of Mayfair. It paid for tonight and a few other things." Paul smiled to himself. "I ran through the graveyard and through a few back gardens and stashed them on the Metro lines then went back the next night."

"Aye it was me," said Carl "Always nice to spread the joy. I'm getting bit old for that shit now. Good crack, though, and an easy score. No chase or anything. Straight in and straight out."

"Do you do the robberies as well, like?" Paul asked sheepishly, immediately unsure if it was a good thing to ask someone he'd just met. It wasn't something he would have thought of asking in a million years if he was sober but, seeing as they seemed to be getting on well and that he was extremely stoned, he'd just blurted it out.

Carl's face straightened and he stared at Paul with a look that suggested he might rip his face off.

Paul sobered up as fast as lightening, instantly regretting the question. He now had a big bad lump of a human being who could easily tear him in half with his bare hands staring straight at him.

"What you asking that for?" Carl moved forward to the edge of the settee and put his palms on his inner thighs.

"No, nothing, it's just . . ."

"Go on."

"I was up in Gosforth the other day and I saw something. It might be nothing but . . . er . . . I just thought I'd mention it."

"What's that then?"

"Well . . ."

* * *

Over the next few months, Paul and Carl became closer and closer friends, much to the chagrin of Lindsey who still nagged at him for the time he spent with villains. She worried that his life was on a slippery slope, a slope that had jail or hospital at the bottom of it. They'd started training together a couple of times a week and drinking on the weekends and Paul noticed how people changed towards him: strangers wanting to be friends, offering him drinks and free cocaine and pills when they were out. He reveled in it and liked the attention he got from the men about town and the women that hung around their racy lifestyle. He'd also started making some cash for himself by running errands with drugs for Carl and making a bit on the side collecting his protection money.

Carl had a feeling about Paul, and he liked him. He felt that he was someone he could trust as far as he could trust anyone, and he took him under his wing. He'd even gave him a key for his flat when he went away for a few days so Paul could chill out in luxury and so he had somewhere to take the local lasses that wasn't his mam's house. Carl had known Jimmy from around Shields and had taken protection money off him at the Spring Gardens, but this was something that Paul didn't know. The subject of his death hadn't been discussed but Paul was aware that Carl had known his dad. He hoped that moving in the circles that Carl did would give him a better chance of finding something out about his demise, but he knew it was a long shot.

Another reason Carl kept Paul around him was the discussion that they'd had in Amy's flat regarding what

Paul had seen as a bit of work for Carl and his team of thieves. He knew that if Paul was involved directly then there was less of a chance that he would blab to anyone after the fact or even worse before the job was done. Carl told him to go and double check what he'd told him and, unbeknown to Paul, he'd had someone watch him to make sure he was doing what he was told and to make sure he was telling the truth. There was a big chunk of someone's life on the line if what he was saying was wrong. For the following two weeks, Carl sent one of his squad to watch the building so the same face wasn't seen at the same location twice. Once Paul's information had been confirmed and the dark nights had come in far enough, the plan was set in place and put into motion

3: BANDIT FEVER

Paul stood at the bus stop waiting for a bus he was never going to catch. The rain was falling and the early December Christmas shoppers and commuters were busying themselves in the teatime darkness. He wasn't sure if he was going to be sick or fill his pants but either way it wasn't a pleasant feeling as the knot in his stomach increased in intensity with every tick of his watch. All he kept repeating to himself was *How the fuck did I get into this?*

He knew he was being watched but he couldn't see where from. Somewhere in the drizzly blackness was a three-or-four-man team waiting for him to give the signal. Carl hadn't introduced him to the others but he could guess who they were. He did as he was told and avoided direct eye contact with anyone at the bus stop. With a scarf pulled over his face and the hood of his black Berghaus jacket up there wasn't much of him that could be recognised anyway. Time stood still. It had only been ten minutes that he'd been waiting but it felt like an eternity. This was a day that he knew was going to change his and some other people's lives forever. And as he stood there with the funk of fear deep inside him, he hoped that in his case it would be for the better, though he knew it would change a few others for the worse.

He looked across the road and through the glass window of the target building. It was lit up brightly, the radiant office lights contrasting against the winter blackness. He knew the people inside wouldn't see what was coming and he genuinely hoped that they wouldn't be too shaken up by what was to come. They were just ordinary people unlucky enough to be about to be caught up in a bad situation, but he thought that they'd get over it easily enough. It wasn't their money, so why should they care; they should just give it up without any resistance. He saw a mother with a child who looked around seven or eight walk towards the entrance and he prayed that the kid wasn't going to be caught up in the coming events. For a moment, he thought of walking off to the left, which was the signal that something was amiss or that the police had been spotted. He looked through to the back of the bank, and as the rear door opened, he saw two women of indeterminate age walk out from it, one blonde and one dark. He couldn't see what they were carrying but he knew what it would be. This was it: this was his cue and his time to move.

There was no waving or other obvious signals. He calmly looked both ways to check for oncoming traffic and walked across the road to his right and into the alley beyond. He heard them pull up outside the bank behind him and he heard the car doors open. He heard the crash of the glass and a faint scream as he walked up the alleyway, resisting the urge to run. Bile rose in his throat, and he felt the acid burn in the back of his mouth and did all he could to keep it down, knowing that he couldn't leave any trace of himself behind. He swallowed back hard which made his eyes pour salty tears, which he wiped away with the back of his glove. Walking to the end of the alley, he crossed the quiet residential street whose inhabitants were unaware of the drama that was taking place a hundred yards away and strode into another back lane. Rounding the next corner, he lifted the door handle of the stolen Ford Fiesta and slid into the driver's seat, keeping his scarf pulled up as he drove away.

This wasn't a film where the robbers drive off and meet at the hideout to split the loot. He knew he wouldn't see Carl for a couple of days and he would never know who else was in the car with him. He was perfectly happy with that arrangement. Carl was a bad man with a worse reputation but some of his acquaintances were certifiable lunatics. A few of them were one examination away from being sectioned off and had no business being in any free society, not even a criminal one.

As he drove off in the direction of Newcastle, he thought of the women at the bank and felt genuine remorse for them. Pulling the car over, he emptied the contents of his stomach into the passenger side footwell and continued to throw up with dread until the dry wrenching made his eyes feel like they were going to pop out of his head. He wiped his mouth with his sleeve and then continued the journey to the West End where he would burn out the car before slipping away into the city centre and then home. If the Police were clever enough to link the car to the robbery, they would begin by looking around Elswick for the usual suspects up there.

Around the same time that he burnt out his car, the robbers would be setting fire to theirs, three or four miles away. They'd planned this. Reports of two car fires at the same time a few miles apart would confuse the police in their response. Theirs was a Ford Sierra, four door with a 2.3 litre V6 engine, that wouldn't stand out in the street. They'd discussed using a Cosworth or another flash car, but it would have attracted too much attention while they waited for Paul's signal to pounce.

*   *   *

The robbery had gone like clockwork.

The gang pulled up and were straight out of the car with no hesitation. Two seconds later, a heavy, steel, drain cover was thrown through the glass door and they ran straight in.

When they had scouted the job, they all saw the same thing: two women would walk through the door from behind the safety of the strengthened glass with a large plastic box and open the back of the cash machine. It was in the public area of the bank with the front delivering money to the customers in the street and the back opening into the lobby of the bank. The cash was only vulnerable for a couple of minutes while they opened the back of the machine to top it up for the weekend, but a couple of minutes was a lot more than they needed.

The blonde opened the door to the bank's foyer and walked out with the brunette behind her who was carrying the money that was stacked and counted, ready for the weekend warriors of Newcastle to spend in the city's bars and shops. Each band of one thousand pounds was marked with a stripe on the side for easy counting, which made the robbers' job of splitting it up easier as well. It was the girl's very last job before they closed for the weekend and their minds were elsewhere.

As they unlocked the machine, they took no notice of the car that pulled up outside, and even if they had, the darkness wouldn't have allowed them to see what was coming. The noise of the crash and the splinter of a million shards of glass cascading across the diamond patterned carpet caused them both to jump. The young brunette screamed as she turned to be greeted by two masked figures, both dressed identically in blue boiler suits and ski masks and with one holding a pickaxe handle.

"Get on the fucking floor, now!" bellowed Carl towards the girls.

"Now, now, don't fucking look at me!" the other raider screamed. "Give me the fucking money!"

The second command was pointless because the dark-haired girl had already dropped the money case in fright.

"Stay there! Don't fucking move! Don't fucking move and you won't get hurt!"

The girls were scared stiff, they were too terrified to speak even if they'd wanted to.

The bandits had this all rehearsed; it wasn't the first time they'd done jobs like this and they both knew their roles. Carl was there for the muscle: big, loud and imposing to anyone – the more so considering his dress and demeanor. The other guy was still a big lump that few would have a go with, but he was there to grab the cash. He emptied what he could from the back of the open cash machine into his rucksack then grabbed the cash box and turned to leave. Carl stood guard, holding the pickaxe handle two handed across his body. It would take a very big man to get past him and stop them, which was exactly why he took on that role; he gave the other man a feeling of relative safety. Outside, the driver sat in the car looking out for the police, readying himself to sound the horn if they came as he waited nervously to whisk the gang away. A handheld scanner in his jacket pocket flicked a hundred times a second between several police frequencies, it would let them know the moment the robbery had been called through from central command to the cars on the street.

The young lass curled into a ball on the floor. Eyes screwed tightly shut, she cried among the shards of glass and buried her face into the blond lady's chest. The older woman pulled her in tightly and shielded the frightened young girl from the two masked thugs looming over them.

"Got it, got it! Go, go, go!" shouted the other robber, as he grabbed Carl's arm.

Then, as quick as they came, they left. Less than thirty seconds was all it took, and they were off into the black, wet Friday night of Newcastle considerably better off than they had been the day before.

The car pulled off like it was someone picking their mother up from the shops and with no squealing of tyres. The driver had been stealing cars since he was eleven and was generally considered the best driver in Shields. He'd taken his fair share of chases over the years and was perfectly capable of outrunning any police driver, and often in inferior machinery.

Turning right up Salters Road, the gang was buzzing. They had just executed a perfect score – like taking candy from a baby. When they were planning the job, they'd considered using guns, but then considered that they were only expecting a couple of ladies with the cash. They weighed up that the extra time they would get if they were caught with firearms wouldn't have been worth it at all.

But the easy heist was only half the job. Weaving their way through the residential streets at a speed that was just fast enough not to attract attention, they pulled into a car park behind the art deco flats on Westfield Road where the first changeover car was parked. A common Vauxhall Cavalier had been left under the corner of the shared carport that serviced dozens of flats. A new car wouldn't stand out there. It was just off the main street and by the time they'd swapped cars and someone realised the getaway car was on fire they'd be long gone, lost in the headlights and confusion of the rush hour traffic. At the same time the police combed the area looking for a Sierra and not a Cavalier, a job made much more difficult by the busyness of the roads and the lack of daylight. They maintained a silence between them until they were in the second car and on their way to the next changeover in Fenham. They could just make out the low sound of sirens in the distance.

Just like with the Sierra, they would torch the Cavalier, only this time with the boiler suits, masks and weapons in it so they'd leave no forensics and so the police couldn't remove and plant anything on them that they took from it later.

"We've done it, we've fucking done it!" shouted the second robber from the back seat where he lay.

"Keep your fucking voice down," the driver spat back

from behind the steering wheel.

"Why? Nobody can hear." He looked at Carl who stared back at him with widening eyes.

"Shut up! Now!" Carl told him.

"We don't need any attention," the driver spat back.

"People are more likely to wonder why some bloke's talking to himself while driving a car on his own," said the second robber, laughing. He piped down when Carl gripped his arm.

They made their way to the second changeover and away without incident. There were no witnesses. The second car was burnt out, along with the gear. They'd taken care to leave the passenger window down so the fire didn't burnout prematurely and leave crucial evidence behind. The car they drove back to the coast would have its number plates swapped back and be returned to the secondhand car lot they borrowed it from. It would be sold on at a less than market value to get it off the lot quickly in case the police turned up asking questions. The owner would get a drink on it to more than make up for the difference without ever knowing what it was used for.

They trusted each other, and the money would be put away for a while before anyone was allowed to splash out on anything that might attract attention. They'd just go on with life as normal in case the police were watching and so nothing looked out of place.

Carl did what he always did after a score and made himself scarce for a few days. He worked on the principle that it was best not to be around when the police were kicking in doors and looking for suspects. He would take himself away and hole up in a hotel and there was only one person who would know where he was. She was married, beautiful and a danger to be caught with, but to him she was worth the risk.

*   *   *

Later that evening, Cookie made a call to Mark from a pay phone on the Marden Estate. It was answered on the third ring.

"I need a meet," said Cookie. "You available?"

"Aye, I can be," said Mark. "Where and when?"

"I'll park up outside Hadrian Road Metro on the ATS side and leave the back door unlocked. Just jump in. How does nine suit you?"

"That works for me," said Mark. See you there."

Around an hour later, Cookie pulled up outside the station as arranged and parked up facing away from it and next to the gable end of the terrace. He winced as the bitter, salty taste of the beta blockers hit his tongue and he swilled them down with a mouthful of whisky. Ten minutes later, he saw Mark's white Peugeot 205 GTI pass the bottom of the street and a few minutes after that the rear driver's door opened and Mark jumped in. He stretched out along the back seat so he couldn't be seen.

"What's up?" asked Cookie as he pulled away. "Been a while since I heard from you."

"I've fell out with the Bolton's," said Mark, "and they're making things a little difficult with the drugs."

"Aye, I heard that,"

"They're putting the squeeze on me and Liam. They've kicked us off the doors as well, so it's hard to make a few quid at the minute."

"So that's why I haven't heard from you. But we've still got our little arrangement, don't forget. You should be inside doing a four stretch and it's only because of me that you're not."

"Look, I know but–"

"No buts, Mark. You need to keep your side of the bargain. Info or cash – or both – but preferably cash. Or you know what happens . . . it's a holiday in the big house." He let the threat sink in for a moment. "Listen, I've got a plan for you and your mob and, if you get onboard, you'll end up with a lot more than you have now. And this is it. I'll feed you some info and give you some protection and you and Liam are going to take over George and Kenny's business."

"Go on," said Mark.

"That's if you think you can handle it. I saw him do you in one punch last time."

"You saw that?"

"I did. Or rather *we* did. We were parked up on South Parade when it happened – our little bit of entertainment for the evening. Anyway, this is the plan . . . Get a hold of that Craig Cameron who does the drugs for them first and make him give you their cash and their main stash. Then go around taxing all their dealers and make them work for you."

"And what about the Boltons, Einstein?"

"Well, that's where I come in. They won't do anything

straight away because they know we'll hear about it pretty quickly and we'll be watching them. But when they do grab their guns and come after you, we'll perform some timely raids and get them out the way, and then you'll have no opposition. In the meantime, I'll keep you informed if anyone's looking at you. And by that I mean us or any other police agencies,"

"And what about Carl Liddle?"

"You've got no problem with him, have you? Not yet anyway. But one thing at a time. I doubt he'll get involved unless you piss him off and tax his lot so just be careful whose doors you knock on for now,"

"And what do you get out of this?"

"I can either go on a wage or get bigger lumps as we go along. But you'll have to sacrifice a few of the little fish now and again so I can look good to the boss. I'll give you a heads-up when to start so I can be on duty in case it comes on top and I need to warn you."

There was silence in the car while Mark thought it over. But Cookie knew he'd offered him a no brainer; either he lived his life skint or grew a pair of balls and went for it.

"Ok then, I'm in. And I'll give you a week or so's notice."

"I'm putting myself on the line here and taking a much bigger risk," said Cookie. "So, I'll be expecting a much bigger envelope – don't forget that. And never call me from anywhere except a pay phone and I'll do the same, even if it's life or death. And one more thing . . . not a word to anyone. Not even Liam."

"I'm not that daft," replied Mark curtly.

"That, Mark, remains to be seen."

*   *   *

There was a knock on the door and Carl sat up straight on the king-sized bed in the Copthorne Hotel. As he was staying for a few nights, he'd treated himself to a suite overlooking the river. A video for *Fields of Gold* by Sting played softly from the TV. Carl expected a visitor, but he was still on edge and worried that the police had tracked him down for the robbery. There was always a chance that any soft knock could simply signal today as being the last day he spent on the right side of a barred cell door for many years to come.

As he crossed the room he slid a mahogany chair in under the matching desk before turning to straighten the bedsheets and plump up the pillows. He looked through the peep hole out into the corridor and couldn't help but smile. He leant into the bathroom to quickly admire himself in the mirror and make sure the collar of his shirt was straight before opening the door.

And in she walked, smelling like heaven and looking like an angel. Her long slim legs were wrapped in stockings and black, expensive high heels. She wore a knee length camel coloured Burberry coat tied around the waist with a belt. She paused as he closed the door then reached up with her perfectly manicured hand and took hold of his chiseled, clean-shaven jaw. Kissing him softly on the lips, she left a slight taste of her bright red lipstick behind.

"Nice to see you again." Marie Cunningham said,

before dropping her Gucci handbag onto the sofa as she walked towards the window overlooking the Tyne. She opened her coat and dropped it to the floor, revealing the holdup stockings and black lacy bra, which was all she wore underneath.

"And nice to see you too." Carl smiled and admired her near perfect figure and absolutely perfect arse as he lifted the chilled bottle from the ice bucket. "Champagne?"

"Of course. I didn't come her just to see you." She glanced over her right shoulder, flicked back her long black hair and smiled, then looked straight into his eyes. She pulled back the net curtain and looked out across the river to the Brett's Oils factory on the Gateshead bank. She probably hoped that a worker or two would spot her nakedness from afar. Just for the thrill. A pair of middle-aged male joggers ran along the pathway below but missed what would have been the best thing they'd see all day.

She turned and faced him. He looked her up and down, admiring her tanned body that was hairless from her eyebrows down. He pulled her in towards him and he felt her naked breasts push into his chest. One large hand cupped almost all of her arse as the other handed her a glass of Laurent Perrier Rose champagne, with a strawberry in it, just for effect. She took a sip of the cold pink liquid before placing the lipstick-stained glass on the bedside table. They kissed, and she ran her hands down his thick chest before dropping to her knees and unbuttoning his jeans.

"Missed me?" she asked.

"Oh yes." He looked down and pulled her hair back

into a ponytail before closing his eyes.

Carl and Marie had known each other for a while and met semi-regularly for sex, but it would turn out to be troublesome if they were caught. Marie was marred to Les Cunnigham who was twenty years her senior. It was a marriage of convenience. He had money and wanted a young trophy wife for all the reasons older men do, and she wanted a nice house, fancy car and plenty of money to spend without having to lift a finger to get it. Les had an inkling she strayed now and again, but as long as she kept it quiet, he didn't really mind. It would have been hypocritical anyway, considering the number of ladies he had on the side. He knew that at forty-eight he couldn't match her prowess in the bedroom and accepted that she needed to get her needs met elsewhere, but if he found out it was Carl who was meeting them it would be a big problem. For one thing, they were friends, which made Carl feel bad, but if it became public then Les would have to do something about it; he couldn't lose face.

Les owned a casino, a few bars and a nightclub in Newcastle, and had his fingers in a lot of pies, some of which were very hot to handle. He was first cousin to the Fraser family from Newcastle's West End who were one of the biggest crime families on Tyneside. His unofficial nickname was Tommy, after the ultra-violent Joe Pesci character in the film Goodfellas, although nobody called him that to his face. He was around five feet nine, but what he lacked in height he more than made up for in stature. Word on the street was that in order to raise the loan to open the casino, some members of his extended family kidnapped the regional manager of Barclays Bank. They politely requested that he assist in approving the loan, or in future he would have difficulty signing cheques without any fingers. There were also rumours that he'd killed a couple of people in his younger days, but the bodies were never found and the police couldn't charge him or his cousins. As hard a man as Carl was, he knew he wasn't bulletproof, and if Les found out it was him that was playing around with Marie, then a bullet would be a godsend after the torturous beating he would receive from Les's firm.

The hush-hush lovers spent the remainder of the afternoon and half of the evening fucking, only taking a break to rack up another line of cocaine and to replenish the champagne. But then she had to go. Les wouldn't be in until the early hours but she still needed to be sober and not smell of sex by the time he returned.

She kissed him on the cheek as she left. He watched her slim, little arse walk off down the corridor and get into the lift. She didn't even turn her head back to smile before the lift doors closed.

Carl lay on the bed alone, sexually satisfied but still alone, physically and in his head.

* * *

Mark and Liam were almost skint. Since George and Kenny had put the word out that anyone who dealt with the Taylor's was out of favour with them, there were fewer and fewer people who were prepared to take their gear and they were having trouble themselves finding anyone willing to supply them. They were in a sticky situation and, like all cornered animals, all they could do was lash out and hope for the best. Mark believed he had the strength and ambition to make it to the top, and now Cookie had given him a plan and a strategy to elevate himself and his brother to the pinnacle of the coastal underworld.

"What we going to do Mark?" Liam asked his older brother. "We're running out of cash – and fast."

"I'll tell you what we're going to do . . ."

"What's that?"

"Go robbing,"

"Like an armoured car?"

"No, you daft twat. Taxing. I'm not doing robberies. Too much jail for me."

"Who we gonna rob, like?" Liam seemed somewhat confused.

"All the dealers. Then we make them work for us."

"Like who? George and Kenny won't be happy."

"Fuck George and fuck Kenny. I could probably do Kenny anyway and I *will* do George one day. I haven't worked out the finer details yet but I'm not spending the rest of me life with fuck all just cos of them two."

"Aye but–"

"But nothing. Don't worry little brother, I nearly have it all worked out." Mark picked up two dumbbells and stared at his reflection in the mirror. He curled them up towards his chest in unison, determined to be on top one day and to crush the Bolton's in the process. He believed he could pull it off, but just to make sure he needed another maniac with a mad reputation onboard, and he had just the person in mind.

4: ROCKAWAY

"Paul, wake up, it's for you!" said Lindsay, slightly louder than normal.

"Eh? What?" He opened his eyes, adjusting himself to his surroundings, and came to the swift realisation that he'd woken up on Lindsey's settee and not in his own bed.

"The phone. It's for you."

"OK, two seconds," he mumbled, swinging his legs out from under the duvet that Lindsey must have spread over him after he'd fallen asleep the previous night. He made his way into the passage where the cream, plastic phone handle sat next to the receiver.

"Who is it?" he whispered to her, covering the receiver with his hand.

She shrugged her shoulders and pouted out her bottom lip as if to say she didn't know. She didn't look particularly happy.

Paul picked up the phone. "Hello?"

"You got a passport?" It was Carl.

"Er . . . aye, why?"

"Right, what time is it now? Er . . . 8.30." Carl answered his own question. "OK . . . I'll pick you up at nine at the bottom of the street." Then he hung up.

Paul laid the phone back on the receiver and looked at Lindsey. In his hungover and fuzzy mind, he wondered what Carl had planned and hoped that it wasn't anything heavy.

"What did he want, calling at this time of the

morning?" she enquired suspiciously.

"Nothing. He just wanted to know if I fancied a breakfast somewhere. He's going to pick me up in half an hour."

She shook her head, a mixture of annoyance and frustration, perhaps.

He said goodbye to her. She stood in her dressing gown as he walked off down the path, leaning with her left shoulder against the door frame while Jason clung to her right thigh.

"Bye Paul!" Jason waved his little hand.

"Bye mate." Paul said back, and smiled at an unhappy Lindsey as he closed the gate behind him.

* * *

Carl pulled up in the lane behind the photo shop at the bottom of Alnwick Avenue so that he couldn't be seen from the main road. He had to wait a minute or two for Paul to arrive and he left the car running. Over the hum of the idling engine the radio played *Ain't No Doubt* by Jimmy Nail.

"Woman like you's no good to me . . ." Jimmy sang, which made Carl think of Marie.

He knew she was no good for him. He didn't need Jimmy Nail to tell him that.

The passenger door of the Escort saloon opened and Paul jumped into the seat. He closed it behind him and dropped the window a few inches to let in some air.

"Alreet?" asked Carl.

"Aye, think so," said Paul. "Apart from the heed – a bit hungover. What's happening, like?"

"I thought you'd like a bit of a holiday. Fancy a few days in the Dam?"

"Aye, fucking right I do. When we going?"

"Today. Flights at three if you're up for it. I've been onto Jemma at Thomas Cook and she's booked the flights already. I presumed you'd have a passport."

"Aye. Only got it a year or so ago. Swing by my mam's and I'll run in and get some clothes and pick it up. Where we going for breakfast?" said Paul, buzzing at the thought of seeing the windows and coffee shops of Amsterdam.

"We'll go to yours and then stop at the Priory café," said Carl. "Then we'll pop to mine and grab me stuff and then get a taxi up the airport. Couple of pints then offski." He made aeroplane noises and laughed.

"Have you got some money from . . . that thing?" asked Paul. "I'm a bit skint."

Carl looked at him seriously and put a finger over his mouth. There was always a small chance that the car could be bugged, and it would be case closed for the prosecution if they were taped talking about the robbery.

"Sorry." Paul looked decidedly sheepish as they drove off towards his house.

"And have you got that key for mine?" asked Carl. "I'll lend you the flat again when I go away next time. I just don't like having spare keys kicking about, that's all."

"Aye, here is." Paul removed the key and chain from the ring that held his house keys and passed it to Carl, who dropped it in the ashtray in the dashboard.

They pulled up outside Paul's mam's house and he ran in. Carl got out, took his mobile phone from his inside pocket and dialed a number that he knew off by heart: a 00 31 code for Holland. It was answered on the second ring.

"Alright?" asked the voice on the other end.

"Aye, course," said Carl.

"All good?"

"Sound, mate. See you soon."

They both rang off and the receiver went dead. There was no point saying more than was needed. Anyone with a decent scanner could pick up analogue phone, which was why Carl and most of the bigger villains had traded them in for the first digital mobile: a Motorola 1011.

A few minutes later, Paul came dancing out of the house with his Head bag over his shoulder and waving his passport. He opened the boot and threw in the bag, still dancing and singing as he climbed back into the car. Carl laughed and slammed the boot shut. They'd become good friends lately and Paul was someone whose company he genuinely enjoyed. The fact that Paul's little tip had made them a lot of money helped as well.

* * *

Later that evening, the plane touched down at Schiphol airport. It was Paul's first time in Holland and he didn't know what to expect. He'd heard all about the coffee shops and the hookers who plied their trade in the red windows along the canal paths. He also knew that Carl came over regularly and was well versed with the comings and goings of the city and knew the best places to go. In the back of his mind there was a suspicion that there could be more to this trip than just a few days away, but until that eventuality occurred, he was just going to enjoy the drink, drugs and women that Amsterdam had to offer.

Carl had given him a grand before they left and told him it was a loan that could be paid back when they split the money from the robbery. Paul was perfectly happy with that arrangement and he changed a few hundred pounds into Guilders at the airport. As the train made its way to the city centre, he was disappointed not to see fields of tulips and windmills. He strained his eyes in the darkness to take in as much as he could see, which apart from his and Carl's reflections in the window wasn't much.

Twenty minutes later they exited the main entrance of Amsterdam Central Station, and Paul was surprised by the wide, open space in front of him and the people of all colours and creeds. Compared to Newcastle, where most people were white unless you went up the West End, the inhabitants of Amsterdam were much more diverse.

They walked along with Carl leading the way and past the busy junction at Prins Henrikkade. Paul jumped back when he heard the close ringing of a cycle bell and the shout of an unhappy lady.

"Forgot to tell you,"said Carl, "watch out for the bikes and the cycle paths. They've got right of way and, if they hit you, it's your fault. And they don't slow down."

But Paul was barely listening; he was too busy looking around and taking in the sights and sounds as the tourist boats tied up for the night. They turned left along Oudebrugsteeg and headed into the Red-Light District, and he saw The Grasshopper, one of Amsterdam's most famous hash cafes in front of him.

"You'll see some sights now," said Carl. "This is the Red-Light District – and buy fuck all off this lot on the street." He motioned towards two leather-jacketed men standing on the opposite corner. "We'll get sorted out later on."

"Aye, no bother," said Paul. He stuck close to Carl as he took in the porn shops and the windows and the colourful characters of the street, as well as the predominately black drug dealers who were on every corner, all whispering the same line as they passed.

"Es, hashish, cocaine, LSD, speed, brown sugar?" they asked, as the lads passed.

There were hordes of people from every walk of life: Asian tourists; hookers hanging out of doorways enticing in the punters; old couples, leather-clad bikers; big men who looked like the Dam's version of Carl; pissed up British stag parties; trench-coated middle-aged men who Paul thought looked like stereotypical perverts. Maybe they were, but no-one batted an eyelid in this melting pot of humanity, there for whatever flicked their switch that night. They were mainly there for sex or drugs, but some were just there just for the spectacle.

They turned right, past the Oude Kerk church and crossed a small bridge over the canal, and without Carl saying anything they walked into the foyer of the Queen

Beatrix Hotel.

"Is this where we're staying?" asked Paul.

"Sure is."

A slightly built, spectacled man with thin mousy hair brushed into a side parting appeared at the counter. Paul guessed was in his early fifties.

"Hey, Carl, my friend!" he said, in heavily accented English. "How are you? Good to see you again!"

"I'm good, Jacob," said Carl. "And good to see you too, as always. It's been a while." He took Jacob's wrinkled hand and shook it firmly, like good friends do.

"And who is your friend?" asked Jacob.

"Jacob, this is Paul, a good friend of mine. Paul, this is Jacob. He owns the place."

"Good to meet you, Jacob." Paul, extended his arm and shook Jacob's hand. He wondered why Jacob held his gaze for a second too long. It made him feel slightly uneasy.

"Just staying for the two nights?" Jacob enquired. "That's all I have you in for."

"Aye, just two nights. You got the rooms ready? Hope it's the same one as last time."

"Of course. Rooms with a view." Jacob smiled and let out a dry smoker's cough.

They took the keys and headed off upstairs. Carl handed Paul a key for Room 303, taking the adjacent 302 for himself.

"It's fucking great here," said Carl. "Right in the middle of the action. You'll see some belting sights out the window."

Paul could well believe it; he'd seen plenty already in

the fifteen-minute walk from the train station.

"Right . . . quick shower and I'll see you downstairs in half an hour," Carl said. "There should be a little something for you in the bedside drawer, courtesy of the management." He winked and smiled at Paul before disappearing into his room.

Paul entered and took a quick look around. It wasn't luxurious but it would be good enough for two nights. There was a wooden-framed double bed with clean-looking sheets, an en-suite shower room and a window that overlooked the canal. The TV only had Dutch channels. After dropping his bag on the bed, he opened the small wooden drawer of the bedside table and was pleasantly surprised to find two Es, a paper wrap of what he presumed was cocaine and a small bag of skunk with *Bumblebuzz* printed on it.

He sat down and quickly made a joint as he listened to the faint sounds of a drunkenly-sung football chant from the canal path outside. Kicking off his shoes, he lay back on the bed and lit it. After a few tokes, the extra-strong weed went straight to his brain. It was much stronger than the solids back home and he would have been quite content with lying on the bed all night and enjoying the rest, but he had an appointment downstairs and he'd better get a hurry on. He switched on the shower and, once the steam was rising in the cubicle, he climbed in and ran his head under the hot water, which took away the effects of the skunk a little.

Ten minutes later he was downstairs in the hotel bar, where Carl was in conversation with Jacob, who stood over the small round table. Carl sat back in the booth, sipping a pint of Amstel with one hand while the other arm stretched out along the back. He saw Paul enter and beckoned him over, then motioned to the barmaid to bring across more drinks.

Jacob outstretched his left arm inviting Paul to take the seat next to Carl. "How's the room?" he said. "Did you get the presents?"

"Yeah, I did, thanks. How much do I owe you?" Paul enquired.

"What? No, it's on the house!" Jacob, smiled, showing off his yellow, smoker's teeth.

"Don't be daft. It's a present. Me and Jacob go back a long way," added Carl.

Jacob laid a hand on Carl's muscular shoulder and gave it a friendly squeeze. "Yes, my friend, we certainly do. And if you need anything else let me know. Don't go buying off the blacks on the streets. They will rob you and sell you talc for a hundred guilders if you are lucky or rat poison if you are not. Come and see me and I will make sure you don't get ripped off. Anyway, I must go. I have a hotel to take care of and staff to keep happy." He waved in the direction of the barmaid and may as well have told them they were sleeping together. "Have a good night and enjoy,"

"Aye, I'm sure we will." said Carl.

They both shook hands with Jacob before he left through the back of the bar into what Paul presumed was his office.

"How do you know him, like?" Paul asked.

"Jacob? I've known him for years. Got to know him from coming over here. He's a sound fella and as straight as they come."

"Must be a canny life owning a hotel in the middle of the Dam – with owt you want on your doorstep. So, what's on the agenda for tonight?"

"We'll finish these and head out. I'm not going to them coffee shops, though. Not my thing sitting in a smokey cafe all night. But if you want to pop in for a bit then we can. We'll gan for a wander and find some bars. I know a few good places. Howay then . . . drink up and let's go."

They downed the remainder of their pints and smiled at the barmaid who smiled back. "Veel plezier," she said as they walked out of the bar.

"What's that mean?" Paul asked Carl.

"Have fun."

They turned left out of the hotel and away from the Red Light District, away from the tourists and the hustle and bustle, and away from the red windows where a thousand prostitutes of a hundred nations plied their trade. They stopped at a bar and took a table outside, where they people-watched the evening punters go by and chatted while they enjoyed more beers. Paul took himself off to the toilet to knock up a line of cocaine on the shelf that seemed to be purpose built for the occasion. He snorted it back up his right nostril, shook his head then closed his eyes as the bitter taste hit the back of his throat. Taking a moment to get his head straight, he read the graffiti and the stickers that people from all over the world had deposited on the cubical walls: Helsinki, Tokyo, San Diego, Rio, Tel Aviv and many other places that he thought he'd never get to see. He went back outside and sat next to Carl.

"Fucking good gear that," he told Carl.

"Isn't it just," Carl said.

"I might get some to take home. I'm definitely getting some more tomorrow. So, how'd you get to know someone who owns a hotel in the Dam anyway? Especially someone who'll have a lucky bag of drugs waiting for you in the room when you get there."

"Ah . . . now, that would be telling," teased Carl. "I walked in one day looking for a place for the weekend with a couple of pals and got chatting to him. We hit it off and now it's the only place I stay when I'm here. Keep this to yourself but . . ."

Carl proceeded to tell Paul about Jacob. He'd made his money smuggling hash from India to Holland with a firm of Dutch smugglers until he was caught in a truck coming down from the Punjab with half a ton of Kashmir's finest product. He served a year on remand in an Indian jail that was more like a sty than a prison. Once the case had died down, he bribed the local judiciary to bail him to a hostel outside of Delhi and the prosecutor not to oppose it. He spent six months there while his lawyer paid off everyone he could to delay the case, which wasn't too hard over there.

He'd settled into the hostel, signing on at the local police station three times a week. He was free to spend his days outside the hostel if he returned by 9p.m. Jacob's mother was from Adelaide, allowing him to hold dual

Dutch and Australian citizenship, which in turn allowed him to have two passports, a beneficial commodity for someone in his line of work. He also had another rare commodity: loyal friends who never forgot him. One of them flew to Delhi and, through a few local contacts and with the inevitable pay off's, he managed to get his spare passport into the hands of an underpaid immigration officer who backdated an entry stamp in his Australian passport.

Two days later, Jacob signed on at the local police station and then made for the border with Nepal at Banbassa, dressed as a backpacker. They employed a French girl from one of Delhi's many backpacking hostels as a paid prop, and he crossed over before anyone realised he was gone. Two days later, he was on a plane from Kathmandu to Bangkok and then back to Holland via a few weeks on a beach in Bali. His friends had kept his money safe, and once back in Amsterdam he decided to go straight and bought the Queen Beatrix Hotel. He still did the odd dodgy deal to make his money up, but he was semi-retired and had no plans to leave Holland for the rest of his days.

"Howay, then. Let's go." said Carl, after concluding Jacob's story.

Slightly drunk and sniffing back the way coke-heads do in the cool nighttime air, they went further into the Centrum towards the Rijksmuseum. The streets were becoming more residential than commercial. They turned left onto Lijnbaansgracht for a few hundred metres until Paul realised he was walking alone. He stopped and turned to see Carl about ten meters back and standing on the deck of a houseboat, waving him back and laughing.

"Where you going?" laughed Carl. "I thought you were off for a hooker. There was canny one back there that looked like Dot Cotton!"

"Eh? I thought you were right behind me. What the fuck you doing on a boat?" asked Paul, as he reached the top of the gangway.

"I've got someone I'd like you to meet." Carl wrapped his right arm around Paul's neck and put him in a playful headlock, rubbing his knuckles on top of Paul's head, which caused him to call out in pretend pain.

Carl opened the stable type door of the houseboat. It had a glass top half and white-painted wooden bottom. They walked into an immaculate seating area with a mint green bench seat and a collection of small green cacti lining the right-hand wall. The sweet scent of vanilla filled Paul's nose. There was a 360 degree glass atrium above the old wheelhouse.

Paul shut the door behind them and wondered if anyone else was inside. He felt nervous. The feeling that Carl had bought him to Amsterdam for more than one purpose had returned and he wondered if this was it. Carl went first as they descended a set of steep wooden stairs with a sturdy rope banister into a dimly lit room. Paul's nervousness turned to fear. He felt like turning and running and tried to convince himself that it was the joint and the coke that was making him paranoid. His heart missed a beat as a figure emerged from an unseen doorway. The lights flashed on and a man with the shortest, widest neck that Paul had ever seen let out a loud half cheer as he threw his arms around Carl and hugged him. Champagne spilled from the top of the bottle he clutched in his left hand as Carl hugged him back tightly like a long-lost brother. They broke their embrace and hugged again with Paul not really knowing what to say or do, as he felt out of place.

"Carl, how the fuck are you?" the man asked.

"Fucking mint now," said Carl. "And how the fuck are you?"

They turned to face Paul, who was still lost for words.

"You must be Paul," said the short-necked man. "I'm Regan." He looked up, stretched out his equally short and powerful looking arm and winked as he and Paul shook hands.

Paul put Regan at mid to late thirties, with a large, prematurely balding head that adorned his remaining black hair and a set of overly bushy black eyebrows. To Paul he looked like a bull. Paul wasn't sure if the smile on his tanned and friendly face was genuine or not.

"Aye, I'm Paul. Nice to meet you." He was still not sure about what was going on.

"Carl's said a few good things about you. How you liking the Dam? You been over here before?"

"Nah, first time. It's fucking mint – or it has been so far."

"Aye, you'll love it, we'll gan out in a bit and I'll show you around the place. But first . . ."

Regan motioned to the beautiful white kitchen where he'd lain out an upturned china plate on the bench. On it were six generous lines of cocaine and, next to it, what Paul reckoned must have been at least another quarter ounce in one glistening rock. They snorted a line each and shared out the remaining champagne. The coke was even better than the gear that Jacob had provided.

"Is it OK to make a spliff?" Paul asked Regan.

"Aye, but smoke it on the deck. I don't like the smell of smoke in the boat."

Paul rolled himself a small joint and made his way back up the steep stairs and onto the deck above. He admired the clean linen deckchairs and the glistening glass table. Some restored winching gear had been renovated and left out as a nice-looking period piece. As he smoked the joint and looked towards the stars, he felt safe again, relieved that there appeared to be no hidden agenda. Regan had made him feel welcome, but he presumed that he wouldn't have done anything else, considering Carl had bought him over.

As Paul lay back on the deckchair looking across the canal and wondering what Lindsey was up to, he decided he wasn't going to have sex with any hookers while he was there. Even though they weren't together, he felt that if he did, he would be cheating on her.

*   *   *

What Paul didn't realise was that Carl *did* have an ulterior motive for the trip. Part of it was to have a couple of days away to relax in a way he never could at home, but the other part was to introduce Paul to Regan, so he knew who Paul was.

Carl knew that if the robbery came on top then Paul

was the weakest link, and the most likely to open his mouth when questioned. If that happened and Carl was nicked, then Regan could get involved by getting to Paul or to his family and making sure he never went anywhere near a courtroom.

Regan and Carl had grown up together in Shields and were always going to be somebodies in the criminal world; it was obvious from an early age. Carl was the toughest, even growing up. When he was in high school, he was the hardest kid there, and at thirteen he'd proven it by beating the hardest sixteen-year-old in a straight go.

Regan was no slouch either, but what he lacked in fighting ability he more than made up for in street smarts. He always had money in his pocket from thieving or selling whatever came along. He was making thirty pounds a week at thirteen, selling single cigarettes to the other kids at school. He bullied them into starting smoking and persuaded them that their mothers would never miss the coins he encouraged them to steal from their purses.

As he got older, he would pinch a car radio on the way to the pub and another on his way back to pay for his night out. The other lads, Carl included, would be spending the money they'd made from whatever scam they had going that week and would usually wake up skint on a Monday morning. Not Regan. He progressed up the usual criminal ladder from thieving to joy riding, then to ram raiding and robberies, and always before his peers.

It was common knowledge that Regan was on the run and wanted for skipping bail on a GBH charge back in Newcastle it. Word on the street was he'd beaten a man with a hammer over a drugs debt and broken one of his legs in the process. To Regan, this was par for the course in the world in which they lived. If you sold drugs and messed up then that was what happened. Everyone knew the rules when they got involved, so they shouldn't be surprised if it ended badly.

Apparently, the police and judiciary didn't see it that way and he was looking at four to six years if convicted. He'd told Carl his solicitor reckoned he had a good chance of beating the case, but he wasn't convinced and decided he was better off out of the way. He'd been on the trip with Carl when they first met Jacob and he went to see him in Amsterdam as a stop off on the way to Spain. He never left. He made his money organising drugs through Jacob and his contacts, which he sold on in Holland to his mainly Northeast acquaintances who smuggled them back to the UK. He was a distant relative of George and Kenny, and he'd lent them money to start up their drugs business from a robbery back home, money that they still mainly owed him. It wasn't the money that vexed him; he had enough of that. It was the fact that he rarely heard from them that annoyed him. He felt that they were back home enjoying the high life while he was left alone in Amsterdam.

*   *   *

Below deck, Carl and Regan were getting down to business.

"He's a good lad," said Carl, "but I just want you to meet him so you know his face, because, well . . . you never know . . . " He chopped out three lines from the lump of

Columbia's best marching powder.

"No bother," said Regan. "I'm sure he'll be fine. Seems like a canny kid. Where's he from . . . Whitley or Shields?"

"Whitley. He still lives at his mam's down the bottom end of Whitley Road. You might remember his dad . . . he was the one who got topped in the Spring Gardens a few years back. Jimmy Docherty."

"Aye, I remember him. Weren't you getting a wage off him?"

"Aye, I was. I haven't mentioned it to him cos I don't want to put him on a downer. He's still getting over it I reckon. Look, he's a pal and all that but if it comes on top, I just want you to know who he is and where to find him. I'm not worried really but . . . you know?"

Regan nodded his head. "Youse done a bit of graft like?"

Carl gave him a look that said *yes, but I'm not telling you what it was.*

"Aye, fair enough," said Regan. "I know what to do if needed. It'll be alreet. Now, get that line down you and we'll head off."

*   *   *

Paul returned from the deck to find the pair in the living room reminiscing about exploits past. "What time we heading out?" he asked.

"Now, if you like," said Regan. "Anyone need a piss before we go?"

"Aye," said Paul. Where's the bog?"

"Just through the back of the kitchen."

Paul made his way through the kitchen and into the bathroom, which was just as luxurious as the rest of the boat. As he returned, something caught his attention in the half open cupboard. He paused to make sure that his eyes weren't deceiving him, and they weren't. Stood upright with the magazine installed was a worn-looking AK-47 assault rifle. He didn't know what to do but he thought that the best course of action was to pretend he hadn't seen it. He had a feeling that the cupboard had been left open on purpose so he would see it, as a warning to remind him of the kind of people he was now involved with. People who you didn't mess around with and certainly didn't double cross.

"All done?" Regan said.

"Aye, ready to go," said Paul.

Regan put the remaining cocaine into a ziplock bag and slid it into his pocket, before heading out for a night of pleasure and excitement.

*   *   *

Joe Mayo lay stretched out with his head on the pillow, chilled and smoking a joint. The black Guinness ashtray he'd nicked from Kitty O'Sheas pub was on his chest and his concentration was half on the episode of *The Bill* being shown on ITV, the other half was on making sure he didn't get any bombers on his new Naf Naf t-shirt. Joe didn't have much, but as long as he had food in his belly and a roof over his head, he was content. He was a bit of a loner and spent most of his days stoned.

There was a knock on the door, and he reached down with the ashtray and put it on the floor. Lifting himself up, he grabbed two tenner deals of hash from the coffee table. Some of his punters were friends and came in for a spliff, but some of them he only knew by sight, so he served them at the door. He tied his long unkempt, black hair into a ponytail and walked down the passageway. As he opened the frosted glass door to the porch, he saw three figures standing outside. He unlocked it and was greeted by the Taylors and their friend, Matty McKay. All three just stood there and said nothing.

"Alright lads, what's happening?" Joe asked, sensing this wasn't going to be a beneficial visit.

"It's taxing time," said Matty. He pushed past Joe and into the passageway, followed by Mark and Liam.

"Eh? You fucking what?" A sense of how *un*beneficial a visit this was likely to be was growing.

"Lock the fucking door!" ordered Liam.

Joe did what he was told.

Mark and Matty checked the bedroom and bathroom to confirm there was nobody there and then joined Joe and Liam in the smokey front room.

Joe didn't know what to say or do but, whatever he did, it was best that he didn't upset them; their reputations for violence proceeded them by a long way. His eyes followed Mark as he opened the kitchen door and had a quick look behind it before turning to face him again. Then he looked over to where Matty stood, staring into his eyes and straight down the barrel of a black automatic handgun. Joe had only seen one handgun before. It was an old rusty .22 calibre revolver with no trigger guard that one of the Shields lads had shown him, but this was in a different league and looked reasonably new. He was surprised that he wasn't scared and found it a bit pathetic that these three big lumps thought they would need a gun to scare him. It didn't impress him one bit.

"Right, here's the crack . . ." said Mark. "You're selling for us now. We're taking over and the Bolton's are out."

"I don't get gear off the Boltons," said Joe. "I get it off Carl."

The taxmen all looked at each other. Joe presumed they'd just discovered something they didn't know. Perhaps they were wondering whether they had made a big mistake.

"I don't give a fuck who you get your gear off!" yelled Matty. "You get it off us now, Understand? Want me to shoot you in the knee, you little arsehole? Get your pants off!"

Joe decided that the guy had obviously watched too many films.

"Put it away man, there's no need for that." Joe, shook his head at Matty like a father disappointed with his son.

Liam picked half a dozen deals off the table. "Where's the rest of the gear?" he said. "Don't tell us that's it."

"Thats all I've got," lied Joe. "I swear down." There was another two ounces stashed under the floorboards in the bathroom.

"What, that's it?" Mark slapped Joe then grabbed him and pushed him up against the wall, ripping the cloth on his new t-shirt.

Joe started to get frightened. "That's it. I swear," he whimpered. He wasn't sure whether it would be best to start crying for sympathy in the hope that they'd leave him alone or if it would have the opposite effect and encourage them more. Considering they were the typical playground bullies who got pleasure from making people feel weak he reasoned that it would probably be the latter.

"You're full of shit," said Matty, before hitting him over the head with the butt of the pistol.

Then he cocked it.

The sound of the bullet entering the chamber made Joe switch from being nervous to being completely terrified. Blood began to mix slowly into his matted ponytail.

"Just shoot him in the leg," said Mark, nonchalantly.

"Ok." Matty pointed the gun at Joe's right knee.

"No, no don't!" screamed Joe. "The gear's in the bathroom. Under the floor!" He cried the tears of a petrified man as he wiped the drops of blood from his face.

"Show us, then!" Mark ordered. He dragged Joe into the bathroom where he knelt down, pulled back the carpet and lifted up a floorboard.

"Careful!" Matty hissed, as Joe stretched out his arm for the package.

"Look, I'm out," Joe said. "I can't be doing with this shit. If you're having a war with the Bolton's, or Carl, I'm not getting stuck in the middle of it. Fuck that. Take the hash, but I'm out."

"Why?" said Matty. "You'll sell for Carl but not for us? Here's the crack . . . If you don't take it from us we'll kick fuck out of you and take everything you own. Understand? And every time we see you, you'll be getting a slap as well."

"Ok, ok. I'll take stuff off you," said Joe. "Just go and leave us alone." He was shaking and not wanting to look anyone in the eye. He stared at the floor. All he wanted was to get this trio of maniacs out of the house as quickly as he could.

"Right," said Mark, "we'll be in touch. And don't go making any phone calls. We've still got a few more visits to make." He turned and let himself out, followed by the others.

Joe rubbed his hands down his face and through his hair as he contemplated what to do. He only sold hash to keep himself stoned and to pay for a couple of nights out a month. He didn't fancy getting stuck in the middle of a gangster war. He sat on the settee and looked at the table where a few minutes earlier there was a small pile of hash and wondered what to do next. Reaching down he took the half smoked joint from the ashtray and lit it at the third attempt. His hands shook and he wondered whether he should warn the other dealers he knew or keep his mouth shut like Mark had told him. He decided that he would do as Mark said. But he'd make one call. And that was to Carl.

* * *

It was around nine o'clock when Kenny Reid's phone rang,

and it slightly annoyed him that he hadn't finished his chicken Madras when it did. It was George on the other end, and he was very serious and to the point. He didn't sound angry, just very abrupt and businesslike. There was always something that required their attention from the regular problems thrown up by protection and drug dealing. But this was different: someone was trying to take over. It was the first time that someone had made a serious attempt. They'd had people tax the odd dealer here and there or cause trouble in the bars, but never like this.

Though it wasn't expected, somehow they always knew that this day would come. Every dog had its day and there was always someone waiting in the shadows and dreaming of taking everything from them, just the way they'd done themselves almost two decades earlier. George had fought and beaten Iain Palmer for control of the doors in Whitley and then he'd beaten the gypsy bare knuckle fighter that Iain had paid to get them back. They'd had a half serious attempt on them two years earlier by a couple of brothers from Wallsend, but they backed off after both their houses were set on fire in the same week.

George kept the details off the phone and they met at their pre-arranged place in the car park at the end of the Beehive Road. It was a place they sometimes met when there was trouble, where it was unlikely they'd be seen or heard.

Kenny pulled into the car park and saw that George was already there, sitting on the bonnet of his green 325i BMW. As he pulled up next to him, he looked behind, ready to grab the sword and ammonia bottle from the passenger seat if anyone else pulled in.

"What's happening? What these cunts been up to?" Kenny asked George.

"They've taxed pretty much everybody," George said. "Craig's gone into hiding, so the gear's safe. They went to his first and the lad down the street phoned him to tell him cos he knows we've got a rick, and he hasn't been home since. He's fucked off to the Lakes for a few days to keep out the way."

"Who's been taxed?" asked Kenny.

"Everybody in Whitley. They've even been to the dykes. I'm surprised Emily didn't do the three of them. Taxing birds with guns . . . fucking terrible."

"Three? Who's the three? They pulled a gun on Emily and Tracey?"

"Nah, I don't think they pulled it out on them. But they did with everyone else. And, aye, three . . . Mark and Liam Taylor – and Matty McKay."

"Matty McKay? What the fuck's it got to do with him?"

"Dunno. Probably saw an opportunity to play at being a gangster. You know what he's like – thinks he's Shields's answer to Pablo fucking Escobar. But don't worry . . . we'll do him as well as the other two."

"Any more involved?" Kenny asked.

"Not so far but we'll see who comes out of the woodwork. There's bound to be a few cling-ons turn up as well."

"So, what's the plan, then? There's no point getting the guns out straight away. The bizzies will know by now and they'll be waiting for us to fuck up."

"Aye, you're right," said George. "We'll have to bide our time and see. We'll give it a few days and then go and see everyone and remind them we're not going anywhere. If these pricks want a war, we'll just have to give them one. But we've got to be careful. For one, we can't terrorise all the dealers in case they side with them. For another, we can't put ourselves in a position where we'll get lifted."

"What about Carl? Have they taxed any of his punters?"

"Not sure. As far as I know they haven't, but you never know. There's no problems between them that I know of, but if they do have one then we'll see if he wants to join up with us. But, for now, we'll stay out of their way. Those CID wankers would love to see us in Durham jail and I'm not giving them the opportunity to put us there."

"We could always pay someone to shoot Mark," suggested Kenny. If he's out of the way, the others will just fold."

"One thing at a time. I've thought of that, but let's wait and see. They'll fuck up sooner or later, and when they do we'll be on them. Where you staying tonight?"

"At that bird's flat in Blyth, the one from the Snake Pit last week, remember? She's a straight goer and she knows nobody – and nobody knows her either."

"Aye, nice arse, her, like. Just be careful. And if you see them bastards ring us straight away – and Rob. He'll be along as well."

"Murray?"

"Aye, Rob Murray. I've spoken to him and he's with

us all the way. Knows which side his bread's best buttered on, I suppose. Right, I'm gonna go. Take care and watch out."

The cousins shook hands and parted. They got into their respective cars and locked them from the inside in case any unwanted visitors tried to get in and do them harm. Neither would stay at home for the next few days and the wives, girlfriends, family members and close friends were warned to look out for the Taylors. It was surprisingly easy for trouble to spread to their acquaintances because the people on the other side had no moral compass; but, for that matter, neither did they.

Paranoia set in. No matter how big or how hard they were, in such times it paid to look over their shoulders. Constantly anxious, edgy and nervous, they would look to see who's pulled up outside, glancing through the curtains. They'd keep the car out of the middle lane so they always had an escape route. Doors would be always be locked and they'd be in constant reach of a weapon. They would trust nobody and be suspicious of everybody, wondering if the innocuous comment made in conversation was someone fishing for information to set them up or do them harm. Their circle would shrink but it was small anyway. They still had the trusted few who would never roll over or change sides for the Taylors.

Or did they?

That was the part that they couldn't be sure of as they lay their heads on their pillows that night with the same thoughts swirling around in their brains. What was the best way to deal with this without getting locked up or shot?

Was this the beginning of the end and would they end up with nothing, like Iain Palmer had almost overnight? *Or would they come out on top again?*

They knew the streets were watching, and so were the police.

5: CRAZY ON THE WALTZER

Sharon Manstone loved a bit of action, she'd heard about a regime change taking place in the local drugs world and she was salivating about being amongst the fray, excited at the prospect of nicking the major players. She was hoping to catch them with guns. Her bosses liked getting guns off the street; it made for good headlines, which generally meant promotion for everyone.

There was a buzz in the air in the CID offices of North Shields Police Station that afternoon.

"Right then!" she shouted into the busy office – at everybody and nobody in particular. "What's the latest with the dealers?"

A dozen detectives stopped and looked towards her. Nobody wanting to be the first to speak up. Gibbo broke the ice.

"I've heard the Taylor brothers and their lot have been running around robbing all the drug dealers. They're making a play to take over from the Boltons."

"Where'd you hear that from, Gibbo?" she asked.

"Just around. From one of my snitches and from a couple of informal enquires."

"I've heard the same," added Cookie.

"Good work," said Sharon. So it's not a rumour, then. This could turn nasty. I wouldn't expect the Boltons or Liddle to keep quiet about this one. But when it all kicks off, make sure we're there to pick up the pieces. Getting any of those three off the streets is the main priority at this time and hopefully anyone else who's involved. I've had a word with them upstairs and our strategy is to wait, monitor the situation and see what happens. There hasn't been any complaints or reports of violence so far but that doesn't mean it hasn't or won't happen. And, when it does, we need to be ready to react quickly and nick whoever's involved. Remember . . . the quicker we secure the crime scene and the witnesses, the more chance we have of getting these thugs in a courtroom. Press your informants. Ask plenty of questions. I want all information on this to be as up to date as possible." She could have phrased it another way: Northumbria Police had decided to give them all enough rope to hang themselves with.

"Are we getting any outside help?" Cookie referred to any other branches of Northumbria Police who may be getting involved. Cookie didn't want help; he wanted to know if anyone else would be investigating, and if there would be any information unavailable to him that he couldn't pass onto Mark.

"Not at this time, Cookie," she replied. But if there's anyone we need to liaise with I'll let you all know. There's a possibility that in the future there might be, but not at this time."

"Are uniform involved?" Gibbo asked.

"Again, not at this time directly but they will be briefed. If there's any reports of violence – especially shootings – they must be attended to as a matter of priority and the crime scene secured for forensics. Quickly. After any injured parties have been seen to, obviously."

"Has anyone seen the Boltons or Liddle around?"

Cookie asked for his own information.

"Not as far as I know, but any sightings of them need to be reported and logged, and uniform will be told the same. So, keep your eyes and ears open and report anything you see or hear. This is a golden opportunity to get some very bad people off the streets. Let's go out there and do it. As a team." There was a rustling of paperwork as the chatter of voices returned to fill the room. "And one other thing . . . we will be requiring a two-man nightshift, which will be paid at overtime rate and will not be voluntary. And all of you lovely people will be taking a turn."

Everybody looked at her and collectively groaned.

* * *

Paul and Carl walked out of Newcastle Airport and climbed into a black saloon taxi. Paul would have been happy to get the Metro home, but seeing as Carl was picking up the fare he didn't object. It had been one of the best weekends of his life and he was disappointed that it was over. Now they were back on Tyneside and the life they led.

"You coming back to mine?" Carl asked.

"I was gonna go home. Why, what you up to?"

"Nowt. Just thought you'd fancy coming back to mine for a bit." His tone that told Paul he was coming back to his.

"Aye, why not? Not much else doing on a Monday afternoon."

The rest of the journey was spent in silence. Paul sat in the front seat and Carl in the back. They kept quiet in taxis in case the driver knew people that they did, and in case they were nicked over anything. It was one less witness to recount their conversation in court. Carl always travelled in the back, it made it harder for anyone to see him and it gave him two exits in case trouble arose.

They pulled up outside Carl's flat. Carl paid the driver with a £20 note and told him to keep the change with a smile and a nod. They both looked up and down the street, a common practice when they entered or left anywhere, and Carl unlocked the front door with two mortice locks and one Yale. Some people said he was overly paranoid; Carl called it careful. He purposely lived in an upstairs flat and his reasoning was that nobody could shoot him in his bed while he slept.

Carl dropped his bag and headed through the plush and modernly decorated flat and went to use the toilet. Paul had visited many times and was still impressed by it each time he walked in. This was the standard of living he aspired to. Everything spoke of money and good taste. Expensive furniture from Barker and Stonehouse and top-quality electrical goods, plush carpets and tasteful soft furnishings adorned the rooms of the two-bedroomed flat.

"There should be a couple of beers in the fridge!" shouted Carl from the bathroom. "Get them out!"

"Aye, no bother, man." replied Paul.

He made his way to the kitchen to get them and as he opened the fridge and removed them, he noted the three bottles of Moet & Chandon chilling on the middle shelf.

"Sit yersell down! I'll be there in a minute!"

"Already have," said Paul. He sank into the plush

leather settee and admired the room again.

Having changed his clothes, Carl returned a few minutes later with a big smile on his face and a carrier bag in his hand. He tossed the bag over to Paul.

"What's this?" Paul said.

"Have a look. It's yours." Carl mimed pulling down a ski mask and pointing a shotgun towards Paul. Paul looked back at him and smiled, and then opened the bag and peered inside to see a fat bundle of bank notes held together with elastic bands.

"How much?" he asked Carl.

"Seven and a half. Don't buy anything flash and don't let on you have it. Use it for day-to-day money so you don't have to go out thieving for a bit. But listen . . . there's a few things going on that you don't know about and might get dragged into because you hang about with me. It's nothing to worry about too much, but I don't want you getting caught up in it."

"Like what?" asked Paul, apprehensively.

"The Taylors have taxed all of George and Kenny's punters while we were in the Dam, and they reckon they're taking over. They've taxed Joe Mayo as well and he works for me, so things might get a little heavy. Watch out, that's all. If anyone gives you any grief just give us a ring and I'll be straight over."

"OK, so what shall I do?" asked Paul nervously.

"Nothing. Watch your back, just in case, but I doubt they'll come after you. They'll have to get through me first." Carl gave him a wink. "So, what you going to do with that?" He nodded towards the carrier bag.

"Think I'll get a flat and get out of my mam's. I'll get the social to pay for it, but I'll have enough for the deposit and to do it out nice like this. Nice telly and hi-fi. Probably get a little runaround as well."

"Fuck me, it'll be gone in a week. But seriously . . . don't go splashing out and drawing attention to yourself. Get a flat if you like but spend the rest slowly. Don't start running around town like Billy Big Balls, OK? It'll only bring attention."

Paul finished his beer and phoned a taxi. He was starting to feel uneasy and a little paranoid now. He was still hungover from the weekend's drink and drugs and the thought of being caught up between Carl and the Taylor's wasn't too appealing. He took the taxi to Lindsey's flat, and on the way there he thought about what she kept saying about getting out of the criminal life. The money he carried was enough to keep him going until he found a job – if he could find a job with no skills or qualifications. The news reporters talked of an economic recession, which he didn't fully understand, but he took it to mean that there was little in the way of work or opportunities for the younger generation. He secretly envied some of his school friends who led normal lives and he would love to live one too. But no matter how much he longed for it he couldn't stop thinking about finding out who killed his dad, and he believed that staying close to Carl gave him his best chance.

When Paul entered Lindsey's flat, it was obvious that she knew something was up. She knew him like she knew herself and could tell that he was acting differently, and not because he was on a come-down from the weekend. They smiled and kissed on the doorstep like they always did and Paul followed her into the poorly lit kitchen. He sat down at the plain wooden table on a matching chair, which rocked slightly on its uneven legs. "Where's Jason?" he asked.

"He's at me mam's house. Why? What's up? Come on, out with it. Something's up, I can tell,"

"Listen . . . there's something I need you to do, and you've got to keep it to yourself – you can't tell anyone." He unzipped his bag and removed the carrier bag with the cash.

"What's that?" she asked.

"I need you to keep this safe. I can't keep it at home in case the bizzies turn up, and you can't tell anyone it's here. Promise me." He reached into the carrier bag and showed Lindsey the wad of banknotes, which was more cash than either of them had seen in one place before.

"Fucking hell, how much is there?" she asked.

"Seven and a half grand, but you can't tell–"

"I know. You said. So, what the fuck did you do to get that?" Her voice rose an octave. "Tell me you didn't hurt anyone for it!"

"No, no. Look, I can't tell you, but it's OK. Nobody got hurt. Trust me. I just need you to keep it safe, but I can't tell you where I got it. You understand, don't you?"

"Is it yours? I won't be able to sleep at night knowing that's here." She looked towards the ceiling and bit the left side of her lower lip, something she did when she was nervous.

"Nobody knows I've got it and nobody knows it's here. It's not like you're going to get raided, is it? And I'll give you a drink for keeping it."

She thought for a second and agreed to hide it. Partly, she said, because it was Paul and partly because she needed to pay some bills and buy a few things for Jason.

He counted out two thousand pounds onto the table and split it into two piles: five hundred for Lindsey and fifteen hundred for himself. He knew he was being overgenerous but he wanted to make sure that she and Jason were taken care of. The rest was hidden under a floorboard in the utility cupboard. He reassured her again that it would be OK and they returned to the kitchen, where Lindsey made him a hot cup of coffee, which his head sorely needed.

"So, what you going to do with that?" She nodded her blonde head in the direction of the bathroom.

"Get sorted with a flat and buy a car. I think and have enough to see us until I get a job." He knew fine well that the latter part might not happen. The reality was that, although he'd like a job and to sort his life out, he would most likely spend and smoke his way through it and be back to square one inside a couple of months.

"I hope you do, Paul. You need to get away from all this. I don't know what you did for it and I'm probably best off not knowing, but you need to get away from Carl. I know he's your mate, but he's not going to do your life any good. Not in the long term."

"Don't worry, it's all cush man. And, anyways, I brought a bit of this back from the Dam. Good gear this," he replied, deliberately changing the subject. He smiled and gave her a cheeky wink; it was one of her pet hates and something he only did to wind her up. He showed her a small lump of Afghan hash he'd kept in his mouth going through customs.

"Amsterdam? How long were you there for?"

"Just a couple of nights. Mint place, if you've never been. Howay, get sorted and I'll tell you all about it on the way to Whitley."

As he rolled the spliff he knew she was right and the thoughts he'd had in the taxi continued to swirl around his head along with the THC. They spent the remainder of the day visiting Estate Agents along Park View to look for a flat and found one on Eskdale Terrace in Cullercoats that was happy to take DSS. It was only one bedroom but that was all he needed. He paid two months' rent up front and a month's as a deposit on the spot. It was perfect for him because the street was so quiet that any unwanted police or villains could be seen hanging around the front. There were also plenty of ways back through the warren of streets in Cullercoats village that would make it hard for anyone to follow him home. They lunched at Pane-e-Vinos and shopped at Kings and Dukes, like they were a real couple, then made their way back to Lindsey's flat arm in arm. He'd only had the cash a few hours and his seven and a half grand was down to five after the flat and the clothes were paid for. Perhaps it wouldn't last as long as he'd thought.

But he would leave worrying about money for another day.

* * *

Kenny pulled up outside George's back door in his Audi 80 and he looked into his rear-view mirror. He'd traded in his BMW a few days earlier for the more discrete motor to keep one step ahead of the police and his enemies. He kept the car in gear with the clutch depressed and kept the engine running so he was ready to take off at any sign of danger.

George's back door opened inside a minute and out he came, stopping only to lock the back door. As he got to the gate, Kenny reached across and opened the front passenger door so that George didn't have to. This was something they'd did automatically and had done for years. The seconds it would take to open it could mean the difference between a getaway, a bullet or getting arrested. They were both on edge, alert for the police and the Taylor gang, tooled up and ready for trouble. George had a Rambo knife in his jacket and Kenny had a lock knife in the door pocket along with a Fairy Liquid bottle full of ammonia. There was a baseball bat in the boot, along with a ball to explain its presence.

They pulled away silently into the evening traffic and George adjusted the passenger side mirror so he could see if anyone was following them. They could spot other villains easily, but not always the police. But there seemed to be no tail behind them; no Taylors and no CID.

They drove out of Whitley Bay and up to Blyth, taking the long straight roads, doubling back to see if there were any suspicious cars and to throw off any tails. They drove through Seaton Delaval before continuing to Morpeth, all the while watching and hardly saying a word. After an hour they were sure they weren't being followed and decided it was safe to head back to the coast. With darkness now upon them, they drove off the main road, into Backworth Business Park and straight into the open doors of an industrial unit, which Rob Murray closed behind them.

Rob was from Shields. He looked like Freddie Kruger: tall and slim with a drawn-in, pock-marked face, which held a pair of cold beady eyes and a slightly pointy nose. He had a longstanding friendship with the cousins. He was a few years older than them, and they often asked him for advice because he was a lifelong criminal and jailbird who knew every villain on Tyneside. He had the connections to get you anything you wanted: guns, drugs, hookers, stolen cars. You name it; Rob could get it. He was always tooled up with a knife and quite often a gun.

A young lad sat in a van with a mobile phone watching for any police pulling into the estate. His job was to pull the van out and block the entrance to slow the police down and then phone Rob on his burner phone. By the time the police dragged him out the van, the trio would have escaped across the fields and into Rob's car, which was parked up in a nearby street. The lad wasn't told who Rob was meeting or what for, and as long as he was getting paid, he didn't really care.

They alighted into a dimly lit, dirty lock up, which in a previous life had been a small car repair shop. Oil and grease was all that was left of the previous business, along with a few rusting tool cabinets and a filthy workbench.

"Alright Rob, all good?" said George.

"Yeah, all good, George . . . Kenny . . . How are we

tonight?"

"Not bad," George answered curtly. "You bring the stuff?"

Rob opened the tool cupboard and removed a long blue canvas bag, which made metallic knocking sounds as he laid it on the oily wooden workbench.

"So, what have you heard?" asked George.

"Right. Mark Taylor's supposed to be in love with this hooker up the town. Apparently, he sees her about three times a week and always at night. Some blonde eastern European piece, or so I'm told."

"And you know this how?" said George.

"Let's just say I have it on good authority. You know me . . ." Rob grinned. "I made a few enquiries." *he replied smiling.*

"So, can we get to him?" asked Kenny.

"Aye. It's in a perfect place. When you come out you come down the stairs and into a back alley and you need to walk about fifty yards to the main road. They kick off if anyone parks the car out the back, so they make everyone park away from the flat. It's a very classy joint."

"And you know this how?" Kenny teased, mocking George's previous remark.

Rob ignored him and continued. "At the end of the alley on the main road there's a big advertising hoarding with bushes underneath. It's perfect for someone to hide in and jump out and shoot the fucker. You can't see in at night for the lights on the top and there's plenty of light in the street to see who's walking past. Once he's been done, the shooter can leg it through the park across the road and away."

"And how do we know when he's going to be there?" asked George.

"We don't. What we'll do is just keep driving past, and when we find his car parked up we'll know he's there. He's not in and out, so there should be plenty of time to get someone in place."

"And who's going to do it?" asked George.

"I'm working on that one," said Rob. "It's not like I have hitmen lined up in my kitchen. I have someone in mind, but you're best off not knowing who he is. He's reliable, and he'll keep his trap shut if it comes on top."

"How much?" asked Kenny.

"Fifteen grand – and that's to kneecap him, not kill him."

"Bit steep that," said George. Both he and Kenny knew fine well that Rob would be taking a wage off the top.

"Maybe. But it'll be worth it in the long run."

George and Kenny nodded in agreement and turned their attention to the bag. "Did you bring everything?" Kenny asked Rob.

"Aye, that's the lot. I'll take back what you don't want but that's everything we have."

Kenny put on a pair of bright yellow Marigold gloves, which looked out of place in the dirty lock up and opened the bag. Inside there were two sawn off shotguns and four handguns, two of which were revolvers and two automatics. He took out the two revolvers and passed one to George who now sported a pair of leather gloves.

"Do you want one?" George asked Rob.

"Nah, I've got my own." He lifted the left side of his jacket to show them the pistol he kept in a shoulder harness.

"Might have known," said Kenny with a wry smile.

"Do we need to supply the gun?" George asked Rob.

"Yeah, I'll give him couple of these. He can knock him down with the shotty and put a few in his legs with the handgun when he's down."

"Sound's good," said George.

"Are yous keeping them?" Rob asked about the revolvers.

"Aye. We want to have them close at hand in case we need them in a hurry, and I've got a feeling we will unless we can get to Mark and his mob first."

Rob nodded. "Very wise, very wise," he said slowly. He reached inside the bag and removed a small, black, drawstring pouch and poured some bullets out onto the table. "No good without these."

George moved towards the table, lifted the revolver up in front of him and pressed the release catch with his right thumb. The cylindrical barrel slid open as he flicked his wrist to the left. He blew down the cylinder and then the barrel and then loaded six .38 calibre bullets into the chambers before closing the gun back up with his left hand. He scooped up six more from the table and put them loosely into his left jacket pocket before checking the gun's safety was on. Kenny followed suit and did the same.

"Right, then," said George. "Get these doors open and we're off."

"Keep us posted when it's going to happen," said

Kenny. "We'll need to get an alibi sorted out, even if it's just sitting in McDonald's under the cameras."

"Will do and stay safe," said Rob.

Rob unlocked the doors, and the duo went off into the night. They knew Rob was right: fifteen grand was a price worth paying to bring Mark and his little gang of upstarts down a peg or two. It wasn't just the price of getting Mark out of their hair, it also sent a message to anyone else who was brave enough to try to take what they had spent ten years building. As they drove out of the estate, the lookout turned his head and pretended not to see them, but he knew who they were, even without seeing their faces.

"So, what we doing now?" Kenny asked George.

"We'll have a drive around. See if we can catch any of these fuckers kicking about."

"Right, then . . . where first?"

"Down to Shields and drive past their houses – see if we can catch them out and about. I'm not knocking on doors, but we might get lucky. Drive past Mark's place and then down the bottom end of Shields. I'm not sure exactly where Liam lives but it's down by the Pan Shop somewhere, in one of them streets. Then go by McKay's place in Howdon. Hopefully we can catch that twat out as well. Then we'll try the bars. Matty drinks in the Woolsington and sometimes in the Dun Cow. He's shagging one of the barmaids there, or so I'm told."

"Sounds good to me," said Kenny.

They crawled past each target house, hunting their pray and finding nothing. George went to the Dun Cow and looked around. The punter's faces dropped, and they stared into their pints as they saw him enter, not wanting to be involved with whatever it was that brought him in that night. He stared at the barmaid Matty was seeing, which put the fear of God into her. She couldn't have been more than twenty. Short, red-headed and innocent-looking, she knew what he was doing there and she started to shake with fear. He looked straight through her and left without saying a word.

Back into Shields they went, visiting the locations again, looking at the cars driving by for one they recognised, parking up and staring at the windows of their target's houses, all of which had the curtains drawn to keep out prying eyes. They drove around the adjacent streets hoping to see a familiar car. If they couldn't inflict any damage to a person, a car would be the next best thing.

The clock on the dash flicked to 10p.m. as they cruised slowly past Matty's house for the second time that night.

"Where are these fuckers?" Kenny said.

"Dunno," said George. "Probably in hiding. We'll try the Woolsington, and if nobody's there we'll call it a night."

The stinking incinerator loomed large as they carried on their hunt towards Shields. They took a right at the roundabout, along Waterville Road and through the Meadow Well Estate then right under the Metro lines and past the giant gas storage tanks that cast a moonlit shadow over the surrounding houses. Stopping at the junction, they scanned the road left and right and again in the mirrors before continuing to their second pub stop of the night.

Reaching the bar, they turned left, and parked the car halfway up Appleby Street between the streetlights so that nobody could tell the make or model. The lane was deserted and silent, the yards and industrial units were closed for the night and the only sign of life was from the light that shone out from the windows of the Woolsington pub.

"Should we take the guns or leave them here?" George said. "What do you reckon?"

"Take them," said Kenny. "If he's in there, there's a good chance he's gonna be tooled up."

"Aye, good point," said George. He tucked his pistol into the waistband of his jeans and zipped up his jacket as he alighted from the car. Kenny took his gun from the door pocket, checked the safety was on and slid it into the left-hand pocket of his coat. He looked up and down the street, scanning the dark corners for surprises.

The Woolsington was a haunt of Shields's criminal class and somewhere that was guaranteed to have a lock-in on a Sunday afternoon. The manager was easy going and, provided that drugs weren't openly consumed in the bar, he didn't complain too much. He was smart enough to know that if it wasn't for the criminal clientele then he wouldn't have any clientele at all. Not everyone who drank there was a villain, but the ones who weren't were either on the dole or fiddling it. It wasn't a pub for straight goers and didn't get much in the way of passing trade. There weren't too many people who would drink in a dirty boozer down a back lane on an industrial estate in Shields.

George looked through the windows, scanning for their quarry in the bar, but Matty wasn't among them. They passed under the big blue star of Newcastle Breweries that hung above the main entrance as they walked in.

The bar room smelled of stale beer and was fusty from a lack of fresh air. The long wooden counter stretched out in front of them, curved at one end with a bored-looking barman standing behind it polishing glasses with a white towel. An old Chas and Dave record played from the jukebox. Across from the barman on a long bench sat a variety of punters who looked like they'd been there since opening time. Some were alone and nursing pints of half flat beer, three middle-aged men who looked about ten years older than they were sat discussing the latest goings on at Newcastle United. A skinny grey dog lay on the sticky carpet at the feet of one of them. It looked up at Kenny before returning its disinterested and slender head to its original position. A young couple were in the window seats, chatting away and holding hands as they sipped away at the dark brown liquid in their glasses. The barman looked up towards George and Kenny and gave them a friendly nod.

Kenny moved to the left and through the double doors to the lounge, he returned a few seconds later and shook his head. "Nobody here by the look of it."

"Let's check the bogs then we'll go."

They made their way to the toilets. George went in and found them empty, but he pushed open each stall in turn just to make sure. He returned to Kenny and they made their way back through the bar to the exit, disappointed that their hunt had turned out to be a fruitless one.

"For fuck's sake, that was a waste of a night," George

said to Kenny, as they rounded the pub's corner and walked back towards the car.

"Aye, never mind. There's always tomorrow." replied Kenny optimistically.

Crack! Crack! Two shots rang out, breaking the silence of the night.

Instinctively, they both hunched down. George ran towards the car. Kenny ran left and flattened his back against the railings of a scrapyard gate. He peeked around the corner, looking back towards the pub, as he pulled out the pistol from his coat. George didn't make it to the car; he hid behind a large industrial waste bin. He lay down, looking back towards where they'd come from, and drew his gun from his waistband. Another shot rang out, which just missed George's head. He saw the muzzle flash this time and ran around to the other side of the bin. "The other way!" he shouted to Kenny, who by this time had turned around as well.

Crack! Another shot erupted towards them and they saw the gunman's head disappear back around the corner. George got a shot off, but it missed the unseen sniper and flew away into the night.

Crack! The bullet whizzed down the street causing them to duck again, but they regained their composure and fired back a volley of shots, a couple of which hit the wall close to their would be assassin. That was enough for him; it was one thing doing the shooting, but it was another to be on the receiving end, so he turned and ran. George heard the running footsteps getting fainter. "Let's go!" he shouted, as he sprinted towards the corner and after the shooter.

Kenny ran behind him and stopped at the car, pulling open the door and diving into the driver's seat. He fumbled with the key as he tried to get it into the ignition, his shaking hand managed it at the third attempt. It was the first time either of them had been shot at, and it wasn't like it was in the films, the adrenaline wasn't pumping from excitement, it was pumping through fear.

George ran as fast as his bulk would allow. He sprinted around the corner without a thought to his own safety and almost to the junction with Lawson Street. As he reached the corner, he saw Matty jump into his blue Renault 5 GT Turbo. Unlike Kenny, he managed to start it first time and pulled away with screeching tyres. Kenny pulled up next to George, who ran around the back of the car and threw himself into the passenger seat.

"Left, left, left!" George shouted, as they took off in hot pursuit.

They just caught sight of the smaller and nimbler Renault turning right and back towards the main road. They hid their faces from the eyes which peered out from the sanctuary of their homes as they flew past. The garages and yards could be noisy during the day but by evening this was a quiet part of town. Tonight, it had been caught up in coastal gangster business, and the residents had naturally looked out when they'd heard the shots.

By the time they'd reached the main road, there was no sight of Matty; he'd escaped to live another day, just like them.

They turned left and then right and drove back past the gas storage tanks and away, Kenny flicked on the headlights.

"Fucking hell, that was fun!" George said, as he tucked his pistol away.

"Aye, I'm fucking buzzing," said Kenny.

If truth be told they were both scared but dared not to show it. Thankfully they hadn't been hit and, as far as they knew, neither had Matty. They hadn't seen his face, but they knew it was him and they were glad he was a bad shot. Violence had been routine to them since their teenage years and they'd owned guns since their twenties, but this was the first time they'd shot one in anger and, deep down, they hoped it would be the last.

* * *

Matty didn't go straight home; he stopped at his brother's house to wash his body down with petrol to remove any forensics, change his clothes and get showered. Afterwards, he borrowed his brother's car and headed off to a hotel for a few days in case the police came calling. The clothes he was wearing would be burnt that night and the car sent for a valet to remove any microscopic link to the shooting. His brother hid the gun at his girlfriend's house without her knowing. Matty placed a call to Mark to tell him what had happened. He sounded surprised and impressed at the same time. "It takes a big pair of balls to have a shootout with two people on your own."

"It was just Round One." Matty, imagined he was Tony Montana in *Scarface*.

"Yeah, we'll get these wankers," said Mark. "They

need to realise we're not going anywhere. Whitley's ours now and there's no way they're getting it back."

"I'm going to stay out of the way for a few days," said Matty. Giz a bell if there's any more developments."

"Will do. I've arranged to meet with Carl about taxing that Joe. He can fuck off as well – taking no shit off nobody. Carl can do his thing in Shields and we'll carry on in Whitley."

"You giving him the gear back?"

"Not sure. Depends what he goes on like when I see him. I'll see."

"OK, then," said Matty. "Stay safe."

"You too."

Matty put the phone down and thought about Mark meeting Carl. He knew that if Carl didn't get the gear back and Mark didn't make things right between them then it would be another problem that they could well do without. Trouble with the Boltons was one thing, but having a pissed off Carl coming at them at the same time could be more than they could handle.

* * *

Gibbo and Cookie were on the night shift. It had been a quiet evening and they were the only two CID officers on duty. Ordinarily they didn't work nights, but because of the trouble in gangland they were stuck on the graveyard shift. They got the call around 10pm, a report of a possible shooting down by Lawson Street. This irritated Cookie, as he'd been hoping for a quiet night. Mark hadn't been in touch to warn him something was about to go off and he wasn't happy at all. He felt the anger slowly build inside him as Gibbo grabbed his radio from the charger and made his way to the door.

"Two minutes," said Cookie. "I need to take a piss."

"No bother mate," said Gibbo. "I'll get the car ready."

Cookie took a quick diversion into the men's room and closed the door. He reached inside his jacket and took out an orange plastic pill bottle. Popping the top quietly, he pulled out the sponge that he kept in it to stop anyone hearing the rattle and tipped the contents into his hand. *Fuck!* A single white tablet fell into his palm. He'd forgotten to top up the bottle before he left the house. As he swallowed back the lone pill dry, he hoped that one would be enough to see him through to 7am.

A few minutes later, they pulled out of the station car park and made the short journey to the bottom end of Shields. They weren't the first car to reach the scene; two marked police cars were already there and parked up at either end of Lawson Street. For all they knew, the gunman could still be in the area but, seeing as it was fifteen minutes since the first phone call came in, they both doubted that to be true. There were no witnesses to the actual shooting but some of the residents had heard the shots and had seen the getaway cars and phoned it in. One lady saw the cars fly by but couldn't give an accurate description. Another saw one car and another two. One said they were green and another red. Not much for them to go on.

Most locals wouldn't talk to the police; they'd grown up indoctrinated that the force was bad and not to be trusted. *Always keep your mouth* shut was widely considered to be the best course of action.

Both detectives took a walk down Appleby Street to the Woolsington, past where the shooting had been. The drinkers in the pub "saw and heard nothing", as had the bar manager – they knew better than to make it their business. Cookie and Gibbo scanned the ground with their torches, but to no avail: no spent cartridges, no footprints or tyre marks showed up on the wet ground. As they reached the corner, Gibbo pointed at some marks which looked as if bullets had impacted into the brickwork.

"Looks like there was a bit of action here tonight." Cookie said.

"Aye, it sure does," said Gibbo. "Not very good shots were they? So, what do we do with this, then?"

"Fuck knows. Report it to forensics and they can do whatever they like with it. Not real evidence or a lead so we still don't have much to go on,"

"Even so, it looks like we'll be here for a while," said Gibbo.

"Yip." Cookie was getting more and more agitated by the minute, but he was determined not to show it to his partner.

It took almost two hours for the forensic team to arrive. A uniformed policewoman turned up just after midnight and brought them a cup of tea each, which was scant consolation to Cookie. Gibbo greeted her with a smile and a bit of cheeky banter like he did with most of the female officers, while Cookie ignored her.

"Don't know what the fuck we have to stay here for,"

moaned Cookie.

"Me neither," said Gibbo. "But money for nothing as far as I'm concerned, and it beats running around the streets like headless chickens."

By 3am, the forensic team had left and the area returned to normal. They were just about to head off back to the station when the Chief Inspector tapped on the window of their car. They both straightened up.

"Evening, sir," Gibbo said.

"Evening, officers. Right, then . . . Seeing as we've had a shooting tonight and we don't know who shot at who or who the target was, I need you two to keep an eye on things. I want you to spend the rest of the shift watching for the usual suspects. I take it you know where they all live and that if not you'll find out quickly. Drive past and stop and watch their houses for any movement. I want to keep a lid on this – we can't afford to let it escalate. Do you understand?"

"Yes, sir," they both answered.

"OK then. Thanks for the quick response – and keep up the good work, gents."

They pulled away knowing where to go and who to keep their beady eyes on. If they saw anyone entering or leaving their houses they'd give them a pull, or call in a firearms team if need be. Showing their faces would be enough to deter any further trouble, a quick drive past and a wave would put them off their plans, even if it didn't result in an arrest.

Their first stop was Matty's abode. It was a downstairs flat in Howdon, which was technically

Wallsend's patch, but they went there anyway. Cookie parked up at the bottom of the street and Gibbo went out on foot. He crept up the driveway and slowly and quietly disappeared around the back. After around three minutes, he reappeared and climbed back into the car. "No signs of life there," he said. "Place is disgusting, mind. Piles of dishes . . . greasy walls . . . The front room's not much better from what I could see. What's the matter with these fucking tramps? Designer gear, flash cars and yet their homes are like shitholes."

"Where next, then?" Cookie asked.

"Let's go past Mark Taylor's in New York. If there's nothing going on there, then we'll head down to Whitley and take a look at the Bolton's gaffs."

It was a mile or so to Mark's house and the streets were quiet. Apart from the odd passing taxi, they didn't see a soul. They parked up on the opposite junction to the entrance of Mark's cul-de-sac and discussed the plan. They knew he had a dog, so they decided that it wasn't a good idea to creep around the house like they had at Matty's flat. Gibbo would go out on foot again and walk a loop of the street to see if anything looked out of place. What they decided to do next would depend on what he reported back. He turned his radio down to a minimum and tucked it into his inside pocket as he embarked on his mission.

Ten minutes later, he was back. "Nothing out of the ordinary there," he said.

"OK," said Cookie. "Kenny's next, then." He was about to pull away when he spotted a man in a shellsuit and a Berghaus jacket who walking from the direction of

Mark's house. They could tell he was in his twenties, carrying a rucksack and had a hat rolled up on his head. "Look..."

"What?", said Gibbo.

"What the fuck's he doing at this time of the morning?" Cookie put his hand on the ignition key. "Looks dodgy as fuck to me. Time for a pull." He started up the car.

The roar of the ignition and the illuminating headlights caused the lad to look up. A few seconds later they had pulled up next to him at speed and Gibbo jumped out as fast as his tattooed bulk would allow. "Police! Don't move!"

The lad panicked when he saw the huge body builder jump out of the car with something in his hand. Startled, he took off and ran. Gibbo ran after him, but the lad was quicker. Cookie reversed the car and turned back down Aldwych Drive with every intention of knocking the lad over if need be. He sped after him but he darted through a cut between two houses, with Gibbo in hot pursuit. He was getting away. Cookie knew where he was headed, and he floored the car to the end of the cul-de-sac and bailed out. He ran through another cut and onto the grassy area between the houses just before the runner arrived. The lad was in full flight and Cookie timed it perfectly. He tackled him to the ground as he was about to escape through another walkway. He tried to struggle but it was no use; Cookie had him. Gibbo arrived a few seconds later, puffing and panting. They dragged him up and pinned him to the wall, just inside the alleyway where nobody could see.

"What did you run for?" asked Cookie.

"I dunno," he said. "I didn't know who you were."

"Yes, you fucking did," said Cookie. "He shouted 'Police' when he jumped out."

"I didn't hear," the lad said.

"What's in the bag?" Gibbo asked.

"Nowt, mate. Just me bait and that for work."

"What do you mean, *and that*?" Gibbo removed the rucksack from the lad's back and started rummaging inside.

"What's your name?" Cookie asked him.

"Gary Milburn." The lad was shaking. Cookie reckoned he was mid to late twenties, possibly a young-looking thirty.

"What you doing skulking around here in the early hours?"

"Nowt, mate. I'm just on me way to work. I get picked up in the bus stop at four."

From the rucksack, Gibbo pulled out a Thermos flask and lunchbox and took a rummage. Then he opened the zipped compartment at the front and pulled out some cigarettes, Rizla papers and a small ziplock bag with a little brown lump of marijuana in it.

The rage in Cookie grew. He was edgy, his heart rate rose, and he felt a tic in his left eye for the first time. He'd thought he was risking his life chasing someone who could be armed, but in the end it was just some fella with a little bit of hash. "You're fucking joking me?"

Gary looked terrified. Perhaps he'd never been pulled by the likes of Cookie and Gibbo before. Perhaps he'd just not been pulled by the cops before. Cookie held him tightly with his left hand and pushed him against the wall. He pulled back his right arm and slammed his fist into Gary's stomach. He let go, and Gary fell to the pavement gasping for breath. He curled up, and Cookie bent down and delivered another punch as hard as he could into his left kidney. Gary whimpered on the floor, struggling to breathe. Gibbo looked away and watched for the neighbours but thankfully for them there were no windows that overlooked the lane.

"Let's go," Gibbo said. "I mean, we're just wasting our time here."

"One minute." Cookie went in for another punch – but Gibbo pulled him back with his tattooed arm.

"Come on, let's go," said Gibbo. "Leave him." He led Cookie back towards the car and they left Gary to lick his wounds. Cookie stood on his sandwiches as he walked away.

On the walk back to the car, Gibbo turned to Cookie and showed him the hash. "What we going to do with this?"

"Just give him it back," said Cookie. "I can't be arsed with the paperwork." He snatched the bag from Gibbo's fingers and turned back towards Gary while Gibbo continued towards the car. Gary was bent over and picking up his flattened lunch when he saw Cookie return. A look of terror came over his face.

"You forgot something." Cookie threw the ziplock bag towards Gary. For a split-second, Gary looked relieved – almost grateful. He straightened up to catch the hash as his eyes followed the moving bag. Cookie punched him with his right fist. Gary hit the pavement again. He curled up in a ball, expecting to receive a few more punches.

But Cookie had his sadistic head on now. There was a swish and a click as he extended his truncheon, which he brought down on Gary's left arm. Surprisingly, Gary didn't shout and scream like most people would as the blows rained down upon him. Cookie pummelled him a dozen times, pausing between each strike to make sure he didn't hit his head as he squirmed around on the ground. Cookie trembled with fury and he sweated profusely from the effort he was putting into the beating. When he stopped at last, he pushed the bulbous tip of his truncheon into Gary's left cheek, bent down and then calmly whispered into his ear.

"Next time, don't fucking run."

* * *

A week later, Kenny gulped down the last of his early morning cuppa and burnt the back of his throat as he swallowed it. His wife, Francesca, gave him a look that said, *hurry up and get your arse out of the house.* Nikki, his nine-year-old daughter, was standing at the front door in her school uniform and motioning to her dad to hurry up so she wouldn't get told off for being late – again. She plainly considered that it generally wasn't her time keeping that was the issue, it was her dad's.

"Come on, get out, you're going to be late!" Francesca scolded.

"Alright, alright, I'm going." He grabbed his car keys from the table.

Nikki smiled and reached for the door handle.

"Wait up princess!" Kenny wanted to make sure that it was him and not his only child that went out into the street first. As he walked down the garden path with Nikki behind him, he looked up and down the street. He saw nothing out of place. He unlocked the door of his Audi, and she slid her schoolbag off her shoulder before jumping into the passenger seat. The wipers began automatically when he turned on the ignition and swept the early morning dew from the windscreen. Kenny looked at Nikki and gave her a smile, aware that the innocence of childhood prevented her knowing what her dad was involved in and how dangerous his life could be.

It was only a short drive to the school gates, and they could have walked it, but he was aware that his enemies knew that he took her to school and walking back home would make him an easy target. As he rounded the corner and stopped outside the school he reached over and released the seatbelt catch.

"Giz a kiss then," he said.

"Aw, Dad . . . no."

"Why not, like?" he teased.

"Because. Someone might see."

"OK then. Bye darling. Have a good day at school."

"I will. Bye!"

He chuckled as she climbed out of the car. He'd amused himself by embarrassing her just a little. Then he drove off to meet George.

They needed to discuss the current situation and plan on what to do next. The planning wasn't that complicated;

it just amounted to working out when and how to grab a hold of and hurt the opposition while they waited for Mark to be shot.

Kenny turned left and then right and drove down through Monkseaton towards George's house.

* * *

Kenny didn't see the Ford Orion following him in the school run traffic. The driver was dressed as a woman and wore a long brown wig. His balaclava-clad accomplice lay under a blanket on the back seat. Kenny turned left along Queens Road and cut down Kew Gardens, avoiding the traffic lights at the bottom of Marine Avenue. They didn't follow him. They were sure of where he was going and, if they timed it right, they would be able to catch both Boltons at once.

A few minutes later Kenny pulled up outside of George's corner house. He saw George at the window watching him arrive, he opened the front door at the same time as Kenny reached for the gate catch. The Orion travelled over the traffic lights and turned left along a road that was unseen by George or Kenny.

"Wind the window down!" ordered Liam to his brother in the back.

Mark did as he was instructed and Liam slowed the Orion down so he could have a better shot. They both prayed that the timing was right. They approached the crossroads while Kenny was at George's front door. So far, neither of them had spotted the Orion – but then Liam turned the corner a little too fast and Mark had to steady himself as his head and shoulders leaned too far out of the window. "Down!" George threw himself to the ground, pulling Kenny down as he did so.

There was a cloud of blue grey smoke and two loud bangs as hundreds of tiny lead balls ejected from the barrels towards the doorway. The smell of burning cordite filled the air as the pellets shattered the glass in the door and the surrounding vestibule and a hanging plant pot fell from its mount and lay broken on the ground next to Kenny's head. Mark pulled his body back into the car as it turned along the back lane and away from the scene of the crime.

"What the fuck happened there?" Mark asked Liam.

"What the fuck do you mean?"

"I had them. I fucking had them. Could you not keep the fucking car steady?"

"What the fuck you on about? Did you hit them?"

"Dunno. I fucking hope so, Get the fuck out of here. Get to Earsdon and we'll torch the car."

They sped off to burn the car out that Matty's brother had stolen the day before. Fifteen minutes after it had been torched, Mark switched on his phone to wait for a potential call from Cookie, his early warning signal for trouble.

* * *

Kenny and George picked themselves up from the glass-covered garden and looked at each other. This was the second time someone had tried to kill them, and it had to be the last. In a few minutes time, the street would be crawling with police and this wasn't the time for planning revenge. As they dusted themselves down, they knew that the contract to shoot Mark needed to be completed quickly. If it wasn't, then they might not be around to pay. They had the money ready and Rob had passed on the guns so there could be no more delays, but if they couldn't get to Mark soon then a message had to be sent.

Now the gloves were off.

It was one thing shooting at each other in a back lane on an industrial estate in Shields but letting off shotguns outside a family home where children lived was another. This was school run time in suburban Whitley Bay, where innocent people could easily be caught up in the crossfire – and the police weren't going to like it one bit.

Five minutes later a police car pulled up and a fresh-faced young constable was the first on the scene. He parked his car across the junction to prevent traffic coming from any direction over the crossroads. This was the exact spot that Mark had let off the gun, and the last place he should have parked the car.

"You got anything in the house?" Kenny whispered to George.

"Fuck all, stashed it last night," replied George, referring to the revolver he'd taken from Rob.

"Me too, thank fuck."

The young copper walked towards them, surveying the crime scene as he went, as if making a mental note of everything he saw. As he neared George's front door, Kenny clocked his name and number.

"Hello, lads," PC 4711 Reynolds said. "What's gone

on here? We've had reports of a shooting."

"Shooting?" said Kenny. "Here? Nah, just kids throwing stones."

"Like I say, we've had reports of a shooting. Is anyone hurt?"

"Nah, nobody's hurt."

"Can you give me your names for a start, please?"

George lifted his chin and puffed out his chest. "George Bolton."

"And you, sir . . . what's your name, please?"

"Kenny Reid."

"Is this either of your houses?"

"Aye, it's mine," said George.

Kenny noticed that a second marked police car was pulling up.

"And is there anyone else at the property?"

"No," said George. "The wife's out and the kids are at school."

"Do you mind if we look inside?"

"Got a warrant?"

"No, but because this is a crime scene and there's a possibility that someone could be injured inside, then we have the lawful right to enter and look around."

"OK," said George. "But just you, and I'll be right there with you – I'm not having anything planted."

PC Reynolds gave him look as if say *why would you say that?* and the pair went into the house. Another uniformed officer stayed outside with Kenny while a third began to cordon off the area with blue and white police tape.

*   *   *

When DI Sharon Manson stepped out of the silver Nissan Bluebird ten minutes later, the first thing she noticed was the marked police Fiesta sitting in the centre of the junction and back towards the house. She looked at Gibbo and shook her head. From the damage to the house, she had a pretty good idea of where the shots had come from. "Really?" she said, as they walked towards George's house.

They surveyed the broken windows and the damaged framework of the door. Sharon and Gibbo looked at George and Kenny, who looked back without saying a word. There was no need for introductions. "Early morning alarm call, George?" Sharon said.

George repeated what he'd told PC Reynolds earlier. "Nah, just kids with stones, Sharon."

PC Reynolds looked confused, no doubt due to George and Sharon being on first name terms.

Sharon picked up some lead shot from the flagstones. "Lots of little kids with lots of little stones?"

"Aye there was a few of them," added Kenny. "With catapults."

"Right then . . ." Sharon turned to the two uniform coppers. "Who was the first on the scene?"

"That would be me," said PC Reynolds. "I attended and saw these two gentlemen in the garden and–"

"Constable, can you tell me why there is a car parked in the middle of the crime scene. Right where the best forensics will be?"

George and Kenny sniggered, and PC Reynolds's face

flushed. "I'll move it, ma'am." he stuttered. He made his way down the path, closely followed by Sharon.

As they neared the car, she said, "What was going on when you arrived?"

"Nothing much. Just Mr Bolton and Mr Reid in the garden looking at the damage."

"How long you been out of training?"

"Four weeks, ma'am."

"Well next time don't park the car in the middle of a bloody crime scene." She did her best to stop herself from exploding. "It could make the difference between a conviction or a walk out at court."

"Yes, ma'am."

"And constable . . . was anyone else in the area when you arrived? Any witnesses?"

"No, ma'am. I take it the gentlemen in the garden were the targets?"

"Very perceptive, constable. You'll go far."

Cookie arrived a short while later and asked her what the latest was. She informed him that there were no witnesses apart from the Bolton's who were saying nothing. There were a few neighbours who'd heard the gunshots and looked out and saw a car speed away, but the statements they provided were pretty much useless. The forensics team arrived a short while later, but they didn't hold out much hope of them finding anything that would be useful in court.

*   *   *

George and Kenny claimed not to know who or why anyone would want to kill them. They answered "No reply" to all their questions at the station and, after a few hours, they were free to go. They both returned home and settled in for the night with nervous partners. George's wife left town the next day with the kids until things had blown over, but Francesca said she would stay by Kenny's side forever.

*   *   *

The following night, a green Kawasaki Ninja prowled the streets of North Shields, looking for the same three suspects that Kenny and George had hunted previously. Rob was behind the dark visor. The bike had been stolen from Newcastle six months earlier and had false plates that matched an identical one he'd seen outside Ken's motorbike shop on Westgate Road.

He parked the bike behind the Phoenix pub, removed the black rucksack from his back and took out the sawn-off side-by-side shotgun. Clicking the catch open he loaded it with two shiny red cartridges. He took four spare cartridges and slipped them into his right-hand pocket, then slid the weapon into his jacket and walked along holding onto it with his left arm across his chest to prevent it slipping down. The estate was like a ghost town and he didn't see a soul on the short journey that took him through the alleyways between the council houses. Anyone who passed him would have thought it odd to see a helmet-wearing motorcyclist out for a late-night stroll.

He rounded the corner and saw that the street was quiet. It was late at night and there were few lights coming from the dwellings, only the glow of the streetlights illuminated him. He unzipped his jacket, removed the gun and pointed it towards the ground, pulling back both hammers with his thumb to cock the barrels. He crept stealthily along the pathway, looking at the houses for anyone who could disturb his mission. Crossing the road, he paused behind a white Ford Transit van then looked towards the stars and drew in a deep breath.

He stepped around the van as he exhaled, aimed at the downstairs window and let off two shots, which obliterated the window and the half-glass front door. He pressed the lock across and opened the gun, catching one spent cartridge while the other fell to the grass at his feet. Reloading quickly, he let off two more shots towards each upstairs window. A cascade of glass streamed down while the curtains flapped outwards and a woman's scream was heard from the room above. Again, he reloaded, catching both cartridges this time and retrieving the one from the grass. He put all three into his pocket. Rob was a career criminal and levelheaded enough not to panic and leave spent cartridges behind. The last two shots were for defence, in case he was ambushed or someone came out the house after him. Then he turned and ran. By the time he reached the motorbike the estate had returned to its previous silence except for the barking of dogs. He started up the bike and headed back to his lock-up. *2–1* he thought as he sped away.

Crazy on the Waltzer

*   *   *

Mark and his girlfriend, Lynn, were both shaking as they stood in their kitchen with no windows – Lynn from fright but Mark with rage. They surveyed the damage that had been left behind: the dozens of holes in the walls from the pellets and broken glass strewn all around. Plant pots and a family photo frame lay broken in the mess on the floor.

Mark didn't know who the shooter was but he would do his best to find out, even if it meant hurting a few people on the way. But part of him thought *fair's fair*. You couldn't expect to go around shooting at people and not have them shoot at you back. By now there were lights were on in almost all the neighbouring houses, with a couple standing on their doorstep looking towards Mark's house in disgust. They clearly knew he was a criminal but, for them, this was too much. The sirens were getting louder and eventually drowned out the barking dogs that Rob had disturbed from their slumber along with the residents. And soon the street was filled with blue lights and was cordoned off, changing it from a normal residential street into yet another North Shields crime scene.

*   *   *

That same evening, Carl relaxed in his flat alone. He was thinking about Marie and her beautiful body and hoping it wouldn't be too long before he had his hands wrapped around it again. He was bored, and flicked around the Sky TV channels, trying to find something worth watching that would occupy the rest of his night. He liked to get to bed early during the week so he could get up and train each morning. The weekends were for business and always would be, so long as his business was drugs and protection. He was virtually nocturnal from Thursday to Sunday, so he liked to keep a steady routine during the week.

When his car alarm started wailing, he jumped up from the settee, switched off the lights and plunged the room into darkness. He moved tentatively into the kitchen with his back against the wall and peeked around the closed curtain. He wasn't stupid enough to fling open the door and run outside where a gunman could be hiding in wait or throw the curtain back and make himself a silhouette for a well-aimed bullet.

He saw nothing.

*   *   *

Concealed inside Carl's car a black-clad man pushed a screwdriver into the right side of the radio before prizing it out of the dashboard. He ripped it out from the wires and put it on the passenger seat before rummaging through the rest of the car.

6: A TORTURE TATTOO

Paul looked around his front room rather pleased. He considered himself to have good taste, and as far as he was concerned the decor he'd chosen proved him to be correct. He'd hung plain wallpaper on the bottom, and flower patterned on the top, separated by a dado rail, which he'd stained the previous week. Lying back, he admired the LED lights of the Sony Midi hi-fi, Super Nintendo and front-loading Panasonic video player positioned in the media unit he'd had specially made. Spending money installing something like that in a rental place may not have been financially worth it, but he didn't care; he had the money so why not spend it on the things that made him smile. He'd decided on a brown leather three-piece suite to avoid the ribbing he'd get from Carl if he bought a black one identical to his. His glass top coffee table matched the three-piece in style. A gilt-edged mirror hung over the fireplace. His carpet was cream with a red flower pattern and he'd had curtains hand made to match.

But the cash from the robbery was running out faster than he thought, and he still hadn't looked for a job. Maybe tomorrow. Maybe after the next spliff. Just like always.

The phone rang and he picked it up.

"Alright?" Carl asked.

"Aye, what's happening?" Paul said.

"Nowt. I was going to pop in. Just seeing if you were there first. I'll not be long."

Ten minutes later, he appeared in Paul's back yard

and knocked on the sitting room window. Paul saw him come in and lock the gate behind him. He opened the kitchen door and let him inside.

"What's been happening today?" said Carl. "Getting stoned again?" He wafted away some pretend smoke in the room, which still smelled of ganja.

"Aye, not much. Just having a chilled day. You?"

"Some arsehole broke into my car last night and nicked the stereo."

"Really?"

"Aye, really. So, if you hear of anyone selling a Sony one then let me know. I've just been to Halfords to get a new Blaupunkt flip front. Looks the business, like."

"Aye, If I get offered one, I'll let you know. Any ideas who?"

"None at all. Presumably somebody who doesn't know who the car belongs to."

"Probably not." Paul said.

Carl looked around the room. "You've got it nice in here. I like it."

"Cheers. Cost a few quid though." Paul wondered if Carl recognised his good taste of was just buttering him up before asking him the question he'd really come to ask.

"I'll bet it did. Looks good. Listen . . . I have a meeting with Mark and Liam later and I need you to come along. We're gonna sort out what happened with Joe when they taxed him."

"You need me to come along? What am I going to do if it all kicks off?"

"Look, it's not like that. I just need someone there who can watch me back. I'm not arsed about those two plumbs. I'll punch their fucking faces in if they start."

"Aye, but what about what they did to George and Kenny? They're probably tooled up."

"That's why I'm meeting them in the Vic in Whitley. Nobody's going to start shooting a hundred yards away from the bizzie station in the middle of the afternoon are they? It's sound. Don't worry. I just don't want to be walking in there on my own, that's all."

Paul gave a sigh. His gut told him no, but he didn't want to let Carl down. He was one of the few close friends he had and he was starting to see him more like the older brother he'd never had. And in the absence of his father, he was the closest thing he had to one of those as well. "Ok, I'll come. But don't expect much from me if it all kicks off. I can hold me own but not against that lot. They're too much for me."

"Don't worry," reassured Carl. "It'll be alright."

"When you meeting them?"

"Three bells. I'll pick you up about 2.30."

"Aye OK. I'll look forward to it," Paul said sarcastically.

"Sound. I've got to go. I'm meeting this bird in a bit."

"Who's that like?" Paul asked, as a smile came over his face.

"Ah, now that's a secret," Carl teased.

Carl departed for his early morning rendezvous and Paul sat down on his leather armchair that still had its new furniture smell, dreading the thought of the meeting later on.

The pickup time came and went and as the clock passed 2.45 Paul hoped that Carl had made other arrangements and that his presence was no longer required. He knew Mark and Liam by sight, and they knew him. He would sometimes nod hello as he entered whichever establishment they worked at, but he kept his distance, like most people did. Few people had a good word for either of them, and he'd heard enough bad stories to know they weren't the sort of people you could consider to be friends, even if you knew them well. They took liberties with people, and most of the dealers who now worked for them wished they didn't. They'd all been given the same options: start selling for us or take a kicking and get robbed of everything you have.

A few minutes later the phone rang and it was Carl. Paul's hope turned back into dread.

"You ready? I'm out the back."

"Aye. Two minutes." Paul put down the receiver and picked up his coat. A feeling of unease swept through him and he considered taking a knife from the kitchen drawer. He gave his head a shake and went outside to meet Carl, who wasn't driving his usual RS Turbo, but a rusty old blue Mini.

"What the fuck's this?" asked Paul.

"Thought I'd leave the RS at home in case owt happens."

"I thought you said it'll be fine."

"It will be. Nowt's the bother. Nothing's going to kick off. It's all good, man."

This didn't do much to calm Paul's nerves. "OK, then .

.. if you say so."

They left Cullercoats and drove to the centre of Whitley Bay. There were plenty of daytime shoppers around, which was good for their security and put Paul more at ease. Carl parked the car in the back lane of Oxford Street and they took a short cut through the urine-smelling alley under the closed Fire Station and past the dirty public toilets on their way to the pub.

When they entered the bar, they looked around. There were a few daytime drinkers in there as usual. The window seats were taken up by the slow drinkers who watched the world go by, staring through the glass into the goldfish bowl that was Whitley Bay town centre on a Wednesday afternoon. Paul ordered the drinks: a pint for him and a diet Sprite for Carl. The barman had been told that a meeting would be taking place in the pool room and he'd cleared it of patrons. He told them that it was closed for cleaning and got twenty pounds for his trouble. "Has anybody else turned up yet?" Carl asked him.

"Aye, Carl," he said, as if he'd known Carl for years. "Mark and Liam are already in there."

They took their drinks and walked through the archway and into the pool room. It was deserted apart from the brothers. Two bench seats were fixed to the back walls with a fire exit door between them, above one sat a barred window with frosted glass that Paul guessed led into the rear yard. Each red seat had matching square tables and two loose chairs. The tables were adorned with fresh beer mats. A strip light hung above the pool table, showing up a beer stain on the green baize cloth and sepia pictures of

Whitley Bay from eras past hung on the patterned wallpaper walls. The pool table took up most of the room, leaving just enough space around it to stretch out and take a shot. A rack of cues was screwed to one wall.

Mark and Liam stood up as they neared.

"Mark . . . Liam . . ." Carl extended his right hand and shook theirs in turn.

"Carl, how you doing?" Mark asked.

Liam said nothing.

"Not bad," said Carl. "This is me mate, Paul,"

"What's he here for?" said Liam. "This is between us. I don't want any fucker knowing my business that doesn't have to."

"He's just driving me," said Carl. "It's alright. He'll wait at the bar."

"Aye, no bother," said Paul, who turned and walked back to the main bar area, glad that he wasn't directly involved so he couldn't be implicated in any fallout.

*   *   *

The three men sat down, the brothers with their backs to the wall on a bench seat, Carl facing them from a single chair. Carl took a sip of his Sprite as he weighed up the situation. He was sure that if it came to it he could beat both of them in a fight. But as they were going up against the Boltons he knew that they meant business, and he also knew that they had access to firearms and weren't afraid to use them. Carl also knew that having him as an enemy along with Kenny and George would be more than they could handle and so he expected an acceptable outcome.

Mark sat back, relaxed, but Liam looked on edge, eyes like saucers, staring at Carl while he licked his lips. Carl could tell he was off his nut. He'd heard the rumours about Liam going off the rails in the last few months, about him hammering the coke to cope with the stress of the Boltons and the police.

Carl broke the ice on what was going to be a delicate subject. His disdain for the brothers caused him to skip the usual small talk and get straight down to business. "I hear you've been having fun and games with Kenny and George."

"Aye we have," said Mark. "And are you going to get involved on their side?"

"Your problems with them two are your own. They're nowt to do with me, unless you want to involve me . . . which you have. Taxing their punters is one thing, Mark, but taxing mine's another,"

"What? That daft Joe?" said Mark with half a smile. "We only got two ounces off him."

"My two ounces. It's not necessary the amount, Mark. it's the principle."

Liam smirked. "Well, it's our two ounces now."

Carl looked intently into Liam's face. "No. *My* two ounces."

"Listen, Carl . . ." Mark seemed inclined to calm the situation down, but Carl was having none of it.

"It's my fucking hash and I want it returned," Carl growled. "Do you understand?"

"Here don't fucking talk to us like that!" said Liam.

"We're not your fucking errand boys."

"It's OK, Carl." Said Mark. He's just had a line in the bogs – no big deal."

But it was big deal to Carl. He was no longer interested in what they had to say and was starting to lose his temper. He looked Mark straight in the eyes and spoke slowly and deliberately. "Get the fucking hash back to Joe. Today. I'm not interested in listening to your bullshit. Right? He told you he worked for me when you went in, and you still robbed him. And I'm not fucking having it. OK?"

"Who the fuck do you think you're talking to?" Liam spat back.

"You, ya cunt." Carl leant forward and pointed his finger into Liam's face.

Liam reached for his back pocket. Carl pushed himself up and back with the speed of a panther and at the same time he threw the table to his left. The sound of breaking glass and crashing furniture made the whole pub go silent as the three men faced off.

Liam swung a blade towards Carl's face, but he ducked it. Before Liam had time to take second swipe, Carl shifted his weight to deliver a short right uppercut, which connected perfectly to Liam's jaw. His unconscious body hit the pool table before coming to rest on the claggy pub carpet.

Mark jumped up and threw a right at Carl, which caught him just above his left eye. Carl felt the weight of the punch, but it didn't slow him down. He bobbed and weaved and moved a step back to get himself out of danger.

Following in with a left jab, he dipped left then landed a perfect left hook to Mark's chin, which caused him to reel backwards and land on the bench seat he'd been sitting on a few moments earlier. It was a move he'd studied many times before, watching Mike Tyson's training videos and practicing them repeatedly in the gym. Before Mark could respond, Carl landed two rights into his face that caused his nose to snap and split open the skin above his left eye. Mark was beaten, and it was best to stay down. He'd come to the meeting with good intentions and to sort things out because he knew that falling out over two ounces of hash was a bad idea. It was Liam and his ever-growing coke problem that had led to this.

* * *

Paul heard the commotion and looked into the pool room to see Liam out cold and Mark on his back holding his hands up as if to say, *that's enough.*

Carl was silent as he strode past Paul, his ripped shirt splattered with Mark's blood. Paul turned and walked out behind him, he would ask him what happened later once he'd calmed down and the adrenaline had subsided.

But, whatever had happened, he knew that no good would come of it.

* * *

The following day, Cookie met Mark in a car park in South

Shields, out of the way of the prying eyes that lurked on the other side of the Tyne. Mark had requested the meeting and Cookie presumed that something was amiss. As Mark neared, Cookie could see that something was different. At first, he thought Mark was wearing a mask. As he came closer, Cookie clocked the two black eyes, the cut above the left one, and the badly bruised face.

"Had a bit of trouble, have we?" Cookie asked.

"Just a bit."

"What's the other guy look like?"

"To be honest, not a scratch on him?" said Mark

"So, who's filled you in then?"

"Me and Liam had a bit of bother with Liddle. To be fair to him, he did the two of us and we only landed one punch between us. Liam's jaw's fractured as well."

"Oh dear, oh dear," Cookie mocked. "Is this going to be a problem for us?"

"Yes and no."

"Go on."

"We taxed one of his punters when we went for George's, and he wanted the gear back. I don't think he'll come after us, but he wants it returned."

"And?"

"We can't. We'd lose too much face if we did. So, it leaves us with two options . . . shoot him or bend over."

"Be careful, Mark. There's a lot of heat already about the shootings, and we don't want to upset the apple cart any more than we have already. Then, the Crime Squad takes over. If that happens, I won't have access to all the information and our little arrangement will need to be terminated. You'll be on your own. You won't last long without my help, and you know it."

"Aye, I know. I'm not sure which way to go with this,"

"There is another option," said Cookie.

"What's that?"

"Set him up. Plant drugs in his house. I'll say I've received a tip and set up a raid. Make sure it's enough to get him remanded straight off and then he's out of your hair."

"And how do you propose I get the gear in his house? He's hardly going to let one of our lot through the door is he?"

"So, who's close enough to him to do it. There must be someone you can pay or threaten,"

"Now you mention it there is someone. That Paul he knocks around with . . . he'll do it if I make him. Little fucking hanger-on."

"Who's he?"

"Paul something. From Whitley. I don't know his last name. He's always with Carl these days."

"Well, it's simple, then. Grab him, terrify him, give him some drugs and make him set up Carl. Tell him Carl will never know. A couple of ounces of smack should do it."

"Sounds like a plan."

"So, what have you got for me then?"

"A grand."

"Is that it? I was expecting more than that. Any info to go with it?"

"Things have been a bit quiet. It's difficult to get much done with all the filth that's about at the minute. No offence, like."

"None taken. But next time I'll be expecting at least double that. And don't let me down."

"Don't worry, I won't."

"No info at all then?" Cookie asked.

"I'm working on it. We've been getting the Es off a couple of people, and I have one in mind for the set up, but I have to be careful and not to make it look too obvious. Give us a couple of weeks and once we've had a few of parcels off him I'll let you know the where and when and you can grab him. He sorts his gear out on a Wednesday or Thursday ready for the weekend. And don't worry, I'll give you plenty of warning."

"How many?"

"A thousand. Maybe more. You got anything for me?"

"Not really. We know that it was your lot that shot at the Boltons but there's no witnesses and no forensics to link it to anybody, so I can't see you getting pulled in for it and definitely not charged. As long as you keep your trap shut if you get nicked, there's nothing we can charge you with. And no signs of anyone outside of Shields looking into you for now, but if that changes, you'll be the second to know."

"Who's first?"

"Me."

*   *   *

Rob placed the twelve brown bars of hash into the rucksack

and shoved it down into the footwell behind the passenger seat before he drove out of his lock-up. He'd wrapped them up into parcels of four for easy handling and now he was off for the handover. He was paying £1,800 a kilo and getting £2,300 back off each one. £1,500 for a few hours work. Not bad.

He wasn't overly paranoid about getting caught with the gear; he'd get longer inside if he was caught with the .22 automatic he carried in the holster below his left armpit. But, even so, he was on the alert for the police and looking out for an ambush from anybody brave enough to try to take it from him. Few people would try to rip him off because they knew what the consequences would be if he found out who they were. He wasn't the hardest man around, but what he lacked in fighting skills he more than made up for with a high capacity for violence, which was enough to put most people off him.

He parked his car around the back of High Howdon Social Club and walked with the hash over his shoulder to the rendezvous a few streets away. He knocked on the door of a ground floor flat, which was opened by Matty who ushered him inside.

"Matty . . ." Rob said.

"Alright Rob?" Matty greeted. Just go through."

Rob walked into the dirty front room and was disgusted by the state of the flat. He wondered how anybody could live that way. The carpet looked like it hadn't been hoovered in months and dirty plates and cups sat on top of weeks old newspapers. The smell of an unemptied bin wafted in from the kitchen making him almost gag as he entered the sitting room. The tinny sound of some loud and bad rave music came from a cheap ghetto blaster in the kitchen.

"Can you turn that shit off?" asked Rob. Everybody knew the scene in *Scarface* where the TV was turned up before the Cuban cocaine dealer got chopped up with a chainsaw in the bathroom. The louder than normal volume made Rob a little nervous. Matty did as he requested and went into the kitchen to turn it off.

"Don't mind if I look around, do you?" Rob didn't look forward to seeing the state of the rest of the apartment but he needed to make sure there wasn't an ambush team waiting for him in the bedroom.

"Feel free," said Matty.

Rob made his way into the small passageway and wrapped a hand around his gun, ready to pull it out if need be. He checked the bedroom with its unmade bed to confirm that he was safe and then had a quick look in the filthy bathroom before returning to the front room and to Matty.

"Happy?" Matty asked.

"Aye, I am now."

"Take a seat," Matty said.

"It's OK. I'd rather stand." Rob thought he catch something if he sat. "So, shall we get down to business then?" he said.

"That we shall," said Matty.

Rob opened the bag and removed the three taped up parcels of hash and put them onto last week's newspaper that lay on top of the round coffee table. "Three key so that'll be £6,900 for cash."

"Bit steep that, Rob. I was thinking more like £6,300 to be honest."

"Look, Matty . . . the price is twenty-three a key. No more, no less. If you don't want it, I can take it back, but good luck trying to find anybody that will serve you with decent hash at any price."

"I know it'll be good gear," said Matty, "but the price is a bit high. Can you not come down a bit?"

"Nah, sorry. Maybe next time, but not right now. And, anyway, I know you've been getting gear that's much shitter this and paying just about the same for it."

"And how do you know that?" asked Matty.

"I have my ways. So do you want it, or shall I take it back?"

Matty looked poker-faced at Rob, but Rob knew he had no choice. Matty and the Taylors had been getting lower grade hash because hardly anybody would do business with them. Rob also knew that if they continued to serve up more of the same it would destroy their business in the long term.

Matty knew that too. He took a deep breath in and then breathed out for theatrics' sake. Then he nodded. "OK' I'll take it." He reached under the settee's cushion and removed a carrier bag. He then removed a bundle of cash and counted out a hundred pounds, which he slid into his back pocket before passing the remainder of the notes to Rob. "There you go. There's £6,900 there. Count it of you like."

"Nah it's OK," said Rob. "I'll trust you." He wrapped

the notes back up in the carrier bag, which he dropped into his rucksack.

"So, I take it George and Kenny don't know about this?" said Matty.

"And what do you think?"

"I think they'd be pretty pissed off if they did."

"Well, they're not going to find out, are they? And neither's anybody else. Because if they do then you'll be back to buying dink hash at an even shittier price. And that's if you can find anyone who'll do business with you after I've had a word with the few people who'll give you the time of day now."

If Matty caused any problems for Rob then he'd be cutting his own throat in the long term, and it was doubtful if the Bolton's would believe anybody's word over Rob's anyway – and certainly not Matty's. But it turned out that the drug deal wasn't the only reason that Matty had sought Rob out.

"So, you don't fancy changing sides, then, do you?" Matty asked.

"The only side I'm on's me own, Matty."

"Aye, but you're still with Kenny and George, aren't you?"

"For now. But that could all change if I felt like it. But for now, I don't. So, let's just keep our little arrangement between ourselves and see what the future brings. OK? And, besides, what could you put on the table that I can't already get from them?"

"We could give you a wage off everything we do . . . the drugs . . . the doors and all that."

"You don't have the doors, Matty. And there's nothing that tells us that your little firm has . . . er . . . what shall we say? Longevity. Know what I mean? But if that all changes then I might get onboard one day."

Matty nodded, as if the response he'd just had from Rob was as positive as he'd expected.

*   *   *

They shook hands, and as Rob turned to leave, Matty got a glimpse of the handgun in his jacket. He hadn't brought one to the meet himself, but he considered that he would for the next time. He let Rob out and called Mark.

"Alright?" asked Mark.

"Aye, all good."

"So did you ask him about teaming up with us?"

"Aye, but he wasn't too receptive. He says he's happy enough as is, but he did suggest that if things swing our way, then he might get onside. You know what he's like. He'll go wherever suits him. He's got no real loyalty to Kenny and George."

"He's got no loyalty to nobody. We'll have to keep using him for now, but make sure he's not setting you up the next time you meet. He's a snake in the grass that fucker."

"He sure is. Anyway, I'm getting off. I need to get this out of the house before wor lass comes in."

"OK, later," said Mark.

"Aye, laters."

* * *

Mark sat back and thought about the Rob situation. They needed him for now, so he couldn't throw him over to Cookie just yet. Rob's name had come up a few times as the shooter at his house, and although there was no real proof that it was him, he was still at the forefront of Mark's thoughts for a set-up.

"His time'll come," he muttered to himself. "Just like for George and Kenny."

* * *

Three days later, Paul returned home from his daily workout at Ivy Court. It was a pleasant enough day: the sky was clear and the air was crisp. He'd decided to give Proflex a miss. By now, the entire coastal criminal fraternity had heard about Carl chinning Mark and Liam and they also knew that he'd been there. He couldn't be arsed with the questions and he didn't want to be anywhere the Taylors' pals frequented, as most of them would be happy to tip them off to his whereabouts just to curry favour. He tried to get the events in the Vic out of his mind but it was a struggle. He took the bottom way from Whitley to Cullercoats, where it was less likely that he would be spotted. It paid to be careful.

He walked past the tennis courts and the bowling green and again he thought of how to get away from this life. While he'd waited in the Vic, he'd chatted to an old school friend who was heading out to the alps for the winter as a ski chalet host and he told him about life in the mountains. Sure, the job wasn't the best paid, but the partying and girls more than made up for it and he was tempted to give it a go. It seemed like a colder version of the Med: sun, ski and sex instead of sea and sand. If he could have walked away and boarded a plane right then he would have done it, but he would have to give up the flat first, and it would mean leaving Lindsey, and Carl as well, his two closest people after his Mam.

Reaching home, he put his sweaty gym gear into the washing machine and opened the fridge to see what he had in for dinner. The pickings were sparse: just one chicken breast and some veg inside. He considered ordering a Chinese takeaway but there wasn't much point in going to the gym and then filling himself up with high calorie food straight afterwards. Taking out the chicken and the veg, he cut them both into strips, removed his wok from the cupboard and placed it on the gas stove. The oil crackled as he poured it into the hot pan. Then there was a knock on the door.

He wasn't expecting anyone, and so he prayed it wasn't the Taylors. He'd locked the back gate when he returned, so whoever it was they must have climbed quietly over the wall. His stomach cramped but he knew he had to answer; the unexpected visitor would have seen his shadow moving in the kitchen. It couldn't be Carl; he would have rung first and wouldn't have climbed stealthily over the wall.

A shadow appeared in the glass and knocked again – louder this time. "Paul? Open the door. I can see you're in there."

That gave him no option. He took a step towards the door and knew it was one of the Taylor lot, even though he couldn't see a face or recognise the voice. His hand shook as he turned the key and he opened the door on a battered and bruised Mark Taylor. "Mind if I come in? I'd like a word." If Mark's smile was intended to put him at ease, it failed.

"Eh, not really. I'm just away out."

"Away out?" Mark nodded towards the stove. "You're cooking your tea."

"Oh, aye . . . yeah. I was just about to turn that off."

Mark pushed past him into the kitchen. "It'll only take a minute."

Paul felt more vulnerable than he'd ever felt before. He managed to prevent himself shaking but he was scared, and he knew that Mark would know it.

"Anybody else here?" asked Mark.

Paul shook his head.

Mark walked past him like he wasn't there and looked in each room to double check.

"Look . . . about the other day . . ." stammered Paul. "I was just there with Carl. what's going on's nowt to do with me. He just asked us to come along and watch his back."

Mark laughed. "Watch his back? What the fuck would you have done? Fuck off. Well, it's got something to do with you now. You got yourself involved. You want to hang around in our league then this is where it gets you." He opened his jacket and removed a rusty-looking gun.

Paul looked at the ancient weapon and wondered if he'd have more chance of dying from the bullet wound or septicemia if he was shot with it. It looked like an old Webley revolver left over from the second world war, but the .45 calibre bullet would put a big hole in anyone it hit. "Your problems with Carl or anybody else are between yourselves," he said. "Leave me out of it."

"No, no, no," protested Mark. "This is what's going to happen . . . I'm getting rid of Carl and you're going to help me. Whether you like it or not. What you're going to do is hide something in his flat and I'll do the rest. And if you don't, I'll do you, your mam and that daft bird whose house you're always at." He took the revolver and pressed the end of the barrel under Paul's chin.

"Look, leave them out of whatever the fuck this is. It's not fair."

"Fair? What's fair got to do with fuck all? And, by the way, I know where your mam lives – just over there." Mark motioned in the direction of her house with the gun. "All you need to do is take what I give you and hide it in his flat the next time you're there. I'll give you me number and you can tell us when it's done. And then I'll leave you alone. I might even give you a job when it's over." He fished a plastic-wrapped package from his pocket with his free hand.

"What is it?" asked Paul.

"It's smack. Three ounces. And he'll never know. I'm hardly going to tell him, am I?"
He put it back into his pocket.

"But he'll know it's me?"

"How? It could be one of his birds for all he'll know. And he's not going to think it's you, is he? You're about as far up his arse as you can get, aren't you? You fucking worship him."

"Nah, fuck that," said Paul. "I'm not setting him up. No fucking way. Whatever I am, Carl's me pal…"

Mark grabbed Paul by his throat and pushed him back over the kitchen bench. "I came here to be nice, but if that's the way you want it . . ." His face was so close to Paul's that he could smell Mark's bad breath.

"No Mark," Paul stuttered. "It's just . . . I'm no fucking grass."

Far from being mollified, Mark seemed stung by what Paul had just said. Then he turned almost white with rage. It didn't help when the hot oil in the wok bubbled and spat onto Mark's arm. He fliched and turned to look at it. Then he grinned. He pushed the wok from the burner and laid the gun on the bench behind him. Paul considered making a lunge for it but Mark grabbed him by the back of the neck and spun him around, pulling one arm behind his back. "Never mind shooting you, I'll just burn your fucking face off!" Mark forced him over the cooker and pushed his head down.

"No, no, please . . ." begged Paul, "Don't!" His body doubled over as his face was forced closer to the flame.

"This'll hurt more than getting shot!" Mark had a look of savage determination on his face.

Paul used all his strength to push himself back upright, but it was futile. One arm and his back muscles were no match for the bigger and more powerful arms and body mass Mark bore down upon him. Paul's face inched down towards the hot, blue flame. He felt the heat sear up and he smelled the burning ring as he closed his eyes and waited for the pain to come. The sound of hissing gas increased as he pushed back with all his might.

"No . . . please . . . don't," pleaded Paul.

"What? I can't hear you. Down?"

"No, don't!" cried Paul. "I'll do it. I'll do it!" And now he was really crying, shedding tears down his scorched face. Mark let go and Paul straightened up. He stood with his back against the bench and stared down at the floor. He felt weak, useless and pathetic, ashamed that he wasn't man enough to stand up to Mark. The reality was that he stood no chance; this was a fight he couldn't win and any attempt to get out of it was pointless.

"Look at me!" ordered Mark.

"What?" Paul whimpered back.

Mark took the parcel back out of his pocket and put it on the bench. "There's the gear and you're responsible for it. If anything happens to it, you'll be paying, so you better do what I say and put it in Carl's flat."

Paul resigned himself to agree to whatever Mark wanted just to get him out of the house. "Just leave it. I'll do it." He stared at the package, scared of both Mark and of what Carl would do to him if he found out.

"Good lad," said Mark, smiling now. "Canny flat, this. It would be perfect for knocking out the hash. Come and see us when Carl's out the way and I'll sort you out." He picked up a pen and scribbled his number onto some empty food packaging and looked across at a broken Paul. "Keep in touch." he said, before leaving.

Paul slid to the floor and pulled his knees up to his

chest. He buried his face in his hands and cried uncontrollably as his body shook. He sat on the cold lino, distraught and unable to move. A short while later, he picked himself up and turned off the gas. His face was still red and hot from the heat of the stove. A fear came over him and his mind told him to get out of the flat. He reasoned that if he wasn't there then maybe he could convince himself that it hadn't happened. But it had. In the last few months, he'd been in situations that he thought he never would be in, but now he was out of his depth and he knew it, stuck between betraying his friend and saving himself and the people he loved the most. He put the smack in the kitchen drawer. If the police came knocking then it could be a godsend: prison might be the easiest way out of this situation. He grabbed his coat and a half smoked joint and headed out of the door, pausing as he exited, scared in case Mark was still hanging around. But he was long gone.

As he walked the streets of Cullercoats, Paul passed the houses where the "normal" people lived. His mind turned to his mam and thoughts of Mark doing her harm. Whatever he came up with, he had to make sure that she was left unharmed and that nobody ever went to her door. She knew more about his life than she let on. She knew plenty of people around town from her years in the pub trade and he was sure she asked around about him, just like his dad had done. It wasn't that she was nosy; she just wanted to make sure that her only child was safe and not in any danger. If only she'd been a fly on the wall that night, she would have realised how far under he'd sunk. It wouldn't have stopped her, though; she would have stood up to anyone for him, Mark and his revolver or not.

As he walked on, he looked through the windows of Cullercoats Club, thinking how the people inside lived in another world, and he felt alien as he passed. Why couldn't he be like them, with their jobs and their families, enjoying a game of darts or snooker and a few drinks with their friends, never worrying about who was knocking on their door or who was in the car that had just pulled up? He was willing to bet they didn't sleep with a bat under the bed or live their lives paranoid and anxious.

Along the sea front he went, cutting down the bank and walking the length of Long Sands beach. The surf crashed on a high winter tide, throwing salty spray onto his lips. His thoughts turned to Lindsey and to Jason. They were "only friends" but he loved that boy like his own and couldn't bear the thought of anyone turning up at their house. He wouldn't be able to forgive himself if he put them in danger.

He weighed up his options as he walked. He knew he couldn't betray Carl for Mark, but at the same time he couldn't put his mam and Lindsey at risk. He needed a plan, and quickly.

He could leave town, run away and never come back. He could sell his car and his electricals and, with the money he had left from the robbery and Mark's three ounces he could set himself up somewhere else – get a flat and a job, down south, somewhere nobody would ever find him and somewhere he would never bump into anyone he knew. The risk was that Mark would be true to his word and go after his mam and Lindsey. He reasoned that even a psycho like Mark wouldn't go after a middle-aged woman and a single mother, but he couldn't rule it out. Not completely. If he left town with the smack, he could never come back. Not ever.

Fuck it . . . he'd just go through with it and set up Carl. He was closer to Carl than almost anyone else and the guilt of putting him in jail would stay with him forever. Carl wasn't daft – far from it. He'd know it was Paul, even if he tried to convince him that it wasn't. But he couldn't lie to Carl's face. The ability to lie and make it convincing was a trait that many successful criminals had but, unfortunately for Paul, he wasn't one of them. If Carl was locked up, he would be on the top of his visitors list and, when confronted, his guilt would be written all over his face. A five stretch might sound like a long time but the years ticked by and it wouldn't be long before Carl came knocking – and that was if Regan and his other pals hadn't found him first.

He considered heavily cutting the gear, and the bit he creamed off the top would make him some money. If he did set up Carl, the heroin that was found would be the worst on the street, which would at least mitigate his sentence.

The ideas came fast as he walked past the Gibraltar Rock towards the priory and down the bank towards the North Pier. The long stone structure was deserted except for the torch lights of a few fishermen. They stood in the cold night air with their thick winter coats and hats on to protect them from the elements.

He could get a gun and ambush Mark. If he took him out, then the others would fade away. Maybe. But what would he do if they came after him? Shooting Mark was something his pals wouldn't forget. The only person he could ask for a gun was Carl and he'd want to know why he wanted it for a start. But, deep down, he knew he couldn't shoot anyone; the odd punch up was about as far as he would go. Maybe he could use a tool to defend himself, but he couldn't pull a trigger – he knew that in his heart. And the jail time you got for just having a gun was enough to put him off.

He could go through with it and plant the skag in Carl's flat. But first he would change it out for something that looked the same. The police would try to nick Carl but the gear would test negative. No real harm done. But, even so, Carl would still be furious. But he would forgive him eventually – wouldn't he? He'd tell Mark that he must have been ripped off, and that it wasn't his fault the gear was snide. That way he'd have done what he was told and caused the minimum of damage. It was risky plan. Even Mark, who wasn't exactly known for his brain power, would know he'd had him over and be back on his case again in no time.

He reached the end of the pier and lit up the joint. With his back to the wind and his head inside his jacket, it still took him five attempts. Looking out over the river and across to the bright lights of South Shields funfair, he couldn't work out the best course of action. It was only an hour before that he was inches away from being disfigured for life and being threatened with a gun.

He was still scared, no longer crying and breaking down but scared nonetheless. He was alone. The next nearest human was a hundred yards away at least and he contemplated something for the first time in his life. As he stared down into the murky black water, he knew how to free himself from his troubles. It would be easier if he jumped. The bitter cold sea and the weight of his sodden clothes would see him off in minutes, if not quicker. Then there would be no more suffering, not for him or for anyone else, and his mam and Lindsey would be out of the firing line too. If it all worked out, the Taylor's would be accused of drowning him. Someone must have seen Mark at his flat and it wouldn't take long for the police to catch up with him after his body was washed up. If it was washed up. Or would it be lost in the cold, grey expanse of the North Sea forever?

He took one last toke of the joint, flicked the roach away into the wind then climbed the first rung of the old iron railing. He stopped and looked down at the waves crashing violently against the pier and then closed his eyes. Pictures of his dad, his mam, Lindsey and then Jason flashed through his mind. Would they miss him? Would anyone miss him? He hesitated, wondering what it would be like in his final moments on earth. Drowning was supposed to be quick and painless, or so the myth said. The sound of the wind and the crashing sea was interrupted with an unknown voice crying out through the late-night sky.

"Oy, what you doing up there you daft bastard?" it shouted. "Get down!" He hadn't seen the fisherman on the lower part of the pier, not ten yards away from where he now stood precariously. And in true North Shields fashion the man hadn't minced his words; instead of asking what the problem was he'd just told him straight. He stood there shaking his head in Paul's direction, shrugging his shoulders and gesticulating with his arms. Paul stepped back off the railing and onto the safety of the concrete below. He gave the fisherman a sheepish wave, turned and walked off down the pier. He didn't look back.

Walking home, he couldn't believe that he'd considered suicide as the answer to his problems and the realisation of the impact it would have on his loved ones came over him. How could he be so selfish and consider putting them through so much pain? Fuck Mark and fuck the lot of them. They weren't worth doing himself in for. His family was worth more than those pricks.

As he lay in bed that night, he still had no firm answer, but he knew that whatever came along he'd be alright. The fisherman's shout was a sign to him, a sign that he had plenty to live for. One thing he did know was that he needed to be straight with Carl. But that was for tomorrow.

7: TUNNEL OF LOVE

Jesmond was quiet for a Monday night. It was half term at the universities and the bars and restaurants of Osborne Road were half dead as Liam drove his Astra GTE at his less than usual breakneck speed through the well-to-do part of Newcastle. Mark was riding shotgun. Neither of them particularly liked Jesmond, nor a night out in Newcastle. Up there they were much less known, if they were known at all. They frequented the bars of Whitley Bay, Tynemouth and North Shields, where they had a reputation and people knew their names. It gave them a sense of worth, a feeling that they were somebodies because they could walk straight in and quite often receive free drinks from the manager or from the small army of arse lickers and hangers on that gravitated around them.

Mark strained his neck as he passed the bars to see if he knew any of the doormen huddled up outside, their cold gloved hands thrust deep into their pockets in a futile attempt to keep warm.

"So, what's the crack with these hookers?" Liam asked Mark.

"What do you mean . . . *the crack*? You give them some money and they let you fuck them." Mark laughed at the naivete of his younger brother.

"Aye, but . . . you know . . . what they like?"

"Why? You never shagged a hooker before?"

"Aye, aye. Well . . . nah, actually. I haven't."

"Really? I'm sure you'll have the time of your life,"

said Mark, with more than a hint of sarcasm.

"What's the crack then? Howay. Where they from? Russia?"

"Ukraine, I think. Wherever the fuck that is. Who knows? just as long as they give good head then that's me happy."

Mark's mind was elsewhere, and he was half ignoring Liam as he stared out into the night. It was on the gunman who'd blown his windows out and haunted his thoughts ever since it happened. He realised by now that he'd never find out who it was, but it wasn't for the want of trying. A good few people had been paid a visit and a couple of names had been thrown up but nothing that was concrete. He knew that the longer it went on the less chance he had of finding out the truth. He was also thinking about his visit to Paul. If he didn't hear back from him in a few days then he'd make another visit to remind him of his obligations. If that didn't work then he would just have to pay the price for insubordination, just like anybody else.

"So, what's the crack with you and this bird then?" Liam asked.

"What bird?"

"The hooker. You know, the one you're in love with."

"Her name's Katina. Means *pure*, apparently,"

Liam burst out into a belly laugh. "Pure? Funny fucking name for a hooker. Anyway, I reckon you're in love."

"Aye, aye. Fuck off. In love? My arse."

"Aye, you are," sniggered Liam. "How many times have you been up here lately? Twice this week that I know of. You'll be setting up shop with her shortly."

"Just drive the car and shut the fuck up," said Mark.

They drove on through the late evening traffic with Mark giving directions. He glanced in the mirror to look at a car that he thought had been behind him for longer than was normal. Sometimes he told Liam the street to take and sometimes he just pointed.

"For fuck's sake!" said Liam. "It's no use pointing your fucking finger. Give us some proper directions What if we get pulled over? I've got a gun taped under the fucking dashboard!"

"Turn right here then park up at the end," said Mark.

Liam shook his head. "Here?"

"Aye, just here on the right."

"Is it here, like?" Liam asked.

"No, it's through the park and across the road. They don't like cars around the flat cos it attracts too much attention. So I just pull up around here somewhere."

"Makes sense, I suppose. How much is it again?"

"Two hundred quid for the lot. You'll get a massage an all if you want one."

"I've got a hard on already."

"Like I really needed to know that." said Mark, as he shook his head in feigned disgust.

They got out of the car and Mark cocked his head to indicate the direction of travel and Liam followed on behind. They puddle--hopped their way through the unlit park and out of the other side to the busy main road. Mark looked across to the picture of the fat balding man looking down from the hoarding above to advertise Regal King Size cigarettes. The advertisement illuminated the pavement before them and their road to paradise, or the closest thing they'd get to paradise that night. Neither of them smoked and Mark especially found it a disgusting habit, a thought that was generally shared by most fit people he knew. He considered smoking to be for weak people who didn't have the discipline or the drive to be fit and healthy, qualities every fighter needed, and that he had in abundance. As they walked down the dimly lit alley, he reflected that even the back lanes in Jesmond were a cut above the ones in Shields.

"Here we are," Mark said.

"What, here?"

"Aye, here."

Liam looked like an excited school kid about to nick sweets from the corner shop as he followed Mark through the gate which he closed quietly behind him. They alighted the staircase and Mark knocked gently on the door that was opened by the stunningly beautiful Katina.

Her long blonde hair reached halfway down her back and the white knitted dress she wore hugged her perfect figure and showed off a pair of long, slim, toned legs. Her makeup looked like it had been applied by a professional on a movie set. Liam looked lost for words as he stared into her piercing blue eyes. Mark knew what he was hoping: that this was Katina's friend, who he was going to be seeing naked very soon. He looked crestfallen when Mark kissed her on her cheek and introduced them in their immaculately clean kitchen.

"Liam, this little beauty is Katina. Kat, this is my little

brother, Liam."

"I hope he's not too little!" an unseen female voice called out from further inside.

"Well, I've had no complaints so far!" said Liam. Despite the bravado, Liam's nervousness was obvious.

"Well, come in and make yourselves comfortable," said Katina, in heavily accented English. "Anya will be through in a minute. She is just making herself beautiful for you, Liam. Would you like a drink? Beer or Vodka?"

"Beer for me please," said Liam.

"And the same for me," Mark added.

"And what has happened to your face?" Katina took Mark's chin gently in her hand and gave him a concerned look.

"Nothing much," said Mark. "You want to see the state of the other guy."

Katina went back to the kitchen and returned with two ice cold beers, which they both took a sip of as they looked at each other with conspiratorial eyes.

No expense had been spared on the decor and this wasn't a low rent flat that served anyone looking for a cheap thrill. New looking, black leather couches lined two walls of the sitting room and tasteful paintings of semi-naked women hung on the green-patterned, flock-wallpapered walls. An unusually designed oblong glass coffee table was the centrepiece of the room, above which hung a cut glass chandelier. A pair of thick, black velvet curtains covered one wall, which led to the girl's private seating area that was off limits to the punters. The carpet felt spongy and new. An unseen hi-fi played hushed music, which Mark always thought sounded like something you'd hear in a department store lift.

The girls didn't advertise in the *Daily Sport* and pull in the dregs of society; this was a high-class establishment with top end girls and it was word of mouth only. The clientele was a mixture of businessmen, wide boys and villains who all had one thing in common: money. It was two hundred quid for a full service and that was four times the going rate. But you got what you paid for: top class women in a clean and discreet environment. It was more if you wanted to stay longer or do anything other than straight sex. They would accommodate most requests and pulled in at least a grand a day each. There were operating costs to account for, which was basically protection, but they wanted for nothing and if things got out of hand, back-up wasn't far away. Any sign of trouble, and a few stamps of the feet later, a gorilla of a man would appear from the downstairs flat and eject the unruly punter, but thankfully that didn't happen too often. They would keep an apartment for six months or sometimes longer, depending what the neighbours were like, and then re-locate before the police caught on. Same number, same clients.

Mark first frequented the cathouse a few months earlier after being put onto it by one of his drug contacts and he was smitten by Katina from the moment they met. Each time he climbed into bed with Lynn he would shut his eyes and think about Katina, her eyes, her smell, her beautiful body. He spent five or six hundred pounds a week there, but it was worth it to him, and sometimes he didn't get charged. Mark had an inkling that Katina had a soft spot for him too. He wasn't the best-looking guy around and a bit rough around the edges, but he tried to treat her well. She'd told him most her clients were overweight, middle-aged businessmen, and she'd told Mark her story.

She'd met Anya a couple of years earlier when they'd worked at the same strip club in Manchester. Both of their boyfriends were big players in the Moss Side drugs world, and after one shooting too many they finished work one night, jumped into their car and headed north, never to return to Manchester. No goodbyes and no Dear John letters. Another strip club and a few private clients later, they were turning tricks together and making a good cash. They both sent money back to their families in Ukraine. They would never tell them where they were or what they were doing, but Katina supposed her folks guessed the latter part anyway.

"So, you must be Liam? I am Anya." An elfin girl with brown eyes and dark curls walked into the sitting room and sat on Liam's lap. She gave him a peck on the cheek, letting him take in a nose of her perfume.

"Aye, that's me," he said nervously. "I'm Mark's brother." Mark and Katina looked on in amusement.

"I know, and I have been looking forward to meeting you all day," Anya teased.

"Mark, shall we go next door and leave these two alone?" Katina asked.

"Aye, sounds good to me," replied Mark.

"Have fun," Mark said, as he and Katina left the room.

*   *   *

"So, Liam, what would you like?" asked Anya.

"Er . . . just a suck and a fuck."

"You mean the full works." She smiled back. "That will be two hundred pounds. Is that OK? And you need to pay me first."

"Aye, that's fine, pet. Here you go." He took a wad of twenty-pound notes from his back pocket and counted them out onto the table.

"Thank you. Now, you come with me." She took him by the hand and led him into the bedroom next-door.

He kicked off his trainers and felt the soft plush carpet under his feet as he looked around the room. The bedroom was spotless, just like the front room. A dimly lit lamp with a dark red shade illuminated the boudoir and a super-king-sized bed with a wooden frame sat in the centre of the left side wall. The rose-smelling sheets looked freshly pressed and a set of handcuffs hung from each bed post. The ceiling was mirrored and a set of blackout curtains stopped any daylight from entering and the neighbours from seeing the shadows of any figures inside.

"Why don't you make yourself comfortable and I'll be back in a minute," she purred. You can put your clothes on the chaise longue."

He did as she suggested and stripped off his clothes. Lying naked on the bed, he looked at himself in the mirrors above, as excited about being in a brothel for the first time as he was about the upcoming sex.

When Anya returned, he opened her satin nightdress

and showed him what he was paying for. His heart started thumping at the sight of her perfect tanned body contrasting against her white lacy bra and G-string. She moved over to the bed and lifted a leg, which she placed on his bare chest.

He reached out and stroked her smooth calf and stared into her big brown eyes. When he had entered the flat, he thought Katina was the most beautiful woman he'd ever seen, but in less than ten seconds with Anya he'd fully changed his mind.

She sat on the bed and lent forward, brushing her soft hair against him as she placed a kiss on his cheek. He turned to kiss her mouth but she pulled away, which Liam thought strange. Turning away from him she took his cock in her hand and seemed to admire it while he ran his hands over her toned body. He hadn't been near a woman who was half as nice as Anya before and she was much better looking than the women that he pulled down the coast, the ones who hung around him for free drink and drugs. He knew he was averagely good looking at best and had no illusions that, without paying for it, he would never touch a woman like her. He could also see how easy it was for Mark to fall in love with Katina next door.

Lying back, he hardly moved. Anya stared straight into his eyes while giving him a blow job and he had to summon all his willpower not to come there and then.

"How would you like to fuck me?" she asked, as she removed her bra and knickers.

"I want you to ride me while I watch you do it," he said.

She took a condom from the drawer, rolled it onto Liams rock hard penis then threw her right leg over him. She lifted herself up and slid him inside her. He lay there with his arms outstretched and his hands on the outside of her thighs as she fucked him, gyrating, up and down then rocking back to front. As he watched her fake breasts bounce up and down, he thought about how long it would be before he could afford another visit. He decided and that this was going to be his regular haunt as well as Mark's. His eyes closed as he came, and he pulled her down tightly as the condom filled with semen. She looked at him, gave him a low playful growl, then reached forward and kissed his cheek before climbing off and wrapping her robe around herself. "You can put condom in the bin," she said.

"Er . . . aye, OK."

*   *   *

Mark was in the other bedroom talking with Katina. They lay naked in bed but hadn't got around to having sex yet. For Mark it wasn't just the sex that he came for, it was to see Katina too. She'd told him of her childhood in Ukraine, and if Mark thought that his rough upbringing in North Shields was bad then it was nothing compared to hers. She told him of the depressing, Soviet built, five-storey apartment block she grew up in, of the rats and the rubbish and where people had nothing that wasn't supplied by the state. Every apartment was the same: same TV, same furniture, same problems. Nobody was prosperous and there was no chance of her ever being so unless she left, which she did at the first opportunity and using the only resource she had available: her pussy.

After sleeping with enough men to be able to afford a flight, she boarded a plane and had no plans to return. Even though Mark knew she made good money he looked after her and told her that if anyone ever hurt her all she had to do was call him. He knew she worked for the Frasers, but he didn't care; he would be there for her no matter what. But he would never leave Lynn for Katina even if she asked. Lynn was rough as old boots, but they'd been together since they were fourteen and they genuinely couldn't live without each other. She knew he played around and Mark guessed she had an inkling it was with a hooker, but she seemed to put it to the back of her mind and pretended it didn't happen so the boat wasn't rocked and life could continue as normal. He gave her a decent life and they didn't want for much, but all that could all change in a heartbeat if he was locked up, or worse.

Mark and Katina heard Anya make her way to the bathroom and they paused mid-conversation. They looked at each other for a second before Mark said, "Fuck me, he didn't last long."

They both burst out laughing and Katina bit the pillow to stop her from being heard.

"Liam!" Mark called out.

"What?"

"Come here!"

Liam peered around the adjacent door having clearly just pulled on his jeans and t-shirt. Katina hid her face and turned away to stop him seeing her amusement at his short performance.

"So, how was it?" asked Mark.

"Aye, canny." A smile came across Liam's face and his cheeks reddened.

"It must have been."

"What do you mean?"

"Well, you didn't exactly break any fucking records did you?" Mark and Katina burst out laughing again.

"Fuck off, you fucking knob!" As he left the room, Liam closed the door a little harder than normal.

* * *

Across town, another North Shields villain was in a sexual encounter that he shouldn't have been but, just like Mark, he couldn't stay away.

The concierge at the Copthorne Hotel greeted Carl politely as he handed him the room key that Marie had left for him behind reception. The staff were starting to recognise him as a regular guest, and he'd decided it was time to find another hotel for their secret trysts. It was one thing him being recognised, but if someone cottoned on that it was Marie he was meeting and tongues started to wag, then it could lead to a big problem for both of them. An innocuous comment about seeing them together could get around quickly and if it did it might get back to Les. There were plenty of "it" girls in Newcastle who hated Marie because of her lifestyle, and plenty who would spread jealous gossip just to split them up. There were also a few who would run back to him just to get in his good books.

He opened the door to Room 423 and stepped inside to see Marie in her regular sex outfit of a black bra and hold up stockings. She was lying on her back, propped up against the pillows with a glass of champagne in one hand and a vibrator in the other. She slid it slowly in and out of herself, pausing for a second as the clit tickler hit its spot. As usual, for her own cheap thrills, the curtains were wide open and the light was left on so the world could maybe see in. "Where've you been?" she sighed. "I got sick of waiting so I decided to start without you."

"Fuck me, you don't mess around, I'm only ten minutes late." He said, glancing at his Rolex watch. He put his car keys and phone on the table, unbuttoned his shirt and walked over to the bed with the intention of kissing her.

She held up a finger to stop him. "Ah, ah! You're late. You can't just expect to rock up when you feel like it and get stuck in. You'll have to wait your turn. Sit over there, and when I'm ready for you I'll let you know."

He paused and looked at her, unusually lost for words. She had him wrapped around her little finger and they both knew it. No matter what she did, he would still come back for more. She was the only person in his life that had any hold over him and, if the truth be told, he loved every second of it, and so did she.

He did as he was told and sat in the chair, kicking off his shoes and socks and sliding his jeans over his muscular legs until he was naked. He sat there, slowly masturbating as she closed her eyes and brought herself to orgasm.

"Now get over here and clean me up!" she ordered.

He knew what she wanted, and he did what he was told. He lifted her thighs and pushed them back, and then buried his face between her legs.

They spent the next hour having sex, only pausing to drink from the champagne that was customary on their hush-hush encounters. And when she was done, it was over. It didn't matter if he wanted to carry on; when Marie was satisfied, that was it. He wanted to wake up with her, but he knew he never would. Even if something happened to Les, she would never be his. She would find herself another millionaire to pander to her needs and whims. She would never shack up with what she considered Carl to be and exactly what he was: a glorified street thug that had done alright out of life.

Smiling at him, she dressed and straightened her tight leather skirt before kissing his cheek and making her way home again.

He lay on the bed and considered staying the night, but he had business to attend to and, as much as he felt like falling asleep on the huge soft mattress, he knew he couldn't stay. He showered and left, making his way down to reception.

"I'd like to check out please."

"Certainly, sir," said the receptionist, "change of plans? Let me take a look. Ah – the lady has already checked out, sir. The room was in her name."

"Aye . . . eh . . . course it was." Carl glanced towards the greying forty-odd-year-old who looked back at him with all-knowing eyes, eyes that told Carl that he knew exactly who the lady was, and who she was married to.

As he drove down the car park exit ramp and away along the bustling quayside, Carl decided that he was using somewhere else next time.

*   *   *

Liam was getting the feeling that he'd outstayed his welcome and he wanted to leave. He could tell that Anya no longer wanted him around, and why would she after their paid-for sex was over. He was running out of polite conversation, but it was her one-word answers that were making him feel like it was time for him to go. He put his ear to Katina's bedroom door to see if he could hear them having sex and double knocked gently.

"What?" Mark answered.

"Nowt. I'm wanting to get off, what you doing?"

"Stopping here for a bit. What you leaving for?"

"I just am. You coming or what?"

"I've just told you, I'm staying for a bit."

"Well, I'm going. How you gonna get back down the coast?"

"Fuck knows. I'll get a taxi, I suppose. I'm not gonna fucking walk it am I?"

"Aye fair dos. You sure you don't want to come?"

"For fuck's sake, I've just told you twice! I'm stopping. Just take the car and I'll catch up with you tomorrow."

"Alright, calm down. Enjoy your night. See ya later." Liam put his trainers back on and made his way to the back door. "Right then, Anya, I'm off," he said.

"Goodnight, Liam."

"It was nice to meet you and all that. Er... I'll come up again some time."

"Yes, yes," she said. "It was good to meet you too, and hopefully I see you soon." She smiled and Liam decided that she genuinely liked him, despite the way she seemed distant and disinterested only a few minutes earlier – but then women were like that, so his mates always said. Looking at her now, he had no doubt that she thought he was somebody really special.

He walked off down the back lane and towards the main road a happy and satisfied man. He'd just had sex with the most beautiful woman of his life, and he pretended to himself that he hadn't really paid for it. It was expensive for the few minutes he lasted, but he thought it was worth it and planned to get the number off Mark the next day so he could pop up whenever he was horny.

The clock struck eleven and the streets were quiet as he walked up the lane with his head still in the clouds. He wondered if Mark would stay the night or return home to Lynn. As he reached the junction, the light of the advertising hoarding illuminated him, and he squinted slightly. It was a sharp contrast from the dark back lane of a few seconds earlier. There was a rustle from the bushes behind him and he froze. Then his head snapped around and he picked up his hands, waiting for the attack to come. Quick as a flash, he turned to see a mangey looking stray dog emerge from the foliage and walk off down the alley from where he'd just emerged. He shook his head and composed himself as he crossed the main road and walked back through the wet park towards his car.

Fumbling in his pockets for the car key, he didn't see the figure dressed in black holding the silver revolver who'd been waiting for his return, nor did he hear the two shots that rang out into the night.

The first slug struck him in the back, piercing his heart before exiting his chest and lodging in a wall. A split second later another was pumped into his dying body as it fell to the pavement, making sure that Liam Taylor was no longer of this earth.

*   *   *

When Mark Taylor heard the shots from his whorehouse bed, he knew that his brother was dead; a sixth sense told him that. He pulled on his jeans and trainers and sprinted out towards the car. He ran up the lane and through the park with the puddles splashing his jeans. Swinging himself to the right using the entrance post as an anchor, he turned the corner to be greeted by the dead and bloody body of his brother.

Liam lay on his front, head to the side and with his eyes open and with two small holes in his back. At first Mark though he was alive because there was very little blood, but the paramedics later told him that a direct shot in the heart stops it quickly and reduces the blood flow. He knelt and turned his brother over. He hugged and held his body, but he knew that he was gone. The exit wounds were huge where the large calibre bullets had left Liam's chest. Mark pulled his head in and cried like child. He had lost his brother and his best friend, and an instantaneous wave of grief swept over him. "No, no, no," was all he could say, again and again as the ambulance pulled up with the police arriving a few minutes later. They tried to resuscitate Liam but their attempts were futile; he'd died when the first bullet struck.

Mark was taken to Pilgrim Street Police Station, which he was told was for his own protection. This was partly true, but it was also so he wouldn't grab a gun and go on the rampage while still in a state of shock. The city centre police didn't know much about him offhand, but a check of his record and the intelligence they already had on him made sure he wasn't going anywhere that night.

The park and the immediate area were cordoned off and the forensic team began their painstaking search for evidence while the murder squad interviewed the residents. There were no direct witnesses but there were plenty who'd heard the gun shots, and a couple who glimpsed the gunman as he took flight. It didn't take them long to locate Liam's car as being foreign to the street, and not much longer to find the .38 calibre automatic that was taped behind the dashboard.

When Mark first entered, he was put in an interview room, but as soon as the gun was found he became a suspect, not for the killing, but for possession of the gun. That was enough to keep him in custody. He was cautioned at the desk and led down the steps into the Victorian era cells, which had a feint smell of urine, their white brick patterned tiles adorned with the names of people who'd called them home for a few hours or days of their lives. As the custody sergeant led Mark down, he wondered how many people had "accidentally" taken a fall down those steps over the years. They paused at the bottom while his name was chalked up against his new temporary home: Cell Six. When he was told to take his shoes off, he baulked at the idea of walking in stockinged feet on a floor that had been covered in human fluids many times over. But he did as he was asked. He wasn't in the frame of mind to kick off that night. He just wanted answers that he knew he wasn't going to receive right then.

A few hours later, he was interviewed by two Murder Squad detectives who tried all the ways they knew to get him to admit the gun was his and to put someone in the frame for the killing. He kept his mouth shut, knowing that he couldn't have any paperwork in existence that proved he was naming names or he would be finished in the underworld forever. And he also knew that any fingerprints on the gun could only be Liam's. So providing he denied it, then he was in the clear.

At the crime scene the forensic team was hard at work under the watchful eye of the local press who were looking for the next big headline. The police were keeping any information close to their chests at such an early stage of the investigation. The Chief Superintendent of Northumbria Police went on TV to reel off the usual lines about how it was an isolated incident and that the public shouldn't feel afraid; the trouble was in gangland and it wouldn't affect the law-abiding citizens of the city.

A six-person forensic team was combing the street and the undergrowth with their long white poles in a painstaking inch by inch search and leaving the proverbial no stone unturned.

As SOCO officer Janice Cartwright prodded into the undergrowth, a small metal object caught her eye. She bent down and brushed back the wet grass to take a closer look while taking care not to disturb the immediate area too much. A police photographer was called over who carefully placed an L shaped marker next to it and took a series of photos. Once the photos were finished, she called over a Detective Inspector of the Murder Squad who picked up the item with a pen using his latex glove covered hand and dropped it into a clear evidence bag.

"Think it could be something important?" Janice asked her superior.

"Not sure. Maybe it is or maybe it isn't, but it's a good find. We'll log it and take it back to the station. I doubt it's from the gunman, he's a sloppy operator if he's left that there, but stranger things have happened."

"Thanks. Always good to do my bit." She smiled back at him before replacing her paper mask and carrying on her search.

"Have you found anything else?"

"No, sir. A few footprints, but they could be from anyone. Ground's wet in places and there's plenty of people who come through the park – dog walkers and such."

"OK and keep up the good work."

Later that day, doors were being booted off their hinges all over North Shields as the police went looking for the hitman. They knew who'd fallen out with who, but the list of enemies that Mark and Liam had was a long one.

George and Kenny had a rude awakening at 5am, as did Rob, Carl and all of Liam's close associates. Each of them was taken to a separate police station for questioning to stop them encountering each other before their interviews. Over the coming days, more people would be dragged into the net, but considering how many people the Taylors had taken liberties with, it was doubtful everyone would get a visit.

*   *   *

Carl sat on the black plastic chair in the interview room in Byker police station with his solicitor and he knew they had nothing on him. His eyes moved from the plain blue walls to the panic strip on the wooden rail that surrounded the room. His mischievous mind considered hitting it to see what the reaction time would be before the room was filled with coppers. If he wasn't sitting facing such a serious charge, he probably would have, just for a laugh. He sat in silence with ganglands' favourite solicitor, Mr Edgebaston, waiting for the interview to commence and mulling over his situation. Sure, he'd fallen out with the Taylor's, but then again who hadn't? Apart from himself and the Bolton crew it could have been anyone who'd shot him. They'd taxed at least a dozen people in the last few months, some of whom they'd battered in the process. Then there were the ones they'd taken liberties with as doormen. It could be one of them, or their mates, or their brothers looking for revenge. He was nervous as he sat there but confident that if he kept his mouth shut then he would walk.

There was a knock on the door then a pause before Detective Inspector James Douglas and Detective Sergeant Liz Wood entered the small, square room. They carried with them some paperwork and two blank cassette tapes, which they placed on the wooden table along with a bag, the contents of which were unseen. DS Wood unwrapped the tapes and wrote on both before inserting them into the black Neal tape machine. It started with a buzzing alarm and whirred as the tapes turned simultaneously.

The interview began.

"For the benefit of the tape, we are conducting this interview in relation to the murder of Liam Taylor in Jesmond, Newcastle last night, 24th January 1994. Present are myself, Detective Inspector James Douglas . . ." He pointed his pen in turn to each person in the room. " . . . Detective Sergeant Liz Wood . . . Gary Edgebaston, Solicitor representing Carl Liddle . . . Carl Liddle." DI Douglas put his elbows on the table and laced his fingers together. "So, Mr Liddle, can you tell me where you were last night at 11p.m?"

"No reply," said Carl.

"Can you tell me of your movements yesterday evening leading up to 11p.m?"

"No reply." Carl glanced towards his solicitor in a swift check that he was answering as advised.

"Can you tell me why you are refusing to answer questions, Mr Liddle? This is a very serious matter. You see, Liam Taylor was murdered last night, as I'm sure you are aware, and we believe you may know something about it."

"No reply."

"Mr Liddle, if you are not guilty then you have nothing to be afraid of. If you tell us where you were then we can eliminate you as a suspect."

"No reply."

"Mr Liddle, were you in Jesmond last night around 11p.m?"

"No reply."

"Mr Liddle, were you in Newcastle last night at or up to 11p.m?"

Carl looked between the two sets of eyes looking back at him across the table. He knew he was in Newcastle, but did the murder squad know that too? Even if they did, it wouldn't put him at the scene, but being in the vicinity could be enough for a slender conviction and he knew it. "No reply."

"Mr Liddle, I will ask you again, were you in Newcastle last night at or up to 11p.m?"

"No reply."

DI Douglas reached into the bag on the table and removed a clear plastic evidence bag containing a key and keychain. "For the benefit of the tape, I'm showing the suspect a key and keychain that was found at the scene of the murder of Liam Taylor. Can you tell me, Mr Liddle, if you have you have seen this key and chain anywhere before?"

Carl's heart sank. The key that he was looking at was the one he'd lent to Paul, the same one he'd put in the ashtray of his RS turbo a few weeks before. He'd forgotten it was in there. The car stereo wasn't what the thief was after, he was looking for evidence that he could use to frame him for the killing. He kept his composure, but he was frightened inside. This was a set up, and one he would have difficulty talking his way out of. He was in shock as his mind raced, thinking who could have taken it. He tried to remember if he'd ever left anyone alone in the car when filling it up or at any other time, but he couldn't. Truth be told, it could have been taken by anybody, and from where Carl was sitting it was doubtful he would ever find out.

"Mr Liddle, I will ask you again . . . have you seen this keychain before?"

"No reply."

"Mr Liddle, when we attended your house, we tried this key in your back door and it unlocked it straight away. I put it to you that this is your house key. Could you explain how it was found at the scene of the murder of Liam Taylor?"

"No reply." was all he could say.

It was obvious that Mr Edgebaston was as caught out by this development as Carl could tell he was shocked. "In light of this evidence," he said, "I'd like to speak to my client in private, and I request that the interview is suspended."

"Mr Edgebaston," said DI Douglas, "this is a murder enquiry, and I have some further questions for Mr Liddle."

"I appreciate that, Inspector Douglas, but if I can speak to my client in private, I may be able to shed some light on the matter of the key."

DI Douglas scratched his chin for a moment and then agreed. "Interview terminated at 11.10am," he announced to the voice recorder. Then he and DS Wood left the room leaving Mr Edgebaston and Carl alone.

"So, how do you explain the key?" asked Mr Edgebaston.

"I don't know. It's mine, but I wasn't in Jesmond when he was shot. I don't know how it got there. It must have been planted."

"Who had access to the key? Did you lend it to anyone?"

"A mate of mine but he gave us it back. It was in the car, but someone broke into it and nicked the radio a few weeks ago. It could have been taken then, or someone could have lifted it from the ashtray."

"And did you report the theft to the police?"

"What do you think?" said Carl.

"And can you explain your whereabouts at the time of the killing? It's well within your rights to no reply the interview, but a piece of your property has been found at the scene. So, unless you can prove where you were at the time, the evidence points to you, unfortunately."

Carl sat with his elbows on the table and his face in his hands. If he told them he was at the Copthorne with Marie then the police would go there first, and then to Marie's house. Les would want to know why she was booking hotel rooms and who she was going to see. A few discrete and not so discrete enquiries would follow, and it wouldn't take long before he found out that it was Carl, his friend and business associate, who wouldn't be either for very much longer. If Les found out about them, it was the end for him. He could, and possibly would have him killed either inside or outside of prison, and the thought of that wasn't particularly appealing. Even if he didn't, he would make sure that nobody worked with him again. There was also no guarantee that Marie would make a statement. He knew how devious she was, and she might just deny it to save her own hide. He'd have to front it out and hope the key wasn't enough to convict him or that they would find the real killer another way. It was a risky strategy but the only one he could see available. There was nothing else that put him at the scene because he wasn't there – no gunshot residue and no weapon – so he knew he had a chance of beating it. But he also knew where he was going in the coming days: on a one-way van ride to Durham Jail

8: SING ABOUT THE SIX BLADE

A beam of early morning light radiated through the gap in the partly drawn curtains, piercing the darkness of Paul's bedroom as it shone into his face. He opened his eyes into the blinding glare and rolled over on the double bed, pulling his duvet in tightly before closing them again. He hoped to force himself back to sleep so he could ignore the events that were occurring around him.

Carl was locked up inside the Victorian era cesspool that was HMP Durham. He'd lost his friend and protector, and it made him feel uneasy. Now he had nobody to turn to if things got heavy, and he no longer had access to large amounts of drugs on tick. He needed find another way to make money – and fast. There was still a little left over from the robbery, but it wouldn't last much longer if it wasn't supplemented with a steady income. As much as he disliked the idea, he was going to have to go cap in hand to Craig or Mark as another source of drugs or start thieving again.

The only contact he'd had with any of them was when Matty turned up wanting Mark's smack back. He hadn't asked any questions and Paul decided it was best not to mention why he had it in the first place. Matty offered him the opportunity to start dealing hash from his house, but he declined, mumbling something about going straight and getting out of the life.

Mark hadn't been seen. He was no doubt holed-up and plotting revenge against the Bolton mob. Paul had been told he'd convinced himself that it was them and not Carl that was behind Liam's murder. Carl had no reason to shoot either Taylor because he'd just chinned the pair of them. He'd do what he needed to if attacked, but they hadn't done that and he had no need to pick up a gun. It wasn't his stamp, and everyone knew it.

As he lay there trying his best to ignore the realities of life, the phone rang in the front room. He ignored it at first but It rang and rang, so he jumped out of bed with the warm duvet still wrapped around him and ran to catch it before it rung off. He picked up the receiver apprehensively, unsure who it was going to be.

"Paul?"

"Who's this?" he asked, as he stretched out along the settee and reached out to stop the phone being pulled from the table as the handset cord reached its full extension.

"It's your friend from the Dam." Said Regan, not mentioning his own name over the phone.

"Oh, Aye. How's it going mate?" Paul rubbed the sleep from his eyes and took a sip from the glass of water that had been lying on the table since the previous night.

"Not bad, not bad. And you?"

"Aye, I'm alright mate. What's going on?" Paul had no idea how Regan had his number and it never ceased to amaze him how people found out where he was, or how to get in touch.

"Not much my end. What's happened to Carl? I've been told he's been remanded for killing Liam Taylor."

"Aye he has. How do you know?"

"News travels fast, mate. Even over here. Have you

spoken to him?"

"Not directly. All I've heard is they've found something of his at the scene. Apart from that, just what I've seen on the news. Carl wouldn't have shot him. It's just not him."

"I heard the same."

"How'd you hear?"

"I hear all sorts, me. He'd just chinned the two of them, hadn't he?"

"Aye, I was there. He made a proper mess of Mark and put Liam to sleep. He didn't really need to shoot them if you ask me. That's if he did it at all." Paul reached out to the table and picked up the Rizla papers that lay on top. He removed three and started to make a joint as he chatted away.

"That's true," said Regan. "It's bad shit this. So, are you going to see him?"

"I'm going up on Thursday. Me names on the visiting order with his sister and her fella."

"You got a pen?"

"Aye, I've got one here."

"Take down this number – it's a Dutch burner – and let us know what he says when you see him. If he needs owt, let us know and I'll sort it. But don't worry, he'll be alright in there. He's a big lad."

Paul jotted down the number that Regan reeled off on the top of the previous night's *Evening Chronicle* then tore it off and tucked it under the phone.

"So, what's the crack with you?" said Regan. "You had any visits from anyone?"

"Nah, no police and no radgies, thankfully," Paul lied. "I thought I might get pulled in cos I was there when he chinned them, but I've heard nothing at all. Nowt from Mark and his cronies either, thank fuck. Not sure which one's worse."

"You'll be fine. If you haven't had a tug by now, I doubt you'll get one. Mark's head will be too far up his own arse to bother about you and the bizzies think they've got their man."

"Aye, I can't be arsed with them crackerjacks paying us another visit."

"Listen, I've got to go. But if you hear owt or Carl needs anything just gis a bell."

"Will do." Paul put the handset down on the receiver, lay back and lit the freshly rolled joint. He stared at the ceiling as he pondered what to do next.

*   *   *

Kenny had returned from taking Nikki to school and was settled down at his kitchen table. He drank his early morning coffee as he waited for his cousin and Rob to arrive. He'd had a good grilling from the Murder Squad and was glad he hadn't had anything serious in the house when they came. The only thing they took was the baseball bat he kept next to the bed. He could prove his whereabouts around the time of the killing. He'd returned home around ten and then ordered a takeaway. The police had checked his story with the taxi company and the delivery driver, so he was in the clear. As he sipped his coffee, he pondered getting the money together for Rob.

This was his share of the shooter's fee for Rob to pass on. Then Kenny had second thoughts: now wasn't the best time to be caught with a big lump of cash. The police could say that it was to pay for the shooting, which was technically true.

Before he was halfway down his cup, he heard a big-engined car outside. He made his way into the front room and peeped around the blinds.

Outside was George's Carlton Gsi 3000. The 12 cylinder engine fell silent and out stepped George, followed by Rob from the passenger door. Kenny let them in and the three of them gathered around the small kitchen table.

"Cuppa?" asked Kenny, as the newscaster on the portable radio talked of Michael Jackson settling his lawsuit allegation for molesting a thirteen-year-old. Kenny turned the volume knob down and topped up the kettle with water from the tap. He tutted as some water splashed onto his jeans, which made him look like he'd wet himself. This triggered a small laugh and a raise of the eyebrows from his cousin.

"Aye, please," said Rob. "Don't suppose there's a chance of a bacon sarnie as well is there?"

"I do believe there is," said Kenny. "You want one as well, cuz?"

"Aye go on then," said George. "And one sugar in the coffee."

Kenny leaned back on the fridge with his arms crossed. "So, then . . . I see they've got Carl for doing Liam. At least it takes the blame off us."

"Certainly does, thank fuck," said George. "What did they say to youse two?"

"They just kept on and on about the shooting at yours and played on the fact you'd smacked Mark outside World's End," said Kenny.

"Aye, apparently they saw the whole thing," said George. "They were plotted up down the street just by chance."

"They never mentioned that to me," said Rob. "They mentioned blasting Mark's windows out, though." He wiggled to adjust his holster and gun to stop it digging into his ribs.

"Where were you?" Kenny asked Rob.

"I was having a meal in the Rawalpindi in Tynemouth. How about youse two?"

"With who?" asked George, as he looked over at the statues of the three wise monkeys that Kenny kept on the windowsill.

"Just a couple of lads from over the water," Rob replied vaguely. "You won't know them."

"I'd just got in and phoned a takeaway," Kenny said. "And George was in the Berkley Tavern. Apparently the CID had seen him around the same time, so they knew it couldn't be him."

"Not like them to put a word in for any of us," said Rob.

"Guess it must have been logged, so there's nowt they can do," said Kenny.

The kettle clicked and he poured the steaming water into two matching red cups and put them on the table then lifted the lid from the sugar bowl and stuck in a silver teaspoon. The bacon was spitting on the grill, and an occasional flame shot out from under the glowing element. Kenny removed it and put the browning bacon onto the bread buns he'd already laid out, burning his fingers as he moved the sizzling rashers which drew a tut and a shake of the head from George.

"You not use a fork like normal people? I don't want your scruffy fingers all over me fucking sarnie."

"Scruffy fingers? Fuck off, I just washed them before you turned up." Kenny flipped over the top half of each bun and passed them their completed breakfast. He then removed a bottle of tomato sauce and a bottle of HP sauce from the cupboard above the sink and put them on the shiny wooden tabletop.

"Aye, whatever." George picked up his breakfast bap and tucked in.

"So, when do you want the cash?" Kenny asked Rob.

"Well, here's a thing . . ."

"What's that?" said George.

"It wasn't our man."

"What?" said George. He and Kenny stopped abruptly and looked at Rob.

"It wasn't him that shot Liam," said Rob.

"So, who the fuck was it then?" mumbled George through a mouthful of bacon sandwich.

"Dunno. Carl by the looks of it."

"Eh?" said Kenny.

"It couldn't be," said George. "He's not a hide-in-the-bushes-and-shoot-some-fucker type of fella."

"That's what I think an' all," said Rob. "But it doesn't really matter at the end of the day. They've got Carl for it, and we don't have to fork out ten k for the shooter."

"Fifteen." George furrowed his brow at Rob.

"Aye, fifteen. What did I say, ten?"

"Aye, you fucking did," said George.

They both looked at Rob, who looked back sheepishly. The cousins knew Rob would likely skim off the top but they didn't think it would be by that much.

"I can't believe that Liam gets done and they lock Carl up for it," said Kenny. "Talk about a touch."

"So, who'd you reckon done it, and what for?" said Rob.

"No idea," said Kenny. "Take your pick, they've pissed off enough people."

"Well, whoever did it wasn't our man," said Rob, "and it makes no difference to us who it was or that Carl's in the frame. And at least one of them cunts is six feet under. It was supposed to be Mark, but one's better than none, I suppose." He pulled a small piece of bacon fat from between his teeth.

Kenny looked at him in slight disgust and passed him the kitchen roll. "And what about Mark? What's he saying?"

"I've been told he's not convinced it's Carl either," said Rob. "He thinks it's us, which is almost the truth – or it should have been, any road."

"Always with your ear to the ground," said George.

Rob nodded and smiled.

"So where do we go from here?" asked Kenny.

"What's the plan now?"

"I was thinking about this in the cells," said George. "I reckon we give it a few weeks for everything to die down and then we make our move. If we can get a hold of either Mark or Matty and do them, then there's only one left. And I reckon Matty hasn't got it in him to keep it together himself, so we go for Mark. We do what they did and get everybody back selling for us. But, unlike them, we let everyone keep their gear and don't tax them."

"What the fuck are we going to do that for?" said Kenny. "We could make a fortune."

"Because it keeps everybody on our side and they'll be remembered as bunch of wankers that nobody wanted owt to do with. There's no point in being arseholes with everybody all of the time. Look, they've just took the business off us and now we're taking it back, but they won't be the last to try. Somebody else will come along sooner or later and for the next time we need to keep as many people onside as we can."

"Smart," agreed Rob.

"And what about Carl's punters?" asked Kenny.

"We'll take them on as well. Craig will know who most of them are and we'll just pay them a friendly visit. We can interrogate that lad he hangs about with. He'll be able to fill in the gaps. Anyways, it doesn't look like Carl's going to be around for a while, and if gets a not guilty and wants his business back then we'll just have to cross that bridge when we come to it. But for now, we'll just wait and pick our moment."

*   *   *

Later the same evening, when the sky was dark and the traffic was dying down, Mark climbed into the driver's seat of his Sierra Cosworth and drove off to meet Cookie. He'd been summoned earlier that afternoon and he'd tried to get out of it by telling him he wasn't up for it because of Liam's death. But Cookie was having none of it, and he insisted they meet up. It had been over a week since the killing, and once Carl had been remanded and the visits from the police became less frequent, Cookie deemed it safe enough for them to get together.

They met in a lay by off Berwick Hill Road, the rural back way to Ponteland. Mark pulled into the pre-arranged spot and saw Cookie had arrived before him. He was sitting reading a newspaper in what he presumed was a CID car. Apart from his name and the station he worked at, he knew very little about Cookie, and the times he'd enquired in general conversation drew no firm answers. Not that he particularly cared; he was getting the protection that kept him out of jail and that was all that really mattered. Ending up in prison on the same wing as Carl would be worse than whatever charge he would be remanded for, so keeping Cookie onside was the best thing he could do. Not that he had much of a choice.

Cookie lowered his newspaper as Mark parked next to him and he motioned with his head for Mark to get in his car. If it was a quick meet, they'd sometimes parked up next to each other and talk through the window, but this wasn't going to be a quick exchange of money and a carry on as usual. As he walked towards Cookie, he glanced back and admired the shining paintwork and silver lattice alloys on the car he'd bought himself when things had started to go well. Cookie leaned across and opened the door and Mark climbed inside the unremarkable blue Ford Mondeo.

"Alright?" asked Cookie.

Mark smelled stale whisky on Cookie's breath. "Not bad. You?" He looked around the car and into the rear footwells, which were empty. Even though this was a police car, he wanted to make sure that nobody was hiding in the back.

"Happy?" Cookie asked, then said, "Sorry to hear about your brother. Bad shit that."

"Fucking right it is. But don't worry, I'll get to the bottom of it." Mark looked out across the field in the dimming evening light. He pictured his brother's face and thought of the pain he would inflict on his killer when he found him. His left hand caressed the smooth grey seat cloth as he subliminally made a fist with his right.

"We already have. Carl's banged up. Open and shut case, so I believe. They found his house key at the scene,"

"They told us they'd found something," Mark said, "but they didn't say what it was?"

"That's the rumour round the station anyway. So how was it? Did they ask anything about our little arrangement?"

"Nah, they didn't. It's all good."

"Just checking. If anyone find's out about us then I'll be doing more bird than you."

"Look, nobody asked a thing."

"Sure? No hints, no fishing questions?"

"No, fuck all, like I say. Do you think I'd be here if they did?"

Into the rear-view mirrors, a set of headlights shone from the road behind them: a car travelling faster than the speed limit drove down the lane. Mark put his hand nervously on the door handle in preparation for a quick exit as the sound of the engine approached. He glanced at Cookie and readied himself to run, but the car drove straight past and up the country road.

"What's up?" said Cookie, with a touch of panic in his voice. "You think you've been followed?" His head spun around as he strained to see the car disappear along the lane.

"Dunno. Fucking hope not. But I'm not hanging around if I have been. I took a few precautions on my way here to try and make sure."

"And where the fuck you gonna to run to?"

"Fuck knows. Through the fucking fields I suppose,"

Cookie shook his head. "You're happy that they're not sniffing around us, then?"

"Aye, not a word. I was waiting for it myself. They asked plenty about the Boltons and Carl, and tried to say we were all in the middle of a drugs war, but I just denied it and said fuck all. They'd heard about the fight with Carl but I wouldn't make a statement."

"Fight? He battered fuck out of the pair of you. You're making a habit of it, Mark. It was George Bolton last time, wasn't it?"

"Fuck off." Mark turned to stare at Cookie as the

steroid rage built up inside.

"But, seriously, well done for keeping your mouth shut. Few people do in a murder enquiry."

"What the fuck were you expecting? If I make a statement I'm fucked, and It's not going to bring Liam back, is it?"

"So, what's happening with the business?" Cookie tapped out a tune onto the steering wheel with his fingers while he stared into the middle distance. Something spooked him momentarily and then he let out a sigh of relief. Mark saw a rabbit's scut disappear through a gap in the hedgerow.

"Matty's taking care of things day to day while I deal with Liam's funeral and stuff, and until things die down. I haven't heard a peep from the Bolton's, which is surprising. I thought they'd be going round taxing everyone but they haven't. Not yet anyway. So, aye, all's good."

"They're just a bit smarter than you, Mark, and keeping a low profile until there's less attention around. No point in getting yourself dragged further into a murder investigation if you don't need to be is there?"

"Right enough. It shouldn't take too long till things are back on track, though. And once the funerals over we'll get back to making regular coin."

"Aye, this'll go away eventually, and then things will go back to normal – or as normal as they get anyway. So, what have you got for me today?"

"Two grand. Shame your little plan with the smack didn't come off. I had a kid sorted to plant it on Carl. If he'd been a bit quicker, I'd still have a brother and Carl would still be out of our hair."

"Aye, that's true enough. Who was he anyway?"

"Carl's hanger-on, Paul. Do you know him?"

"I can't say I do. You've mentioned him before and I've heard his name bandied about but I don't know the face."

"He's not a bad lad, really. Just hangs about with Carl, that's all. He's a young 'un that's out of his depth."

"Doesn't know about us does he?"

"For fucks sake! How the fuck is he going to know about us? My own brother didn't!"

Cookie stretched out his left hand, palm up and wiggling his fingers. "So?"

Mark took a wad of twenty-pound notes held together with two elastic bands from his inside pocket, and them into Cookies hand.

Cookie nodded his approval. "I'll count it later."

"Don't worry, it's all there. You got anything for me?"

"It's in there." Cookie pointed to the glovebox.

Mark opened it, took out a small carrier bag and looked at the clingfilm-wrapped parcels inside. "What's there?"

"260 E's, four ounces of speed and a hundred acid. And I want half."

"No problem," agreed Mark. "Anything else going on?"

"Not really. Everyone's delighted that Carl's away, even if it wasn't us that put him there. And apart from that there's not much else. I take it that it'll be you that takes over things in Shields now that Liddle's gone, but don't do it straight away. Keep me posted about what's going on, and if Bolton or anyone else tries to make a move I'll get them out the picture. It might mean an anonymous call to the station to cover our tracks, but we'll work it out, don't worry,"

"I do worry. Especially now I've lost the only person I could fully trust."

"It'll work itself out. Honestly, we've done alright so far. Anyway, I've got to go, places to be and all that."

Mark left the car without either of them saying goodbye, and Cookie reversed out of the lay-by. Once he'd gone, Mark reached into the inside pocket of his jacket and took out a small silver Dictaphone and pressed the stop button. He didn't trust Cookie, and he wanted some insurance in case he was the next one on his set-up list. But until it was needed, he would lock it away in a box in his nana's closet, where nobody knew it was except him.

* * *

The traffic was heavy as Paul travelled across the River Wear with Carl's sister, Jackie, and her husband, Stefan. Carl's brother-in-law drove the beat-up Peugeot 205 that Paul was convinced wouldn't make it to Durham and back.

Usually, they would have a parcel of drugs for whoever they were visiting, but today there was no need. Carl wouldn't take the chance of himself or any of his family being caught taking drugs into a prison, so he arranged for someone else to take the risk. He had an ounce of hash a week coming in via some lad from the West End who was on the same wing. Once the kid had it on the other side, he would keep it hidden and Carl would give him a wage in hash, the rest would be bartered for food or toiletries. That way, Carl didn't take any risk and he didn't have to suffer the indignity of shoving an ounce of hash up his backside in front of his sister. Paul and Stefan watching was one thing, but Jackie was quite another. The last time Carl was on remand, his girlfriend would smuggle hash past the security screws by inserting it into her vagina. She would go to the toilet halfway through the visit and hide it under the bin bag in the women's toilets. Once the visits were over, the cleaner would retrieve it and take it back to the wing.

Paul looked up at the high stone prison walls as they drove up Old Elvet Road. They were rough and uninviting and set against a cold, grey backdrop of a day. He thanked the Lord that it wasn't him that was on the other side. He knew plenty of villains who had spent years behind a door and, once they'd gained their freedom, they romanticised the prison system and told tales from the different ones; some funny, some sad and some genuinely scary. They outdid each other with their stories, the bigger the jail and the longer the sentence often featuring in the bragging rights. They talked like they liked it, but in many cases they were institutionalised, and had been from an early age. The threat of jail meant nothing to them, which was why they committed crime like there was no consequence and often with little remorse. But for some of them it was an escape from the realities of life: no bills, fed three times a day, free gym, no girlfriend on their case and no kids running around doing their heads in.

They parked the car and made their way to the Visitors Centre, where they handed the visiting order to the lady behind the desk.

"And who are you visiting please?" the lady asked.

Jackie handed over the paperwork. "LIddle, Carl."

"That's great, thanks. Take a seat nextdoor and we'll call you when they're ready. And help yourself to tea and coffee."

For Paul, this was always the worst part, waiting in the cold, dreary building to be called up.

Ten minutes and a lukewarm cup of coffee later, they walked up the steep bank to the main entrance block, which was more modern than the rest of the building. Once inside, they emptied their pockets into a blue plastic tray and removed their shoes. They were ushered through the metal detector by a fat and bored-looking screw. Paul held out his arms like Jesus on the cross, and was patted down before a metal wand was waved over him. It clicked as it passed his back. Another screw appeared and ushered them down the corridor and they passed the visitors' toilets, where they were told to wait before the entrance door was opened and they were ushered into the main visiting area.

The room was large, rectangular and noisy from the hubbub of conversations, some loud and some hushed. Laughter mixed with the wail of crying babies. Children played, oblivious to their surroundings on their day out to see their dads. Some couples argued while others hugged in the only loving embrace they would get for a very long time as the anguish of separation tore through their souls, mixed with the regret of being caught. A regret that rarely applied itself to the crime committed. No matter the offence, it was usually someone else's fault they'd ended up inside: the police, the courts, a grass or sometimes even the victim, but rarely theirs.

But in Carl's case it was probably true.

As was the rule, Paul, Stefan and Jackie sat on the black plastic seats and reserved the remaining green one for Carl. A box section, metal frame held all four chairs and the small, round central table in place. Each set of tables sat so close together that it was possible to overhear the next table's conversation over the chatter of the room.

Five minutes later, a door opened, and the latest cohort of prisoners were let in for their visit, with Carl being at the front of the queue. He made his way out, dressed smartly in jeans and a red Lacoste T-shirt, which showed off his muscular physique. He scanned the room for his visitors and a wide smile shone from his handsome face when he laid his eyes upon them. He sat down and shook hands with Paul and Stefan, then reached across and gave his sister a peck on her cheek. Jackie squeezed his hands tightly, no doubt anguished to see her younger brother as a guest of Her Majesty's government.

"How you doing?" Jackie asked, with a look of genuine concern on her brown, wrinkled face, a face that had seen too many sun beds.

"Apart from being in jail on a trumped-up murder charge, I'm fine," replied Carl.

"You all settled in?" Paul asked him.

"Aye, I suppose. As settled in as I'll get. It's hardy five stars but the food's reasonable and I'm getting to the gym twice a day." Carl pushed himself back in his chair and put one foot up on the small round table.

"You got yourself a job yet?" asked Stefan. Stefan had been inside himself.

"Nah not yet. My head's still up my arse with this charge. I can't stop thinking about what happened. How's the kids, Jackie?"

"They're alright. Little shits – you know how they are. They're too young to know what's going on, but they know something's up."

"Well hopefully they won't see Uncle Carl on the telly or in the papers," Carl said.

"It was headline news for about three days," said Jackie, "but it's calmed down now. There were a few reporters at the court but they haven't turned up at mine."

"That's good. How about you, Paul? Had any visitors?"

"Not from the police. Matty came asking us to sell the hash from mine for him, but I said no."

"Good lad. Did he say owt about me?"

"Asked if I'd heard from you, that's all. I said I hadn't. I had Regan on the phone as well. He says if you need owt then let him know and he'll sort it. He's left us a number to get in touch."

"Not much he can do from the Dam, though. If he gets in touch again, say thanks and I'll shout if I need him. No point in getting himself nicked over this shit – he'll only end up on the landing with me. What about you, Stefan?

Anybody been on your case?"

"Nah. Don't think they would anyway. Your business is nowt to do with me. I left all that behind years ago."

"Sensible man," said Carl.

"I'll go and get the teas in," Jackie said. She made her way over to the serving hatch, which was staffed by volunteer pensioners who gave their time selflessly. Five minutes later, she returned with four cups of tea and a few bars of chocolate.

The conversation returned to family and friends and talk of the outside world. When forty minutes of the one-hour visit was up, Carl turned to her and Stefan. "I need to talk to Paul about a few things. You don't mind, do you? Thanks for coming up and all that and for taking him through. I need him do a few things for us that's all."

"No, it's fine," said Jackie.

"Aye, that's sound," said Stefan. "We'll try to get up next week as well. He can can have a lend of the car to come through anytime." Paul decided that he'd sooner get the train than drive Stefan's deathtrap.

"Thanks, I appreciate it," said Carl, "I really do. And I'll make it up to you when I'm out."

"There's no need," said Jackie. "Honestly." She wrapped her arms around him and pulled him in tightly. They hugged and kissed under the watchful eye of the black CCTV balls fixed to the ceiling then Carl and Stefan shook hands

Once Jackie and Stefan had gone, Carl looked over both shoulders to make sure nobody was listening and motioned for Paul to come closer.

Paul leant forward with his elbows resting on his knees to hear what the big man had to say. "So what's the crack? Tell us you didn't shoot Mark."

"Keep your fucking voice down. Did I fuck. I've been set up."

"Who's done that?"

"How the fuck do I know? They've found my back door key in the bushes at the scene. Fuck knows who's planted it, but somebody has. It was the key that I lent you."

"You can fuck off!" Paul hissed. "I haven't fucking set you up!" He sat up and pushed himself back in his seat.

Carl sighed and looked down at the floor before altering the tone of his voice. "I know it's not you. You gave us the key back and put it in the ashtray in the RS. I forgot it was there and it must have sat there for a while. I've had a few people in it over the weeks an' all."

"Like who?"

"You, a couple of birds and the odd other person. But there was only you and me who knew it was there,"

"Look . . . don't blame me or I'm fucking off and you're on your own."

"I know it wasn't you. You've got no reason to set me up and I can't see that anybody else I had in the car would do it either."

Paul thought about the smack he'd been given to do just that. He was glad that Carl didn't know and hoped that he'd never find out. "So, how do you think they got the key?"

"Remember when the car got broken into?"

"Aye..."

"It must have been then. Whoever broke into the car either shot Liam and planted it or passed it on to the person that did."

"And who do you think did that?"

"The only one I can think of is the Boltons, or maybe Rob Murray."

"Why? I thought youse all got on."

"We do, I suppose. Well, more tolerate each other's presence really. They still could have had Liam shot and set us up. I honestly can't think of anybody else." Carl reached forward and picked up a Kit-Kat from the table. He removed the paper cover from the foil wrapper and slid his thumbnail down the thin metal foil. He broke the chocolate bar in half and pushed a full finger into his mouth.

"Have you not got an alibi? Where were you when it happened?"

Carl pulled Paul in even closer and took another precautionary look over each shoulder. "You can't tell anyone this, swear on your fucking life to me." He raised a straight finger up to his lips.

"OK, I swear."

"I was in the Copthorne Hotel – or just leaving it about the same time Liam was shot."

"So, why didn't you just tell the bizzies?"

"Because of who I was with."

"And who were you with?"

Carl waited while an overweight lady chased an unruly toddler past their table. She lifted the child up and carried her away, giving a slightly embarrassed smile as she passed. "Marie Cunningham," he whispered.

"Who?"

"Marie Cunningham. Les Cunningham's wife."

"Really? For fuck's sake, Carl. I though he was your pal." Paul almost laughed. It was scarcely believable that anyone would be brave enough or stupid enough to mess around with Les's wife.

"He is. Sort of. Until he finds out I'm fucking his wife - then I'm a dead man. And don't mention her name. If anybody hears, it'll cause ructions."

"Do you think he's done it and set you up?"

"Maybe. There's half a chance if he knows about me and her."

"Look, it's a fucking murder charge you're looking at here. If you don't explain where you were then you're fucked. Just tell them."

"What? Les is a fucking lunatic. You must have heard the stories? And, besides . . . she's a right fucking minx an' all. I'm not even sure she'd admit it anyway. There's a good chance she'd deny it just to save her golden goose of a husband from kicking her out."

"Aye, but–"

"But fucking what? There's no fucking but!" Carl took a deep breath and let it out slowly. "Sorry. Me head's just up me arse, that's all. But I need you to do something."

"What's that?" Paul was suddenly very apprehensive.

"Get in with the Boltons and Mark. Start getting selling gear for them and worm your way in and see if you can find anything out. If it comes down to doing twenty-five years or breaking up Les's fucking marriage, I'll have to tell them. But if there's another way that doesn't risk getting tortured and shot then I'd rather take it. Know what I mean? People who piss off Les and his family go missing and never turn up. Just get a bit of hash off Mark and the Boltons and don't let them find out you're playing both ends."

Paul looked into Carl's eyes. He knew he should tell him to fuck off, but the look of desperation on his face wouldn't allow it. He had nobody else to turn to in his hour of need and Paul felt proud that he trusted him enough to put his life in his hands.

"Why both of them?" Paul realised that his foot was tapping nervously against the metal table leg, so he moved it further away.

"I just need you to get in with George's mob, really. But if Mark's running things in Whitley, then he'll be on your case if he finds out you're selling the hash for the other side. So, get it off him as a cover. Sell Mark's gear to anybody in Whitley and George's to your close pals who won't let on."

"Look . . . I'll do what I can and see if I can find anything out, but I'm not sure they'll trust me considering how close I am to you. And even if they do, I don't think they'd let on about a murder."

"They'll be a little bit wary at first cos you're my pal. But you have good credentials – they know I don't suffer mugs easily, you know what I mean? But be careful. Don't go pushing it and asking stupid questions."

"Is that it, then?" Paul raised his eyebrows at Carl. "Owt else?"

"Nah." Carl seemed to miss the sarcasm completely. "I've got everything I need in here. I'm as comfortable as I can be but it's doing my fucking head in trying to work out who's stitched me up. I just need someone I can trust on the outside, and you and Jackie are the only people I really can. And I can't exactly ask her, can I?"

Paul looked Carl straight in the eyes. Now was the time. If the bond between himself and Carl was really that strong, there would never be a better one. He'd earned an honest answer. "Carl, I need to ask you something. I've been wanting to ask you for ages and never really found the right time."

"What's that?"

Paul hesitated for only a moment. "Do you know who killed me dad?"

It was the first time Paul had found Carl lost for words. He looked utterly shocked. Then he pursed his lips and clenched his teeth as he shook his head slowly. "Nah. I don't, mate," he said at last.

"Well do you know anything about it? Rumours or owt? It plays on me mind all the time . . . I just need to know."

"I'd tell you if I did. Especially considering what you're doing for me now. There was the usual shite, a few rumours and a few names getting bandied about, but nobody was ever charged with it. A few people got pulled in but that was about it."

"I just need to know," Paul said. "It fucking kills us inside. I don't know what I'd do if I actually found out, like." A shiver of pain and anguish swept through him as he thought of his father's violent demise and he felt a little sick.

"Well, if you ever do find out I'll be there for you, pal," said Carl. "Not just to back you up in case you want to hurt them, but even if you just want to talk about it. When I get out of this shithole, we can."

"Aye, thanks. Anyways, visiting time's over. I suppose I better get myself off. Look, I'll try. I'll do what I can for you, mate."

"Thanks, I'll never forget it you know. And about that bird . . ." Carl, drew two pinched fingers across his lips.

"I know, I know," said Paul.

They shook hands and departed for very different worlds.

On the journey home with Jackie and Stefan, Paul had mixed emotions. On the one hand he wanted to do everything he could to help Carl get off with the murder charge, but on the other hand he was dreading the thought of getting back into the drugs world with the Boltons and Mark on Carl's behalf. It was a dangerous game to play. Carl going away gave him another opportunity to get out of the life and maybe into another with Lindsey. But, for now, that had to wait. He was a man of integrity and a man who kept his word. He'd made a promise that could land him in jail and endanger his physical wellbeing, but it was a promise he had every intention of keeping.

"So, how do you think he's holding up?" Jackie asked, as Stefan weaved the rusting Peugeot through the afternoon traffic on the A1.

"Not bad, all things considered," said Paul. "I'd be in

bits if it was me in there."

"He didn't do it, I can tell. I know him inside out. I would be able to tell if it was him. So, what was he saying when we left?"

"Look, Jackie, I know you're his sister, but I can't tell you. it's confidential."

"Don't give me that shit! He's me fucking brother!"

"Honestly, Jackie, I can't. He made us swear not too."

Stefan seemed to be taking the sensible option of staying out of it. It likely wouldn't have mattered which side he took; Jackie would probably give him hell when he got home anyway. Paul understood Jackie's anger and frustration but hoped that, deep down, she understood that she was best off not knowing and not getting involved. The rest of the journey home passed in near silence until they dropped Paul off in Cullercoats, where Stefan said his goodbyes and Jackie ignored him as he climbed from the back of the car.

He opened the door to his cold flat, flicked on the heating and tossed his coat over the chair before plonking himself down on the settee. He had no plans to do anything except eat and get stoned and veg out in front of the TV. He lit up a half smoked joint and had a few tokes before returning to the kitchen where he put a ready-made lasagne in the oven.

The thought of Carl's plan to weed out the shooter didn't particularly appeal to him, but he decided he would get in touch with Craig the next day. He would spin him a yarn that he wanted to sell a bit of hash but didn't want to get it from Mark and Matty for the obvious reason that they'd fallen out with Carl and he was Carl's mate. He knew that if either faction found out then he'd be on the receiving end of a hiding. He'd faced Mark's wrath once before and didn't want to experience it again.

He tidied the glass coffee table, caught sight of Regan's phone number under the phone and thought he'd give him an update about Carl. After all, he was Carl's best mate and he'd asked to be kept in the loop. Plus, it was always good to keep in with Regan as he might need a favour from him one day – or some back up sometime soon. He called the number and was answered in a couple of rings.

"Hello?"

"Alright, mate. Is that my friend from the Dam?"

"Aye, that it is. How's tricks?"

"Alright, mate. Listen, I've been up to see your pal in the big house today."

"How is he? Holding up alright?"

"All things considered, I suppose he is. Rather him than me, though."

"Aye, me too. So, what's he saying?"

"He swears it wasn't him and I believe him, to be honest. And so does his Jackie."

"Jackie . . . how's that old battle-axe doing? Haven't seen her in years."

"She's sound, mate. You know how she is with Carl. Look, he's convinced that somebody's set him up. Says it was his back door key that was planted at the scene."

"By who?"

"He doesn't know. Thinks it's whoever broke into his

car a while back."

"Sounds like a bit of a tall tale to me."

"Aye, but do you really think he would shoot Liam and be daft enough to lose his spare key at the crime scene?"

"Did he say where he was at the time?" asked Regan. "Hasn't he got an alibi?"

Paul hesitated, unsure whether he should confide in him and tell him the truth. After all he was Carl's oldest and best friend and would do anything to help him get out of jail. But as Carl had told him to keep everything between themselves, he thought better of it. "Nah he didn't say. I asked but I didn't really get a proper answer, he just mumbled something about not being able to say and I didn't press it."

"Strange. So, does need anything,"

"No, mate. He says he's got everything he needs. I'm sorting out some hash each week with some kid from the town, so unless you know who the real shooter is then there's not much you can do, I suppose,"

"You know it still could have been him, don't you. As much as you don't want it to be and neither do I, there's still the chance he's done it."

"Aye, but what for?"

"Dunno. Maybe he thought they would come for him and he got in there first. Fuck knows."

"Ah, don't say that, man. I've been convincing meself it wasn't him. Look. I'm going to get meself off. I was just calling to let you know he's as alright as he can be and I'll bell you back if there's any developments."

"No bother. And thanks for ringing. Same again, though, if you hear or need owt then bell us any time."

"Will do. Cheers. Catch ya dafter."

The phone went dead and Paul lay back, contemplating how he was going to get in with two drug gangs, find out who the shooter was and all the while sell hash for both without either of them finding out.

He was starting to wish he'd opted for a winter in the alps after all.

9: TICKET FOR THE RACES

It was a cold dry morning down the coast and as Paul left the Ivy Court Gym, he pulled his hat down over his ears to protect them from the chill. He was glad he didn't have far to go to meet Lindsey and he was looking forward to treating her to lunch at Pane E Vinos. As far as he was concerned, it was the best Italians in Whitley and somewhere he ate at least once a week. As he approached her flat, he saw her face at the window and when she opened the door Jason was standing there looking cute as a button with his winter coat on and a hat that matched Paul's own.

"Paul!" the bairn shouted, and ran halfway down the path with his arms outstretched.

"Hello mate!" Paul picked him up and they hugged in a warm embrace.

"Hi Paul, remember me?" Lindsey reached up and pecked a kiss on his cheek.

"Erm . . . aye . . . what's your name again?"

She slapped him playfully on the arm. "So, where we going then? Pane E Vinos . . . again?"

"Well, it's either that or Greggs. You decide."

"I'll stick with the Italians, thanks. I need to pick up a few things on the way if that's OK?"

"Aye, no bother." He lifted Jason up and sat him on his shoulders.

On the walk into Whitley, they chatted and caught up

with the latest events of theirs and other people's lives. Paul generally making the small talk and asking about what she'd been up to. He wondered why she hadn't asked about Carl, and he was expecting her to have a go about their friendship again, she'd tried in the past and it would have been just as futile now as it had been then. He'd sometimes thought that one day she would ask him to stop coming around but he reasoned that she cared too much for him to do that. As they reached the door of Poundstretchers they stopped, and Paul lifted Jason down.

"You're going in there?" asked Paul.

"Aye Paul, I'm going in there. We haven't all got as much money as you. Some of us have to watch the pennies, you know."

"Have you spent the money I gave you?" he asked, knowing that he'd spent most of his too.

"Not all of of it. but I'll stretch what's left as far as I can. Can you watch Jason while I nip in here, please?"

"Course I will."

She turned to enter the shop as Mark pulled up in his Cosworth and parked beside them. Matty was in the passenger seat, and he rolled down the passenger window as they stopped. "Oy!" he shouted.

"Eh, alright lads? What's up?" Paul asked warily.

Lindsey looked at them with undisguised disgust, while Matty smiled back at her with undisguised hopes of getting into her pants.

"On second thoughts, I'll take Jason," Lindsey said. She took him from Paul's grasp and led him through the double doors and into the shop.

"Just thought we'd stop and say hello," said Matty. "That your bird?"

"Nah, she's just a friend."

"Tasty." Matty's eyes followed her bum into the shop.

"You heard owt from Carl?" Mark enquired.

"No, mate," Paul lied. "He's only got family going up on visits. I haven't even had a call from him for a while."

"Really?" Matty said.

"Aye, honestly. I expect his heads is right up his arse. I know mine would be."

"I don't really give a fuck about Carl, to be honest," Mark spat back. "But I'm going to do to him what he did to me brother if I ever see him again."

Paul stood still for a moment, unsure of what to say. He decided to change tack and spoke directly to Matty. "Look . . . about that thing you were on about the other day – when you were at mine . . ."

"What's that?"

"About knocking out the hash. If it's still alright, I'd like to give it a go."

Matty looked at Mark for approval. Mark shrugged and nodded his head. "Aye, I suppose we could sort you out, said Matty. "How much you wanting?".

"I was thinking about an ounce to get started."

"An ounce? I'm not running about with a fucking ounce. I'll drop you off a nine bar. But you'll need your own scales to chop it up."

"Aye, sounds good. I'll be in tonight if you want to pop down?"

"I'll be down about teatime."

Matty looked at Mark and then back to Paul, and without another word, they pulled away.

Paul sighed a little and shook his head. He knew he was playing a dangerous game and the thought of it was no more reassuring to him now than when Carl had first floated the idea.

*   *   *

"Do you trust him?" Mark said to Matty as they drove off.

"Dunno. Not a hundred percent, but he'll be OK. I don't believe he hasn't heard from Carl cos he's right up his arse, but I don't think he'll cause us any problems. What's he going to do anyway?"

"Aye, I suppose. But keep an eye on the little twat – you never know."

*   *   *

Lindsey returned and they continued their journey past the Fat Ox and into the centre of Whitley. She didn't ask what Mark and Matty wanted. She had no interest in the coastal gangster patter and would just be glad that they'd left. They stopped at the red brick Post Office and Paul kept Jason amused counting the busses as they passed the window while Lindsey queued and paid her bills. Back into the cold they went and as they neared the entrance to Woolworth's she stopped him for another shopping break.

"I've just got to nip in here for a minute," she said. "And I'll take him – just in case your mates turn up again."

"Aye, OK. I'll wait here."

He waited on the corner, his hands thrust deep into the pockets of his jeans to protect them from the cold as he looked up and down the road.

Bumping into Mark and Matty had been good because it meant he didn't have to seek them out to get their drugs and that made it look more natural. He mulled over the next part of the plan: to get in touch with Craig and see if he could get in with the Boltons as well. He expected that this would take a bit more doing as they might find it a bit suspicious, but he thought he could still pull it off. He would make out that he didn't want to go to Mark and Matty because he was there when Carl battered them, saying he didn't trust them and that the feeling was mutual. Providing they didn't find out it was him who'd sent them to their doors, there would be no comeback.

He would call Craig later. They were friendly through the Whitley Bay bar scene, so there was no need for introductions. They saw each other in Whisky Bends at least once a week and quite often in the Snake Pit on a Saturday night. They'd already done a couple of back door deals with Paul supplying Craig with his fiddle gear from Carl that the Boltons didn't know about. It was dicey because they would both get a good hiding if George and Kenny found out, but they considered that an unlikely prospect and worth the risk.

Craig took care of the Boltons' day-to-day business and made himself a lot of money – and he made them a lot of money too. Craig took all the risk and the Boltons none. But everybody knew the score: without George and Kenny he was just another two-bit drug dealer who was fair game to whatever hard man came along. They gave him the opportunity to get rich – or council estate rich, anyway: cash, nice clothes, fast cars, good-looking women and an almost endless supply of drugs was success to them.

* * *

As Alan Richards sat with his chin in his palms, resting his elbows on his naked knees, he amused himself by reading the graffiti on the dirty cubicle walls and wondered who took the time to write it. *Look left* on the right-hand wall; *Look right – toilet tennis* on the other. "Hardly fucking original," he muttered to himself.

He hated taking a shit in a public toilet, but seeing as he was barred from the Vic, the Ship and the Fat Ox, he was a little short on emergency options. The previous night's curry needed to make a re-appearance – and quickly. Wincing from the cold toilet water splashing onto his backside as his turd left his body, he berated himself for ordering a Vindaloo instead of his normal Rogan Josh. He reached to the right to take some toilet roll from the holder that was adorned with the words *Art Degree* and a downwards-facing arrow. Just as he tore the sheets from the roll, his head turned to the opposite side and he noticed a large blue eye staring back at him through the pre-drilled glory hole. For a split second he thought that it was some better drawn graffiti. Until it blinked. He banged his fist on the cubicle wall and shouted, "Come here, you dirty bastard! I'll fucking kill you!" while jumping up and lifting his tracksuit bottoms as fast as he could. The small brass lock bar flew from the door as Alan ripped it open with all the strength he had. His only thought was on the kicking he would give to the pervert when he caught him. He ran out of the toilet block and into the street, blinking as his eyes adjusted to the daylight. Not knowing which way the man went, he ran left onto Whitley Road.

*   *   *

"Where the fuck is he?" Alan shouted, as he ran up to Paul from the short road that led to the derelict Fire Station.

"Eh, what the fuck you on about?" said a startled Paul.

"That fucking bloke . . . where is he?" Alan scanned up and down the street, looking for the elusive somebody.

"What bloke? What you on about?"

"The bloke. Dunno. Some fucking bloke. I was having a shit in there and I'm just sitting there. Then all I see is a big fucking eye staring through the hole in the cubicle wall."

"What? Really?" Paul fell about laughing.

"Aye. Dirty bastard! I just pulled me fucking pants up and legged it out, but I guess he was faster."

"I hope you wiped your arse!" Paul managed mid-belly-laugh.

"Aye well . . . Wait here. I'll be back in a minute. A couple of minutes later, Alan returned and still with a look of disbelief on his face.

"All clean?" teased Paul, in a pretend posh voice.

"Aye, fucking am now. Dirty cunt. So, how's things with you?"

"Not bad. Apart from the thing with Carl."

"I heard about that. Youse two are pretty close now, or so I hear."

"Aye, I suppose. I don't think he's done it, though." Paul shook his head.

"Mebbe. But you never know, though, do you? So, what's happening anyway? I've got a bit of graft on if you're interested."

"What is it, like?"

"It's a safe on the Foxhunters in one of the garages. Might be a dirty operation but I need a little hand with it. Do the alarm, break in and get it open. Either that or get it out if we can't open it in there. Should be a few quid in it and hopefully a pile of MOT certificates to flog on as well."

"When you thinking about doing it?"

"Sometime midweek, I think. Probably Thursday. A little birdie told us they bank on a Friday so it should be full up on a Thursday night."

Paul mulled it over. He didn't want to get himself nicked while trying to find out what he could for Carl, but at the same time his funds were running low and he could do with a bump up. "Aye, OK. How do I find you?"

"I'll give you a bell Thursday. I'll sort the tools and that out. I just need a hand, that's all."

Paul nodded in agreement.

"Anyway, I'm offski. Places to go and people to see," said Alan, like a man of importance.

"Sound. I'll see you on Thursday. Take care."

Lindsey returned five minutes later with a bag of shopping and Paul was thankful that Alan had disappeared as it avoided the dirty looks and the awkward questions. He took Jason's hand and they walked along in the winter breeze to the restaurant. Once inside, they sat in the window so Jason could watch the people and the traffic go by, which kept him quiet to some extent. They chatted and joked and avoided the subject of Paul's criminality and his dodgy friends. They looked at each other in the same way they always did, Paul hoping that one day he would make her his.

*   *   *

Later that night, there was a knock-on Paul's back window and he drew back the curtain to see Matty in his yard, but at least he wasn't coming to do him harm. Before he let him in, he glanced at the cooker and had a flashback about Mark trying to melt his face off. He opened the door and in walked Matty without being invited. Paul closed and locked the door behind him as Matty removed the cling film wrapped hash from his pocket and handed it to him. He moved his hand up and down, feeling the weight of the dark brown bar before putting it on the kitchen bench.

"Nine ounces," said Matty. "That's eight hundred and ten quid. OK?"

"Aye, sound. Might take a bit to get rid of cos I'm just starting out, but I'll bell you when I've got the readies."

"OK, sounds good. You'll not get any shit off us, and if anyone tries owt then just gis a bell and me and Mark will be straight along," Matty re-assured him.

"Aye, no worries. Look, Carl's away and the bother was between youse lot. I didn't want to come along to the Vic – he just asked us to and–"

"Don't worry about it. Its history as far as we're concerned. We know you weren't involved, really. You were just there. Mark might be a bit funny about you for a while but just try to keep out of his way and I'll keep him calm. It's alright."

"Cheers, much appreciated. I still can't believe it was him that shot Liam, mind."

"Why's that?"

"Dunno. Just doesn't seem like his sort of thing."

"Suppose you're right. But they've got him now, and from what I hear he's a little bit fucked. But anyway, let us out. I've got to go. I Don't like hanging around for longer than I have to."

"Right. I'll bell you soon as I've got rid of that. Laters."

Matty left and Paul's heart rate came back down to normal. He unwrapped the hash and took a sniff of the bar, it smelled good, which surprised him.

He heated up a knife on the gas ring and cut off a bit of personal, which he put on his front room table, then he took the remainder and stashed it up the unused chimney breast, behind the brick he'd previously removed and cut in half. Then he sat down and called Craig, who would be the second of his drug suppliers to arrive that evening, and thankfully one he didn't need to fear.

A couple of hours later, he heard a car pull up and

presumed it was Craig. He took the small piece of personal from Matty's bar and put it in his pocket. He waited with the curtain drawn back and his hand over his brow as he looked out into the yard, like a sailor looking into the sun, so the glare of the room behind didn't impede his vision. The gate opened and his heart sank again. In behind Craig walked George Bolton. What the fuck was he doing here? He let go of the curtain and put his face in his left hand before looking down and drawing it back across his forehead. And for the second time that night he let a visitor into his home that he didn't want to.

He hadn't met George properly, but he knew him by sight and, like the rest of the coastal criminal fraternity, he knew who he was and the reputation he brought with him. He let them both in.

"Alright lads," Paul said. "Howay in. Just go through."

"Course, aye," said Craig. "Paul this is George, and George this is Paul, who I was telling you about."

George hesitated as he moved through the kitchen, pausing to shake hands with Paul. He gave him a forced smile that told Paul that he thought he was beneath him.

"Sit yersel's down," said Paul, trying to make the right impression. "Youse want a drink or owt?"

"No, I'm good thanks," said George.

"Aye, I'll have a beer if you've got one," said Craig.

Paul returned with two bottles of Holsten Pils and gave one to Craig who opened it with his teeth. He took a long mouthful and they all sat down on the three-piece suite. Paul in a chair and his visitors on the settee.

"So, what's the crack?" asked Paul, both eager and anxious to find out why Craig had brought George along.

"Well, I've had a word with George, here," said Craig, "and he's happy enough for us to lay you on some hash, but he's got a little favour to ask first."

Paul knew that whatever it was it wasn't really a favour; George would be asking, and Paul would be doing. "What's that?"

"You're the lad that's been knocking about with Carl, aren't you?" said George.

"Er . . . aye . . ."

"Well, this is the thing . . . Now Carl's away, we're going to be taking over things in Shields and we need a little help from you. In return, we'll give you as much hash as you want on tick, and we'll stand behind you all the way. If anybody gives you any shit, just call Craig and we'll come straight down."

This was the second time in a few hours that someone had said the same thing with virtually the same words. There had to be a *Shit Book of Gangster Patter* out there that all the big-time villains read.

"OK . . . and what's the help?" Paul asked apprehensively.

"We want to know everybody who was on Carl's books," said Craig. "All the hash dealers, speed dealers, E dealers, the lot. Nobody will find out it was you that told us, but to be fair we know most of it anyway. We just need you to fill in the gaps."

"And who do I tell? You? Carl's not going to be happy with us if he finds out?"

"Carl's not coming back for twenty-five years if he gets convicted of the Liam thing," George said. "So I wouldn't worry too much about him."

"And what if he gets off with it?"

"We'll just have to cross that bridge when we come to it, won't we? So, I'll tell you what's going to happen . . . I'm going to fuck off and you and Craig can have a spliff and a can and you can tell him everything we need to know. OK?"

Paul nodded in agreement. He didn't have a choice, but unbeknown to them this was the beginning of the second part of Carl's plan, and now he'd been introduced to George. He let George out and returned to Craig who waived a small bag of white powder towards him when he re-entered the sitting room.

"Grab a plate, wor kid," said Craig. 'This'll cheer you up."

"Coke?"

"Oh yes."

"Just knock it up on the coffee table, mate. It's got a glass top."

Craig did just that. He wiped the table clean with his sleeve and poured out a dirty white lump from the bag. He crushed it with a bank card and separated it into two lines, along with a small pile that he pushed to one side for later. Paul returned with two more bottles of Holsten Pils and handed one to Craig, who handed him back a rolled up twenty-pound note.

"You can do the honours." Craig said.

"Cheers!" Paul snorted up the first line before

handing the note back to Craig, who lent forward and took care of the other.

"Here's that gear for you an' all," said Craig.

"Sound. Nine ounces?"

"Aye. Eighty quid each. just give us a bell when it's gone and I'll bring some more over."

Paul took the hash, but didn't bother to give it the obligatory smell test this time and he put it on the mantlepiece for later. He would hide it in his mam's house, having half a kilo in the house was a bit too much for him.

"So," said Craig, "how's things been with you? Hear you've been getting a bit of shit lately."

"Not really. Carl's away, which is a bit of a nightmare to say the least, but I haven't had any shit off the other lot."

"I heard you were there when he chinned Liam and Mark."

"I was there alright. I didn't see what happened but I saw the state of them afterwards. Liam was out cold and Mark was on his back holding his hands up like this."

He made a gesture like a boxer trying to protect his face with his hands while shaking like a hyperthermic child.

"Wish I'd seen it. I fucking hate those two. They came to mine at the start of all this, but I wasn't in, which I'm pretty glad of. Fuck knows what they would have done if they'd caught me. I used to get on with them. I went to school with Liam and Matty was a pal of me brother."

"How is your kid? Have they been to his too?"

"Nah. He's got fuck all to do with this. He's just a normal lad with a job. Shame about Carl, though. Nice fella. I get on with him, me." Craig separated another couple of lines from the pile and snorted one back.

"It's a fucking travesty," Paul said. "There's no way he did it. I don't care if they found something of his at the shooting – he didn't do it."

"What did they find, like?" Craig asked. "I heard it was his key."

"Not sure," Paul lied. "I just know they've found something."

"I don't think it was him," said Craig.

"Why's that? Who do you think it was, like?"

"My money's on Rob. For as start, he's mad enough, and he's got a gun half the time. George and Kenny are taking over in Shields and he'll make good money out of it when they do. Either that or they've done it and set him up."

"It had crossed my mind."

"Look, this is just me talking here . . ." Or rather it was Craig and the cocaine talking.

"I know." Paul, hoped to put Craig at ease so he could glean more information.

"I'd get into some serious shit if anyone found out, so don't ever repeat this, but I overheard George, Rob and Kenny say something about having Mark shot a while back. It was said as half a joke – you know . . . one of those jokes where everyone's in on it apart from you?"

"I think I know what you mean,"

"I'm not saying it was them, and maybe it's just me putting two and two together and coming up with five, but I didn't think anything of it until after Liam got shot."

Thoughts whirled around Paul's head now, along with the coke, hash and beer, and he didn't know what to believe. He had considered that either George and Kenny were behind Liam's killing or it was Carl all along. Maybe what Craig was saying was true or maybe it wasn't, but at that moment he decided to keep his mouth shut and change the subject. They sat for a while longer discussing the usual subjects of drugs, raves and girls, and Paul filled in the gaps for Craig about the dealers he came to find out about. Then, after an hour or so, Craig stood up to leave.

"Right, I'm off," he said. "Gis a bell when that's sold."

"You be alright to drive?"

"Aye, why not? It's only a few lines and a couple of bottles

"Take care anyway. And stay out of the way of them lot." Paul meant Mark and Matty.

"Will do, wor kid. And don't repeat what I was saying earlier. I'll get into a lot of trouble if that comes out."

"No bother, mate. You know me. I'll take it to my grave," he lied.

Chapter 10: The Roar of Dust and Diesel

Paul met Alan at their pre-arranged spot in Marden Quarry car park and shook hands in silence like long lost brothers in arms. The ground was damp, and the air was filled with mist that rolled in from the bleak North Sea. They were distantly illuminated in patches by the orange glow of the streetlamps from the surrounding roads, and it was close to perfect conditions for what they had planned. The inclement weather and the latened hour kept most people in their houses except for the odd dog walker. The occasional car could be heard passing by behind them on the adjacent Broadway. Not that anyone would see the two black clad figures in the foggy gloom unless they were right on top of them. And that was the idea. Black boots, jeans, jackets, hats and gloves were the order of the night.

Dressed like two identical twins differentiated only by the rucksack Alan carried, and for that you needed to be close. As they walked together, they barely made a sound as they made their way through the undergrowth. Paul heard an occasional dull clunk from the metallic tools they'd wrapped in cloth kept the noise to a minimum.

They paused quietly as they reached the bank top, and surveyed the rugby club field. Alan motioned to take a path over to the left where there was less chance of being seen either from the clubhouse or from the windows of the houses that overlooked the pitches. But tonight, there was only silence. The lights in the clubhouse were out and there was one lone car in the car park. It faced away from them towards the fence that divided the car park from the dwellings' back gardens. Maybe it was abandoned or left by a player who'd drunk too much to drive or maybe it contained an amorous young couple in a late-night tryst. They didn't care. As long as it was pointing the other way and there were no signs of life, they would pass it by and carry on with their plan undeterred.

Crossing the field, they scrambled their way up the hill and through the knee-high grass. Again, they paused and took stock as they scanned the Boy's Club car park, which was empty and still. They looked at each other and nodded a silent agreement then reached up simultaneously and rolled their balaclavas down over their cold, damp faces. Now there was no way of recognising them. Making their way over the crunching ground at a pace that was faster than walking and not quite running, they looked up the road towards the Ice Rink and along the dirt pathway that led the other way to the Marden Estate.

Alan took the rucksack from his back and tossed it over the fence and into the allotments. He climbed a tree with Paul's assistance then helped to pull him up before they both climbed onto the fence and dropped to the dirt path below. Alan kept his footing, but Paul fell backwards into the mud. Alan helped Paul to his feet, gave him a thumbs up and received the same signal in return. Normally they would have laughed and joked but not tonight. Even in a deserted allotment, they needed to move as stealthy as could be.

They followed the dirt pathway through the allotments with Alan leading the way. It was the third time he'd taken this route. Paul had reasonable bearings for where they were despite the weather, he'd come to the allotments with a school friend when he was eleven or twelve to help the friend's grandad with his prize growing vegetables. As they walked, they hopped over any growing foodstuffs where they could; they might be a pair of balaclava-clad thieves on their way to rob someone's business, but they didn't want to destroy some old fella's hard grown veggies if they could help it. They weren't complete animals after all.

When they passed the last allotment, Alan crouched down beside a high palisade security fence and motioned for Paul to do the same and to stay put. He scuttled off, leaving Paul crouched down in the wet grass, before returning with a ten-foot length of wood that he placed between two of the upright posts, just above where they met the lower horizontal bar. "Here's one I prepared earlier," he quipped in a whisper.

After Alan motioned for Paul to help him, they used the wood as a lever and after a couple of good pushes the rivets holding the two sections popped open and their route into the yard was clear. They watched and listened in the fog for any signs of life. Once they were satisfied the coast was clear, the metal picket was pushed to the side and they squeezed through into the yard of the MOT inspection company.

The yard was full of oily bins and cars in various

states of disrepair. Rusting engines stood on broken pallets and a variety of car parts were strewn around the oily yard. Some cars were intact with sale prices painted on the windscreens, and some had missing panels and full front ends. None looked like they would ever run again.

They half walked, half crouched their way between the lines of vehicles until they reached the building that housed the workshop and the offices. The main workshop had a high-pitched roof with the single-storey, flat-roofed office block at the back, painted drab grey. An alleyway wide enough to drive a single car through separated it from the building next door. There was a high, rusting palisade gate at the end fastened by a padlock and chain. A coil of barbed wire crowned the top.

"This is what we need to do . . ." whispered Alan. "Gis a hand to get on the roof and I'll sort out the alarm. Once I'm up there, pass up the tools and you go and keep toot. When I'm done, come back and we'll get inside."

"OK," said Paul.

As quietly as they could, they manoeuvred a large industrial bin over to the building and they both climbed on top. Alan jumped up and Paul wrapped his arms around Alan's legs and pushed him up enough for Alan to lie on the flat bitumen roof with his legs dangling off the edge. He paused for a few seconds to get his breath back and then pulled himself up on top. Paul grabbed the tool bag and passed it up into Alan's outstretched hand, the two of them making themselves as long as possible in order to do so. Alan, who had much more experience at burgling than Paul, motioned for him to go to the front of the yard and watch out for interlopers. Then he hung off the side of the building as he started disabling the alarm. Paul had no idea what he was doing as he flicked between watching the deserted entrance road and watching for Alan's signal to return.

The seconds and minutes ticked by in what seemed like an age as Alan worked away. Paul looked out into the mist and concluded that if the police arrived then they would practically be at the gate before he knew it was them. Generally, the estate was deserted at night since Foxhunters Taxis had vacated their offices, so if any cars drove towards them, they would stop and take off. Eventually Alan gave out a soft low whistle and Paul looked up to see Alan beckon him back to the bin. They lowered down the tools and Paul helped Alan climb back down.

"All done?" Paul whispered.

"Aye. Just got to get in now." Alan opened the rucksack below what Paul presumed was the office window and laid the tools out on the ground. Alan unwrapped a lump hammer and took off his coat, which he instructed Paul to hold over the glass. Then he took a rolled-up towel that had wrapped the tools and laid it out on the ground under the window to catch the falling glass. He swung back the hammer. "This is when we find out if I've done the alarm properly."

Paul said nothing, but nodded his head in agreement.

The hammer swung through the air and smashed the toughened glass in one strike and with a muffled thud. Paul lowered the coat, which caught most of the broken glass. What he didn't catch fell to the towel almost noiselessly. No alarm rang. Carefully, they spent the next five minutes knocking out smaller pieces of the pane and laying them in a pile on the towel then cutting the security mesh out of the frame with a pair of wire snips.

Paul was getting nervous, but the alarm was still silent. He looked through the barred window and into the office below and he could see the safe under the desk, exactly where the young MOT tester said it would be. Alan was quiet and calm and determined to get to the safe and the booty that it held. The thick metal security bars were all that separated the pair from their plunder. Alan got to work with a crowbar and attempted to pry the bars apart from the brickwork that held them in place but no matter how hard he tried the tools he had just wouldn't shift them. Each time he tried, the crowbar would pop back out and the bars wouldn't move. They persevered for the next ten minutes until Alan was making more and more noise with each passing attempt. Their nerves rose along with their collective pulses.

"Is there anybody in there?" an unknown voice called from the street outside.

The burglars flattened their backs against the wall and froze in case their shadows were visible to the voice outside. They heard the patter of dog's feet and the sound of a man who they guessed was elderly by the pitch of his voice. They tried not to breathe as the sound from his shuffling feet echoed in the passageway between the buildings.

"It's OK, Holly. Probably just hearing things. Come on." The old man and his canine companion shuffled away.

They waited a few minutes in silence, listening for returning footsteps or the sound of approaching cars.

"Let's go," said Paul.

"Fuck that," said Alan, "I can see the safe."

"So fuck. I'm not going to jail. If that old fucker goes and rings the bizzies, which is highly likely, they'll be sniffing around in no time."

"Aye, but–"

"No buts," hissed Paul. "I'm off even if you're not."

Alan heaved a sigh. "Ok then, let's fuck off."

They wrapped the tools carefully back up and put them in the rucksack, which Alan handed to Paul. Then they squeezed back through the fence, away from the scene of the crime and back into the muddy allotments. Halfway through, Alan stopped Paul and looked into his balaclava-clad face.

"Right, I'm off this way," Alan said. "I'm going to me bird's gaff in Shields."

"Eh?"

"Aye. It's better if we split up. If we're caught together then they'll defo link us to the break in."

Paul thought about it, and Alan was probably right, but he also considered that Alan's devious mind had quickly weighed up the plausible deniability defence he could use in court if he wasn't the one who was caught with the tools.

"And what about this?" Paul nodded to the tool bag on his shoulder.

"Just stash it. You going to yours?"

"Aye."

"Find somewhere to hide it in the quarry or on the way. There's plenty places round here. We can come back for it tomorrow."

Not exactly happy about the idea of taking the tools with him, he and Alan shook hands and parted ways. Alan turned right and Paul turned left towards the Boys Club and home. He was just as disappointed as Alan about leaving the safe behind, but it was better than getting eighteen months inside and still coming away with nothing.

* * *

"Two shots?" Kenny shouted to George.

"Where?" said George.

"There?"

"Was it fuck! I never touched it." George was trying to hide the fact that he'd moved a ball with his cue as he lined up to pot the black.

"It fucking is, you cheating twat!" Kenny took a mouthful of his pint and pushed in front of George to take his shot. "Out the way!"

They'd drunk their way down South Parade and found themselves in the back of 42nd Street, playing pool for twenty pounds a game. House rules were that the winner stays on, but as it was those two playing then nobody dared to put a coin on the table and the rest of the bar shared the other one between them.

Since the trouble with Mark and his gang started, it had been unusual to see them in a bar together; they had worked on the principle that if one of them was shot then the other one could still get revenge. But tonight it was different. Tonight was Rob's birthday and they were out to help him celebrate. The trio had been drinking for most of the day with a few hangers on thrown into the mix. Some of them went because they wanted to and were proud to be invited, some of them because they felt like they should and to show respect, and some for fear they might upset the Boltons or Rob. Even though they'd lost Whitley Bay's drugs trade from the houses, they still controlled the doors. And if you controlled the doors, you controlled the dealers inside.

The bar was busy but not packed. The DJ played the latest chart toppers, interspersed with the occasional sing along classic. South Parade was busy on a Thursday but mainly with locals from the coast. Friday and Saturday were busier nights but there was more of a mixture of people. Like most other revelers, they'd started at the top and worked their way down the street, ending up in 42nd Street before the clubs.

Kenny potted the black, winked at George and gave him a smile. He was five to one up and now he'd taken eighty quid from him. He felt a buzz in his pocket as his mobile phone rang. He flipped it open and saw his house number illuminated on the screen.

"Hello!" he shouted over the noise of the music and revelers. He recognised Francesca's voice on the other end but couldn't hear what she was saying. "Hello, hello! I can't hear you! I'll go outside!" He pointed at the phone and motioned to George that he was going outside, then pointed at the table and spun his right index finger, indicating for him to rack up the next frame.

At the fire exit he pointed at the door. The doorman pushed down the lock bar and opened it for him to walk through. As the door shut, he waved to his doormen over the road at Rio's before returning to his call.

"Hello, what's up darling?" he said to his wife.

"Nothing. I was just wondering what time you'll be in. I'm starving that's all, and I can't be arsed to cook."

"No change there then," he joked.

"Yeah, funny. So, what time will you be back? Are you going clubbing or not? I'm just hungry . . . and horny."

"Oh really? Well, I was gonna go clubbing but I might change me plans now, especially if you're going to get all dressed up for me."

"Well, if you bring some food I'll see what I can do. And I promise you'll get my full attention when you return."

"So, what are you fancying, madame?" He put on his best French accent.

"Surprise me. I fancy a pizza. Or a chicken kebab with chips."

"Classy bird," he said.

"Fuck off, you. Do you want your leg over or not?"

"Course I do. Anyway, I'll finish me pint, get the food and jump in a taxi. I'll be there in an hour, tops."

"An hour? Hurry up, I'm fucking starving here."

"Really? You haven't mentioned it. I'll not be long. Love you."

"Love you, too. Bye." He turned and knocked on the fire exit door, which the doorman dutifully opened.

George was standing with both hands on his pool cue and shaking his head back at Kenny with a pretend look of disgust on his face. "I guess that will be you, then?"

"What do you mean?"

"The wife's just summoned you, so that means you'll be scuttling off now. You're right under the fucking thumb you are."

"Shut up, man. Am I fuck."

"So, are you off or not?"

"Well, not just yet." Kenny gave a wry smile. "I'll have this game and then go."

George shook his head again.

Kenny started a game and ignored his ribbing. He knew George wasn't bothered if Kenny left early; he just wanted the chance to win his money back. Five minutes later, Kenny potted the black and held out his hand to his cousin. George counted out a hundred pounds and handed it to him as Rob appeared from the front of the bar, bopping along with a vodka and coke in his hand.

"I'm off for a line," said Rob. "Youse want one?"

"I'm alright," said George. "And this soft arse is away. His lass has summoned him."

"Really?" said Rob. "It's me birthday, man."

"It's not that," said Kenny. "I've been out all day and I'm on a promise, that's all."

"On a fucking promise?" exclaimed George. "Like fuck. You'll get in and she'll have a fucking headache or something. You know what they're like."

"Aye, probably. But anyway, I'm off. Gonna get a bit scran and a Joe Maxi."

"Fanny." Rob shook his head. "Letting the side down again. On me birthday as well."

"What youse doing next?" asked Kenny. "Sylvesters after this?"

"Probably," said George. "Then to the Sagar for a curry . . . for a change

"I'll catch up with youse tomorrow, then. Enjoy the rest of your night, boys. Have fun." Kenny picked up his Lacoste sports jacket and he squeezed his way through the crowd. He stopped to shake hands with a few people before doing the same with the doormen outside. He turned left towards the Spanish City, then stopped at Pizza Cottage for Francesca's food order and waited for the drunk guy with his larger-than-life girlfriend to order his food. Kenny looked at her, thankful that Francesca wasn't loud and brash like the girl who stood before him. Francesca was slim, elegant and quiet, until her temper kicked in, and like most women she wore the trousers around the house. It didn't matter who or how big Kenny was, she would stand up to him all the way. And that was why he loved her.

He walked to the taxi rank outside Rio's, and he was glad he didn't see anyone he knew. He'd had enough to drink and all he wanted to do was get home and enjoy the food. The taxi drivers would often complain about having food in the car but this one was fine with it and didn't object. As he sat in the back seat his mind drifted. Kenny thought that it would be great if the sex happened, but he was feeling tired now and could just as easily go to sleep after the food. The older he got, the more he appreciated spending nights in with his girls rather than being out drinking with his pals. One or maybe two drunken nights a week were enough for him these days.

"Just go right and then left, mate," he instructed the driver.

"No bother, mate." The skinny young driver turned into Hillheads estate from Shields Road.

"It's just up here on the left mate, just after the yellow Mini."

"There you go . . . three pounds twenty, thanks,"

Kenny fished about in his pocked with one hand and pulled out a handful of coins as he balanced the food with the other. He looked at the change and reckoned it was just over four pounds and handed it all to the driver. "Keep the change,"

"Cheers, mate. Much appreciated."

He reached across and opened the passenger door to see Francesca at the front room window as he stepped out into the misty street. She smiled and waved and then the curtain went down as Kenny he made his way up the path. The taxi drove off towards Whitley.

They were both still smiling as the door opened, but a split-second later Francesca's face turned to abject horror as she saw something Kenny couldn't. He turned just in time to see a dark figure looming out of the fog and running towards them both. He dropped the food to the concrete as Francesca uttered a piercing scream and the figure made his final few steps towards his target. Kenny stood stock still and stared at what he could see of the gunman's face, swathed in a scarf and a wooly hat so that only his eyes and the bridge of his nose were visible. As Kenny and the gunman stared at each other, the split-second delay was enough for Kenny to think that the assassin didn't have the balls to go through with it, but he was wrong.

*   *   *

Two bright flashes and two loud bangs broke the stillness of the street as both barrels of the shotgun were unloaded into Kenny's chest from a few feet away. He staggered backwards through the doorway where he collapsed onto his devoted wife. Francesca screamed and screamed as loud as she could, she wrestled herself clear and grabbed her husband's lifeless body and held it tight. "Kenny, no, no," she wailed and cried, but she knew he was dead.

He'd died almost instantly, the shots leaving a bloody mess of bone and sinews where his thick, barrelled chest had been.

"Mam, what was that?" asked Nikki, as she poked her head around the top of the stairs. She saw a sight that no child should ever have to suffer as her mother held her fallen father in her arms.

*   *   *

The shooter ran to his getaway car that was parked around the corner and threw the shotgun inside. Scrambling in, he started the car with the screwdriver he'd left in the door pocket and drove off into the smog of the night. Driving briskly, but not fast enough to attract attention, he drove towards the ice rink, cut through the car park adjacent to the football ground then turned right onto the narrow lane of Rink Way.

He slowed as he pulled into the Boys Club car park and turned the car full circle to see if anyone was there. But, tonight, his luck was in and the car park was deserted. This was the risky part: there was one way in and one way out by car and that was back towards the scene of the crime. He switched off his headlights and the lot plunged back to its inky haze.

Out of the car he leapt, at his wit's end as the adrenaline flowed through his veins. He opened the boot, took out a bag and a petrol can and poured the petrol into the car, front and back. He stripped off his clothes and threw them inside before dressing in the new set he had in the bag. Taking out a lighter, he doused his old T-shirt in petrol before lighting it and throwing into the vehicle. It ignited at once with a low roar and he stared into the flames and watched the evidence go up in smoke. He stood a few seconds, mesmerised by the fire that shot up in front of him before turning and running down the hill towards the rugby club and to the lone car that was parked next to the club house.

He'd done it. *No witnesses*, he thought, as he sprinted away into the fog.

* * *

The sound of the engine disturbed the tranquility of the night and became progressively louder. There were no blue lights and no sirens wailing as the beams from the headlights cut through the fog towards Paul. He sprinted across the car park and threw himself into into the shrubbery, pressing his face into the soft earth as he tried to make himself as small and as flat as possible, praying that it wasn't the police. He lay like a statue, scared stiff of making any movement that would give his position away, and pulled his coat over his mouth so his breath couldn't be seen in the cold night air.

The sound of the car door and then the boot opening petrified him further. *Fuck, fuck, fuck. Not a police dog!* He visualised a sharp set of teeth tearing the flesh from his arm, but there was to be no barking and no canine came. Cautiously, he lifted his head and peered through the long grass not ten feet from the car.

The driver removed his clothes and stripped to his shorts. There was little natural light that night, but enough to see the thick swirls and jagged points of the full-sized tribal tattoo the man wore on his back, like the thorns of a dozen roses spiralling across his skin. The man lit something that he couldn't quite see and tossed it into the car, which erupted in flames. The man reeled back and lifted his arm to shield his face as the heatwave from the ignition swept over him.

Paul ducked back down and buried his face into the soil once more to prevent the light from the flaming car alerting the man to his presence. He heard disappearing footsteps and lifted his head to see the man sprint down the bank towards the rugby club. Once he was far enough away, Paul stood up and sprinted down the other bank and across the rugby pitch towards the relative safety of the quarry. As he ran, he heard a car start and presumed it was the man from the fire, but he wasn't hanging around to see. All he wanted to do was put as much distance as he could between himself and the blazing vehicle. He'd almost been caught burgling an MOT station, and the last thing he needed was to be nicked for TWOC and arson for burning out a car he had nothing to do with.

He ran into the quarry, through the trees and the whipping branches, not stopping until he reached the water's edge. He stopped to get his breath back and flung the backpack as far as he could into the night, watching as it disappeared beneath the surface.

He was halfway home now, but he'd only done the easy half. The risky part was making his way through the streets and then home without encountering the police. He crossed the Broadway unhindered and ran on through the silent streets and down towards the Metro station. Halfway along, he saw the lights of a vehicle approach and he ducked behind a car parked on the nearest driveway. He lay prone as it passed, and when quiet had returned, he continued, scaling a fence before the Metro station, cutting across the tracks and the small allotments and then home.

His lungs burned as he lay on his settee gasping for breath, disappointed to be coming home skint, but delighted to be coming home at all.

*   *   *

"Have you shot Kenny Reid" Cookie spat down the phone to Mark.

"No. Have I fuck. Why?"

"Why? Cos he's been fucking shot, that's fucking why!"

"Is he dead?"

"Aye he's fucking dead. Get rid of your phone and don't get in touch again. I'll find you when it's safe. OK?"

"Aye, OK."

The line went dead, and as Mark lay back on the pillow a warm glow of satisfaction washed over him. One down, one to go . . .

Then he bounced out of bed realising he had to act fast; his door would be going in soon and he'd be the prime suspect in a murder investigation. He placated a half-asleep Lynn, dressed and crept downstairs to the kitchen. Before he slipped quietly out of the back door, he removed the battery from the burner phone, flicked out the sim card then wiped the components clean of his fingerprints. The clock struck three, and he didn't see a soul as he walked through the estate to find a suitable drain. He slipped the phone between the grating and dropped it into the murky water where it would be lost forever. The sim and the battery were dropped into different drains around the estate. Then he went home, climbed back into bed and lay waiting for the inevitable visit from the Murder Squad.

They arrived later that morning and, surprisingly, they had the decency to knock. He'd had a few people over for drinks that night, which gave him enough of an alibi to be bailed the next day. Even though there was no evidence linking him to the shooting, the police weren't entirely happy. They knew he could have slipped out and done it and then slipped back in, and the only people vouching for him were his friends. They couldn't prove he was lying, but at the same time they couldn't prove he wasn't.

*   *   *

Paul drew back the curtains and was pleasantly surprised to see the sun was shining and the sky was clear. It was a big change from the doom and gloom of the previous night. He hoped that the weather would reflect his life today and he would have more luck than he'd had the evening before.

Barefoot and in only his dressing gown, he walked onto the cold kitchen floor and flicked on the kettle, then he opened the washing machine to retrieve the clothes he'd washed to remove any forensics from the burglary or the burnt-out car. He thought about how close he'd been to getting nicked for burning out a car that had nothing to do with him as he slid two slices of bread into the toaster.

Rubbing the sleep out of his eyes he flicked the TV on to Channel 3, where the opening credits for the ITV local news were rolling. He reached for the remote and turned up the volume as Kenny Reid's face appeared in the top left corner, with Kathy Secker reporting in a serious voice that he'd been murdered late last night. The inevitable shot of the incinerated car and Kenny's cordoned off house followed, along with an interview with one of the residents. She described how she'd heard the shots at around 10.30 last night, the same time that Paul and Alan had been up to no good.

The realisation of what he'd witnessed in the car park

hit him like a freight train. The man he'd seen burn out the car was the shooter. A knot in his stomach formed quickly and he ran to the bathroom and threw up in the toilet. He'd been right next to the car when it was torched, and he prayed to his porcelain God that nothing had been left at the scene that could be traced back to him.

And then he panicked. What if they followed his footsteps to the quarry and dredged the lake? Were his or Alan's fingerprints on the tools that lay submerged the mud? Could a sniffer dog still follow his scent back home after all these hours? He filled the sink with cold water, thrust his face into it and screamed. As his soaking head left the water for the second time, he heard the phone ring from the front room. He thought twice about answering it in case it was the police, and then dismissed that as being unlikely. He tried to compose himself and lifted the receiver from its handset in a state of apprehension and dread.

"Hello?"

"Hello, mate."

It was Carl.

"Oh, hello – two seconds!" Smoke billowed into the front room from the kitchen.

He ran into through and popped up the toast from the machine, burning his fingers as he threw the blackened bread into the bin before returning to his call.

"How's things?" said Carl. "Much been going on?"

"Er . . . not much." He was unsure what to say because he knew that prison phone calls were recorded.

"What you doing tomorrow? Fancy coming across for a visit?"

"Aye, can do." Paul's mind raced.

"Sound. See you, then. The visiting order's at Jackie's. Come by yourself." Carl then rang off.

Paul dressed quickly, took his wet clothes and trainers from the washing machine and left the house with them in a carrier bag. Then he walked into Whitley Bay and stuffed them under some rubble bags in a full skip in a back lane that he hoped that would be taken away soon. He then returned home and cleaned his flat solidly for six hours.

* * *

"Hello, ma'am, what brings you here?" asked the uniformed copper who was inspecting the site of the attempted break in at the MOT station.

"There was an attempted burglary here last night, PC Reynolds," said Sharon Manstone.

"Yes, ma'am. But surely that's a uniform matter, not something to bother CID with?"

"We were called in to assist, constable. I think it would have been left with you if it hadn't been for last night's shooting."

"And what's one got to do with the other, ma'am?"

"Maybe something or maybe nothing. But the shooting took place over there and the car was burnt out over there, and we're kind of in the middle." She pointed in each direction with her radio.

"And do you think they're linked, ma'am?"

"I doubt it. But you never know. There was a shotgun found in the car, which is believed to be the murder weapon, and I wouldn't have thought that someone would pause mid-burglary and nip off and shoot someone. However, they may have been disturbed by the shooting or the getaway car and saw something. And seeing as they broke in through the allotments and we received a call from a concerned resident of a possible break-in last night, there's a decent probability that they did."

"And was this reported last night, ma'am?"

"No. This morning. The garage reported it when they opened up, and after seeing the shooting on the news, an old guy rang it in. Apparently, he thought he'd heard something when he was walking his dog but dismissed it at the time."

A few minutes later, Sharon found the makeshift entrance to the allotments and followed a set of footprints through the sodden earth from the damaged fence to the carpark, seventy yards from where the blackened shell of the Rover 216 sat. The other set she followed off towards the Marden Estate, but she lost them halfway down the track. As her eyes scanned the car park, she considered that the intruders had seen the shooter, or maybe that they were the same person, using the burglary as an alibi. Deciding that she was unsuitably dressed to scale the fence, she took the long way around and continued her search. When she inspected the perimeter of the car park and surveyed what she presumed was the killers escape route, she noticed the freshly disturbed grass just over the brow of the bank. She stared out over the quarry top. Had the thieves seen the car being torched?

* * *

Paul returned to the table with two cups of milky tea and scanned the visitors room for anyone he knew. He was glad that he didn't recognise anybody, as he couldn't be arsed with the usual questions about how Carl was doing and the murder trial. It was quiet today, and the table he sat at was a few feet away from anyone else. That would suit them just fine.

He was looking forward to seeing Carl to tell him the only real information he'd discovered. Even though it had been a complete fluke that he'd seen Kenny's killer, he still hadn't seen his face. Even if he had, there was no guarantee that it was the same person who killed Liam and set up Carl. When Alan had called at his place the next day, he'd denied seeing anyone or seeing the car getting torched, even though Alan pressed him on it. He'd told him that he'd stashed the tools on the Metro lines and would get them another time because he couldn't think of a plausible excuse for why he'd thrown them in the lake. They both promised to keep the burglary to themselves and to tell nobody else, *ever*. But, as Alan spoke the words and as much as he sounded genuine, Paul still doubted his ability to keep his mouth shut.

Carl had made him promise that if he found anything out the only person he should tell was him, and that was a promise Paul intended to keep. It had been a couple of weeks since he'd last seen him, but when he appeared Paul was taken aback by his weight loss. He was still a big unit, but his shoulders and arms had lost an inch or so and his face was visibly thinner. He didn't want to mention it to him, and he presumed that it was the stress of the charge and the poor prison diet that had caused it. They shook hands and sat down across from each other.

"Alright mate," said Carl. "Thanks for coming through."

"That's alright. How's things in here?"

"Just the usual. Not going anywhere in a hurry, am I? So, what's happening with you? You got any news?"

"Well, as I'm sure you know, Kenny got done yesterday."

"Aye, shame that," said Carl. "He wasn't a bad bloke, really."

Paul didn't know if the reply was sarcasm, indifference or honesty. "And I've got a bit of news . . ."

"What's that?" asked Carl.

Paul looked around and he prayed that their conversation wasn't being recorded. "I saw the shooter."

"Eh? How's that?" Carl's body tensed and he straightened up quickly.

"I was doing a burglary with Alan Richards and it came on top. Sort of."

"What you doing with that prick? Sorry. Go on."

"We were screwing this MOT place on the Foxhunters and it came on top. We got disturbed by some dog walker so we nashed back though the allotments and split up. He fucked off to the Marden and I went back towards mine through the quarry."

"And?"

"And . . . I was just about to go down the bank to the

rugby field from the Boy's Club car park when I heard this car come down from the rink. So I dived in the grass and some bloke got out. He stripped off, changed his clothes and torched the car. I've seen the car on the news, so it's definitely him."

"Fucking hell! What else?"

"I couldn't see his face, but I saw the guy's tats when he got changed. He had this big fucking tribal thing on his back – loads of swirls and pointy bits on the ends."

"Go on . . ."

"He was big. Bit taller than you but not as wide."

"Obviously." Carl tensed into a pretend bodybuilder pose.

"I didn't see his face or what colour hair he had. It was too dark."

They both sat back in silence. Carl racked his brains thinking of anyone who met the description and Paul wondering what was going through Carl's mind.

"And I spoke to Regan," Paul said. "He was asking after you again. He's given us a contact number in case you need owt. I was going to ask him if he recognised the shooter guy's tats."

"Don't!" Carl shot back. "Just keep it between you and me for now. I don't want anybody to know fuck all about fuck all. Not even Regan. So, what happened next?"

"He ran off and I think he jumped into a car in the rugby club car park. I just fucked off out of there. I dumped the tools in the quarry lake and legged it home."

"Did you see the car?"

"Na. It was too far away."

Carl looked disappointed. "Doesn't help us much, though. It could have been anybody. And there's nothing to link this to Liam."

"Aye, maybe you're right. But I did hear a little snippet. I was having a drink and a few lines with Craig Cameron last week. I've been getting the hash off both sides like you asked and he told us something. He said that he heard George, Kenny and Rob talking about having Mark shot."

"Really? Why would they talk about that in front of him?"

"Dunno. But I don't think he was lying. He said it was said as a joke, sort of. It could have been them that's set you up. He also said that his money's on Rob for it."

"Aye, but it's Liam, not Mark, I'm in here for."

"Fuck knows. Maybe they shot the wrong charva?"

Carl pondered and rocked back on his seat for a moment. "Paul, it could have been anybody. I've gone through a hundred scenarios in my head, and I've no idea who it was. George . . . Kenny . . . Rob . . . Mark . . . Les . . . Craig . . . Fuck knows. Even with Kenny getting done, there's nothing linking that to Liam, so it doesn't really help my case much."

"Aye, I thought that. But I'll keep trying for you. I'll do what I can."

"Look Paul, you're the only person that's doing owt for us in here and I'd be lost without you. And I've been having a think. When – sorry, *if* – I get out of here, I'll have an ask around and see if I can find anything out about your dad."

"Really?"

"Aye, really. It's the least I can do. But be careful, Paul. It's dangerous people you're playing with here."

"Don't worry, I'll be fine." Paul kept a brave face in front of Carl, but he could only pray that he would be.

11: Scream and Slam

A month had passed since Kenny's killing and George had vowed at the funeral, and every day since, that he would avenge his cousin's death. Every morning as he climbed out of bed, and for every hour until he lay his head back down on his pillow that vow remained the same. He thought of little else as the pain tore into him, consumed him, ate away at every fibre of his being and sent him into rages that were unusual even for him. His friends and family were worried about his mental state and tip-toed around him. They were scared to upset him and have his temper unleash itself from the cage in which he kept it. He managed keep a lid on it until after the funeral and until the police's interest had melted away.

And then he made his move.

He grabbed anyone and everyone he thought could have the remotest piece of useful information. He'd told Mark and Matty's punters that if they had anything to do with either of them, they were on a one-way trip to hospital. He was fair; he gave everyone a simple choice: tell him what he wanted to know or suffer a hiding or torture from an eighteen stone raging sociopath. But so far it hadn't worked and he was still no closer to knowing who had murdered his cousin.

Paul had received a visit from George, Rob and Craig and was expecting to be quizzed about the burglary and the burnt-out car, but for some reason they were calm and said nothing of it. He wasn't sure if they were sounding him out and leading up a path just to catch him out because it amazed him that a disaster like Alan could keep his mouth shut about where they were that fateful night. They had chatted about the hash business and they asked a few more questions about Carl and his rackets and then left.

And as the raindrops fell and pitter-pattered on the roof of the Transit van, George could think of nothing else except revenge and hurting Mark.

Three men sat in silence on the cold steel floor, each with their own thoughts of the job ahead, and armed with a variety of weapons. Rob was in the front, and if the two who were in the back with George wished they weren't, they wouldn't say that to his face. He'd seen them alright over the years and they both made a good living off his back. With Carl locked up, they'd know that it was only a matter of time before he was back on top. Even with Kenny in the ground he was strong enough to take on Mark and Matty and win back control of the drugs game. George knew that they were there for themselves and not for him, but they would know that at the first sign of disloyalty they would be dropped and replaced with more willing subordinates. They'd be straight off the firm and sink into obscurity.

For the previous two weeks, George had put the word out: "Tell me when you see Mark or Matty and, if I get them, I'll give you a grand."

Word of this must have made its way back to them because they were now extremely vigilant, which made them harder to catch. There had been a few sightings and a few chases, but so far George and his cronies had failed to snare either one of them. Hopefully today would be different.

Mark's car had been spotted in the car park next to Whitley Bay Metro Station and he'd been seen walking into town – and, unusually, he was alone. These days he was typically either with Matty or with one of his hangers-on for safety in numbers, but today was different and they had the opportunity to catch him out.

The timing was perfect for George and his gang; they were already assembled in Rob's lock-up discussing their day-to-day drugs business when the call came through. Rob had a stolen van in the lock up: a Ford Transit that he'd adapted for kidnap and torture.

"They've spotted Mark in Whitley," an excited George blurted out.

"Who has?" asked Rob.

"It doesn't matter who. He's been seen and his car's in the car park next to the Metro. If we're quick we can get him."

Never one to miss an opportunity, Rob jumped into the driver's side and started up the van. George slid the side door open and ushered in the other two who, whether they liked it or not, were now part of a kidnap conspiracy.

The van had been used a few times to hunt Mark's gang. It had been parked up in the streets near Mark and Matty's houses with a squad inside hoping to catch them out. Rob had drilled small holes in each side and in the rear doors so they could peek out to survey their targets without being seen. Ever the professional, he'd put together a "kidnap kit", consisting of several ski masks, gloves, a handgun and a variety of bats, ammonia, handcuffs and rope. It was a kit that he felt a little proud of as he drove from Backworth down to the coast.

They parked the van on the opposite side of the station to Mark's car and George sent Craig through the cut to see if it was still in place. Five minutes later, he returned and confirmed that it was.

"Are we on then?" asked Rob.

"Fucking right we're on!" said George. "Drive down Cullercoats way so we don't go near the bizzie station and we'll park up and wait."

Rob did as instructed and drove the van into the car park while keeping an eye out for Mark's return. They couldn't believe their luck when they saw an empty space next to his car. They parked with the cab against the fence so the sliding door was next to Mark's driver's door. The van's engine was turned off and Rob squeezed into the back with the other three, pulling down his ski mask as he took a spot on the floor. *"Raindrops keep falling on my head,"* he sang, while he peeking through the spy holes that were invisible to the unknowing eye in the early evening drizzle and rocking his head from side to side. Craig looked at him with openmouthed.

A mixture of apprehension and nervousness swept through George as he waited. his left leg vibrated as he sat, revolver in hand, wondering how it'll feel when he pumped six bullets into Mark's body after torturing him first.

"He's here," said Craig.

George jumped up to take one of the peep holes on Craig's side of the van. Sure enough, Mark was strolling through the entrance of the car park, carrier bag in hand.

The gang stood up slowly, hunched over and readied to pounce. Rob laid his gloved hand on the door handle. George was behind him, pointing the gunmetal grey pistol to where he expected Mark's head to be in a few seconds' time. Craig held his hand up to signal. The other lad hung back, likely worried he'd do the wrong thing, mess it up for everyone and have to suffer the consequences later.

George, Rob and Craig hardly dared move, not wanting to make a sound and give the game away. There were footsteps crunching on the gravel outside, and then a beep of the alarm as Mark pressed his key fob to unlock his car door. Rob quickly slid the van door open and Mark didn't have time to react. He turned, perhaps expecting to take his last breath on earth when he saw four masked faces, one of which was pointing a gun at his head. He had to know who they were and why they were there, but there was no point in running; he would have been shot down where he stood.

"Get in!" snarled Rob, as the other three moved back to make more space in the van.

Mark stared at the faceless quartet, and stepped slowly inside. The door to his mobile prison slammed shut.

"Lie down and put your fucking hands behind your back!" ordered George.

Mark did as he was told. George could easily imagine what he was thinking as he the handcuffs clicked tightly around his wrists. He'd be scared alright, but he'd also think that because they hadn't shot him straight away he might have a chance, however slim, that he could live through this. He had to know he was getting a beating and possibly getting tortured, but he would just have to live with that.

"Get his keys and take his car to the lock up," said Rob to the fourth gang member.
He did as instructed and snatched Mark's keys from his hand, delighted that he would miss the coming events. He squeezed into the front and out the passenger door in case any passers by glanced into an open sliding door to witness the scene inside.

"And don't scratch the paint," said Mark, sarcastically. The comment earned him a smack around the head from Craig's rounders bat.

"Shut the fuck up, you!" said George. He then gagged Mark's mouth and pulled a blindfold over his eyes.

Rob slid into the driver's seat and pulled off his ski mask, and they drove away into the early evening traffic. They turned left then right at the traffic lights and back down Whitley Road towards Cullercoats. Craig was silent and apprehensive. Mark made the occasional grunt as the van adjusted speed which varied the weight of George who was sitting on his back, and whose thoughts revolved around the violence he would be inflicting soon.

"Where we taking him?" Rob shouted into the back over the sound of the diesel engine.

"The lock-up," instructed George.

"Can't take him there. I'm not having it covered in forensics from this cunt. And besides, it'll be full when his cars in there – no room for the van,"

"I know," said Craig. "Turn in at the Co-op and we'll take him to Paul's place."

"Good plan," said George.

"Hope he's in," said Rob.

"I don't," mumbled Mark through his gag. The comment that earned him another dig from George, but this time with the butt of his pistol.

Rob parked the van up outside Paul's back gate with the cargo door facing it so nobody would see inside.

"Go and see if he's in," said George to Craig, who slid open the van door once they were level.

* * *

When Paul heard the gate open, he looked out the window expecting to see one of his dope punters. He was surprised to see Craig and a masked-up man sitting astride an unknown and blindfolded body. *For fuck's sake!* He put his coffee cup down on the table. He wondered what was going to happen next. First Mark turned up with a gun and tried to burn his face off and now it was the other mob with a wrapped-up individual.

"What the fuck?" Paul said to Craig as he opened the door.

"We need to come in," said Craig, in a manner that told Paul he had no choice.

"Who the fuck's that?"

"It's Mark. And we need to come in." Craig cocked his head and stared at Paul.

The van door slid almost fully closed again. It was left open just enough for Paul to make out the dark figures inside.

"No, no," said Paul. "No fucking way! You're not bringing him in here."

"Listen," said Craig. "George and Rob are out there and they're on the fucking warpath. So, unless you want to be the next fucker tied up in a van, I suggest you let us in… *Now.*"

Paul had no choice and he prayed that, whatever happened, he wasn't going to take any blame for this – not from the police or from Mark and his gang. It looked like Mark was on his way out, and when all was said and done, it was better to be on the winning side than the losing one. "For fuck's sake. Bring him in, then."

Craig went back to the van and slid the side door open; an excited Rob had reunited himself with George in the back.

"It's OK, it's sorted," said Craig to the other two. "Get him out the van."

"Right, let's get him in. And if you try anything I'll put a bullet in your back," George warned Mark.

Through the blindfold, Mark could just make out the light emanating from Paul's kitchen doorway which helped them manhandle him out and into the downstairs flat. George and Rob kept hold of him by an arm each while Craig kept an eye out for the neighbours. They half walked and half dragged him into the front room.

"Get on the fucking floor now," ordered George, as he kicked Mark's legs away from under him.

"In the fucking corner," said Rob. He dragged Mark across the carpet by his arms and dropped him on the floor.

Paul looked over to Rob and his mind flashed back to the first time they'd met. He was getting stoned in the lesbians' flat when Rob came in to score some hash with a sawn-off shotgun handle sticking out of his sports bag. It was the first time Paul had seen a firearm and he was lost for words, and if he was honest a little frightened, especially considering the lunatic who was carrying it.

"Don't worry, you," George said to Paul. "If owt gets wrecked, you'll get the money for it."

The destruction of his furniture was the last thing Paul was worrying about as he stood in the doorway chewing his bottom lip. He nodded and stared at the pistol in George's hand, wondering how much would need to be replaced if he pulled the trigger.
Surely, they wouldn't kill Mark here, he thought – and prayed. Craig gave him a thumbs up and a smile that was supposed to be reassuring, but for Paul it fell way short of the mark.

Rob seemed to be buzzing over the power that he now had over Mark. It wasn't the fact that it was Mark on the floor; it could have been anyone. But because it was Mark it was a bonus. Having him tied up helpless and bound beneath him seemed to make Rob feel like a king.

From what Paul had heard, this was far from the first time Rob had tied someone up. He'd done it for debt collection, in robberies and sometimes for interrogation, and he knew all the tricks. He'd once tied a guy up in a drugs robbery and his victim threw himself through a first-floor window and into the garden, an act that stopped him from being robbed but earned him a broken back. If he had any rope, he would tie their legs on the bare skin to stop their socks from giving them any wiggle room, with the pain from the course rope adding to their terror. If he had none, he would undo their belts and pull their jeans down over their shoes so they couldn't run away, and that was what he did with Mark.

"Turn the fucking telly up," Rob ordered Craig, who did as he was told.

Paul turned his head away as Rob lifted his bat with two hands, he knew what was coming next. He rained four blows in quick succession onto Mark's back and right shoulder. Mark curled up helplessly and attempted to shout and scream through his home-made gag.

As disgusted as he was with what Rob was doing, Paul had little sympathy for Mark. He'd taken plenty of liberties with people, himself included. He'd been willing to burn his face off and harm his mam, Lindsey and Jason if he didn't do his bidding. *Fuck him.* Part of him wanted to shout for them to stop but a bigger part of him hoped that they hurt Mark badly – so badly that he would never bully anyone again.

"Give us that here!" George grabbed the bat from Rob and laid into Mark's back and legs, smashing him with it repeatedly.

"Do him, George! Do him!" Rob, egged George on while Craig and Paul watched.

"No, no! Please . . ." whimpered Mark through the gag.

A minute later, George stopped and wiped the sweat from his face. He flicked back his wet hair as he stared down at Mark. Nobody else said a word. George was in charge, and he alone would decide Mark's fate. He crouched down and grabbed a handful of Mark's hair. Their faces were just inches from each other. "Now, Mark, I want to know who else was involved in killing wor Kenny, and you're going to tell me. And if I think that your lying, I'll make you suffer, just like my fucking family's suffering now. Do you understand?"

Mark nodded.

"I'm going to take the gag out, and if you scream or shout, Rob here will put a bullet in you, OK?"

Mark nodded again as Rob drew out his pistol.

George leaned the bat against the wall and pulled off Mark's mask. Mark blinked quickly as his eyes adjusted to the light. They stared at each other, one scared and helpless, the other angry and in charge.

"Right then Mark," said George, "who killed wor Kenny?"

"I don't know, snivelled Mark. "Honestly."

"It was you, wasn't it? You fucking killed him because you blamed us for Liam."

"Look, it wasn't me. I swear."

"Gag him again," George said to Rob, who stuffed the cloth back into Mark's mouth.

George gave Mark a few more cracks with the bat while Rob booted him in the torso before removing the gag once more.

"Come on then, who the fuck was it?" Rob said,

through gritted teeth.

Mark did something Paul expected that he hadn't done in years. He started to cry. "It wasn't me," he sobbed. "I mean, it wasn't us."

"Yes, it was!" yelled George. "I swear to God, Mark, this is gonna be a long and painful process if you don't tell us who did it." He continued with the beating.

"Who did you pay?" said Rob.

"Nobody . . . I swear . . ." Mark murmured back.

For the next fifteen minutes, the pattern was the same. George and Rob asking questions then pummelling Mark when he didn't give them the answers they wanted to hear. Mark was in pain – serious pain – but there was no blood flowing, which made Paul slightly happier as he watched on in horror. They were taking care not to hit his head as they didn't want to kill him prematurely. Paul knew these were bad people, but he hadn't realise they were capable of such viscous, brutal acts, and it scared him.

When George finally stopped the beating, he looked like he'd finished a marathon. His hair was matted with sweat and he was panting from his cherry-red face. "That it. I've had enough of your fucking shit." He kicked Mark viciously between the legs.

George looked at Rob and they nodded to each other, a silent confirmation it seemed of a part of their plan that nobody else was privy to. Rob picked up a pillow and handed it to George. George pushed Mark onto his side and straddled him. With his left hand he placed the pillow over Mark's face as he drew the gun from behind his back with his right.

"I've had enough," he said. "You've had your chance. Now you can go and join your piece of shit brother in hell." He flicked off the safety, pulled back the hammer and straightened his right arm.

Rob looked on in interest, anticipating the shot. Paul stood rooted to the spot, aghast at what was happening. Craig looked away. Mark tried to plead but his muffled voice could hardly be heard through the gag and the pillow that was pressed over his face.

"Bye, bye, cunt," said George, as he turned his face away to stop it being splattered with Mark's skull.

"Stop!" Paul shouted.

George paused and turned his head. "Shut up you, you little fucking mug!" He turned to resume the execution of his rival.

"Stop! I saw the shooter! It wasn't him. It wasn't fucking him!"

Mark shook as George lowered his gun.

The whole room looked at Paul. Nobody said a word as they waited for George's reaction.

"He had a massive back tattoo. A big fucking tribal thing. Look . . ." Paul stepped over and lifted Mark's shirt to confirm that he didn't have it.

"So how the fuck did you see the shooter?" Rob's disappointment was palpable.

"I'd been burgling a car place on the Foxhunters, and it came on top. We left it and fucked off home. And on the way back to the quarry I saw the car get torched. In the Boy's Club car park. I was hiding in the bushes cos I thought it was the filth. He got out and torched the car and he chucked his clothes and that in. And when he had his top off, I saw the tat."

"It was you that fucking paid him!" Rob said to Mark, as he booted him in the back of his head.

"No man, no," shouted Mark through his gag, as he shook and cried. Please don't kill me. It wasn't me, I swear."

"You know what, Rob?" said George. "I actually believe him. Get him up. I think me and Mark need to have a chat."

They untied a battered and bruised Mark, pulled his pants up and sat him in a corner chair. He was a broken man, both mentally and physically. He sat whimpering and shaking as Paul handed him glass of water. He was in no state to try anything, but they were taking no chances; George kept the gun pointed at him in case he tried to escape.

"Let's start at the start then, Mark," he said. "Carl's obviously in Durham, but like everyone else round here I have serious doubts that he killed Liam, and I wouldn't imagine in a million years that he would shoot him dead on the street, especially as he did the pair of yous in the Vic."

"Look, George, I swear . . . Kenny's death was fuck all to do with us. It wasn't me. And Matty hasn't got a back tattoo either, so he's out of the frame. He would have told us anyway – you know what he's like. And we didn't pay anybody else to do him. Honestly, I swear."

"So, what about this tat, Paul. What exactly did it look like and why didn't you tell us this before?"

"Look, I just wanted to keep out of it. I'm just fucking

scared that's all. I'm not used to guns and murders and all that. It's just not me."

"Neither are we," said George. "Well, maybe Rob is." Rob put on an obliging smile.

"It was a big swirly tribal thing," said Paul, "with big fuck off pointy bits that covered the whole of his back. It was dark and I couldn't really see much else. He torched the car and ran to the rugby field and jumped in another car, I think."

"You didn't recognise him, then?" said George.

"No, mate. Honestly. I've never seen him before in me life. I didn't get a look at his face anyway."

"What sort of car did he get into?" Rob asked.

"I dunno. It was too far away. I couldn't see. I wasn't exactly hanging around to find out, so I just legged it home."

"How big was he?" asked George.

"Dunno. Six foot? A little bit smaller maybe. I couldn't really tell."

"Hair colour?"

"Dark? He wasn't blonde, that's all I can remember."

"So where does this leave us?" asked Mark between whimpers and gasps of pain.

"Fuck knows. If your lot didn't kill Kenny and we didn't kill Liam – and it's fair to assume that Carl didn't kill him either, then who's doing the shootings?"

"I don't know," said Mark. "I wish I did. So where does it leave me and you

"I'm happy to leave things as they are for now. At least until we get to the bottom of this. If you are that is?"

"I am, George. Honestly. And I'll straighten things with Matty as well." Mark put out his right hand for George to shake.

George took pity on him and shook it gently.

Before they all left, George took out a roll of bank notes and counted out a hundred pounds. He gave it to Paul for the inconvenience of torturing and almost murdering someone in his front room. Then he did something that, by all accounts, he rarely did and apologised for involving him – before chastising him for not speaking up about the shooter earlier, but he then said he understood why he hadn't.

Once Paul was alone and the flat had returned to its previous serenity, he lay back and thanked his lucky stars. He'd been seconds away from a murder charge and it was at that moment he decided that he'd had enough and that he couldn't live in this world any more. He couldn't carry on playing detective for Carl. He'd just have to tell the police he was with Marie and deal with the consequences from Les and his family. He was a big enough lad after all. He'd pay back Craig and Matty, give up the flat and move back in with his mam.

It was time to find something else to do with his life.

*   *   *

An icy blast rushed through the passageway as Lindsey opened her front door and she wrapped her cardigan in tightly to protect her slender body from the cold night air. At first, she thought Paul's eyes were watering from the freezing winter wind, but at a second glance she realised they weren't. Tears cascaded down his crimson cheeks. He sniffed back and lowered his head as he entered the warmth of her flat. Unusually, there was no embrace or eye contact as he passed.

"Are you OK, Paul?"

There was no reply. He'd sounded fine on the phone when he said he was popping along, and she didn't think it was out of the ordinary when he asked if Jason was with her that night. He was staying at her mam's, which gave her an evening of relaxation, or so she expected. Closing the front door, she followed him into the sitting room where he stood, not moving and facing away from her with his head still lowered. She stopped for a moment and stared at his back, knowing that it must be something serious because he hadn't spoken or taken his coat off. In the years that they'd been close she'd seen him in every mood and every state of mind but not this one, and she knew instinctively that whatever it was, it was bad.

"Are you OK?" she asked again, placing a caring hand on his shoulder.

He turned, wiped his eyes and started to sob uncontrollably as he looked back at her.

"Come here," she said, moving closer. She wrapped her arms around him and pulled in his head until they embraced. She felt his cold salty tears tumble down her neck as they stood, entwined like two climbing vines, for what seemed to her like an age until he finally spoke.

"I'm fucking done," he said.

"With what?"

"Fucking drugs . . . villains . . . this shit. I can't take it anymore."

"Good. That's good Paul. What's happened? You can tell me . . . come on . . ."

He lifted his head and looked at her, and she saw the face of a broken man, his dejected appearance telling her that life had truly beaten him.

"Howay, sit yourself down. And take your coat off, will you?" She motioned him to the settee. They sat in their usual positions like an old married couple, Paul at one end and Lindsey nearer the door. She put her hand back on his shoulder and gave him a reassuring smile, which she was glad to see returned. Whatever his problems were, it seemed that he could always raise a smile for her.

"So, howay then . . ." she coaxed, "what's been going on now?"

"You're not going to believe this . . . and don't ever repeat it."

"You know I won't."

"George Bolton was going to murder Mark Taylor,"

"Well, everybody knows that was on the cards."

"Not in my fucking front room, though."

"What?" She was utterly shocked. Just how deep had Paul been suckered into criminality? She couldn't utter another word.

"They came to mine – why fucking mine I have no idea. Craig, George and Rob fucking Murray turned up. They had Mark tied up and started smashing him up in the corner. It went on for ages. In the end, George just lost it and cocked his gun. He stuck a pillow over Marks face, pointed the gun at his head and I thought that was it."

"And what stopped him?"

"Me."

"You? What did you do?"

"Nowt, I just told him it wasn't Mark that shot Kenny."

"And how the fuck do *you* know that?"

"Cos I saw the shooter."

This was proving all too much for Lindsey. She struggled to take all this in. He'd been in her flat for five minutes and he'd confessed to almost being involved in a murder and witnessing the perpetrator of another. She ran both hands through her hair and then looked at him aghast through her fingers, not knowing what to say or do next. "I need a joint . . . and a cuppa," she said at last. "You skin up and I'll chuck the kettle on." At least she could get her out of the room for a moment or two while she tried to unscramble her thoughts.

Standing in the kitchen she contemplated throwing him out and never seeing him again. This was on another level. She knew he was in over his head, running around with the likes of Carl, but as much as her head told her to tell him to leave, her heart still wouldn't allow it.

By the time she returned to the sitting room with the coffees, she even felt ashamed of her thoughts of abandoning him. He looked more relaxed and the crying had stopped but the pink cheeks remained. He looked up into her eyes and she looked back into his. There was hurt and sorrow there, but also gratitude and affection, hope even – perhaps love? She held his hand and smiled as he took a long deep toke of the joint and he squeezed it back as if to say thank you for being there.

"So come on, then," she said. "Tell me the full story."

"Ok then, here goes. Carl didn't shoot Liam. And, by the looks of it, Mark had nowt to do with murdering Kenny either. From what was worked out at mine, nobody knows who this fucker is that I saw or even if it's the same person. Craig thinks Rob might have done it, but he hasn't got a big fuck off tattoo on his back – but that's not to say he hasn't paid someone else. Matty might have something to do with it an all, but I doubt it – he's crackers but he hasn't got the brain power to murder two people and get away with it."

"What tattoo are you on about?"

"I saw Kenny's killer torch the car in the Boy's Club car park. He chucked his clothes in, and when he took his top off he had a massive tribal thing on his back."

"What were you doing in the Boy's Club car park?"

Paul looked sheepish for a moment before continuing. "Me and Alan screwed a car place on the Foxhunters but we couldn't get in so we fucked off. I was on me way home when the car pulled into the car park, I thought it was the bizzies so I hid and then I saw him torch it."

She shook her head slowly in disbelief. "And why would Rob be in on it? He's their pal, isn't he?"

"Well aye, I suppose. But would you trust him?"

"You're asking me? How the fuck should I know about the people you hang around with? But, from what I hear about him, probably not."

Paul flicked a bomber off his jumper. "I certainly wouldn't."

"And what about Carl?" she asked.

"It definitely wasn't him. He's been stitched up. Somebody broke into his RS, found his spare key in the glove box and planted it where Liam was shot."

"Really?"

"Aye, the spare key that he lent to me."

"He doesn't think it was you, does he?"

Paul passed her the joint and she took two quick tokes just to keep it lit.

"Nah. I don't think so anyway."

"So where was he? Why doesn't he just tell the police where he was if it wasn't him?"

"Look, I can't tell you that bit. He says he will if he has to, but he'll be in some serious shit with some very, very naughty people if he does."

"What, worse than George and Mark?"

"Much worse, believe me."

"So, how come they took Mark back to your place?"

"Carl asked me to do a bit of detective work, so I started getting hash off Mark and Craig at the same time to see if I could worm me way in with them and find anything out about the shootings."

"Fucking hell, Paul."

"I know. And I suppose mine must have just been convenient for them. Wrong place, wrong time."

"So what you going to do now?"

"Get out. I've had enough. It's too much for me. I don't mind selling a bit of hash and that, but guns and people getting killed? Fuck that. Honestly, I can't go on. Me head's in bits." He wiped away a tear and looked as if he was doing his best not to break down.

"Come here," she said. She pulled him in close and they embraced holding each other tightly.

Pulling back, they looked into each other's eyes. He took her face in his hands and closed his eyes as she closed hers. Their lips touched and they kissed. He moved his hand to the back of her head and ran his fingers through her hair and she let her hands move over his skin. He slid his hands down onto her hips and then upwards to her ribs, lifting her blouse. She felt a thrill run through the muscles in her belly and her nails dug gently into his sides. She pushed him back and took him by the face, kissing him deeply as she straddled over him then leaned back to remove her top from over her head. Reaching up he flicked her bra straps from her shoulders and freed her aching breasts, which he took in his hands before she lay back down on him.

"I love you, Paul," she said. Then she kissed him again.

"And I love you too."

And they kissed more passionately than she had ever kissed before.

He rolled her onto her side and they fumbled with the belts and buttons of each other's jeans. She stopped suddenly and looked into his eyes again.

"What?" Paul looked suddenly like a dejected child, scolded for something he knew he hadn't done.

"Nothing, it's just . . ."

"Just what?"

She couldn't take his hurt look any longer. "Not here.

Let's go next door. I don't want the first time we have sex to be a quickie on the settee." She closed her eyes and kissed him again before taking him by the hand and leading him into her bedroom.

They lay on the duvet and entwined once more, undressed each other and slid between the cold sheets, which made Lindsey shiver.

"It's OK, I'll keep you warm," he said.

And she hoped it would be forever.

The sex was better than she had ever had. There was no first-time awkwardness and no attempt to hide their bodies from the light that shone in from the passage. There was an electric connection between them that she had never felt before.

"This is it," he said, slipping slowly and gently into her. "I never want to be inside another woman."

And she felt the same. There was no going back, and their friendship would be no more. From now on they were lovers and would be until the end of their days. He was the one for her, and while she wrapped her legs tightly around his back and drew her arms around his shoulders, she berated herself that she'd waited so long for this moment. Once the sex was over, they kissed and lay in silence, satisfied and in total comfort until they fell asleep in each other's arms.

And there they stayed until they were disturbed by the sound of Lindsey's mother braying on the front door.

"Lindsey?" she shouted through the letter box.

"Shit. It's me mam. What time is it?"

"Er . . . ten past nine."

She jumped up, wrapped herself in her dressing gown and made her way to the front door.

A few seconds later, her mam and Jason stood at the bedroom door, both surprised to see Paul sitting upright in the bed with no top on. Her mam looked at her with a raised eyebrow while Jason ran in and jumped on the bed.

"Oh aye?" her mam teased. "Stay the night, did he?"

"Aye he did." Lindsey smiled. "And I think he'll be staying a few more."

"Paul!" shouted Jason, as he gave Paul a big hug.

"Hello, mate," said Paul. "How are ya? Did you have a good night at your nana's?"

"Yeah, I did," said Jason.

"Well, I think I'll be off then," announced her mam. "And it's nice to see you again, Paul." She turned and walked towards the front door.

"OK, Mam. Thanks for having him."

"No bother. Any time." Her mam dropped her voice to a whisper. "And I hope it works out with you two."

"So do I, Mam," Linsey whispered back.

And she meant it from the bottom of her heart.

* * *

Three weeks later, Paul woke up and looked at Lindsey lying peacefully asleep beside him and he thought she was the most beautiful woman he'd ever laid eyes on. She opened her eyes as and moved towards him, resting her head on his chest as he slipped a loving arm around her. She tilted her head back and puckered her lips for an early morning kiss that Paul was more than happy to give her. The kiss turned into a snog and Paul took hold of her bum as they slid further down into the bed.

"Morning," she said. "Ooh, and a good morning to you too!" She lifted up the duvet and looked down at Paul's morning glory.

"And a good morning from us both," said Paul.

Her hand slid down and she pulled back the duvet with the apparent intention of giving him an early morning blow job.

"Mam!" Jason called out from the other side of the door.

"For fuck's sake," she said.

"Aye, perfect timing," said Paul. He swiftly replaced the duvet before Jason opened the bedroom door.

"Mam, can you make my cornflakes?"

"Yeah. Go and sit at the table and I'll be there in a minute." She reached for her dressing gown from the bedroom floor and then made her way to the kitchen.

Paul waited for his erection to go down, got up and dressed in his Ellesse track suit and joined them at the kitchen table. "Morning mate," he said to Jason.

"Morning Paul," Jason replied through a mouthful of cornflakes.

"So, what you up to today?" Paul asked Jason, but he was really asking Lindsey.

"I think we'll take a walk down to the Spanish City and then to the beach," said Lindsey. "Sound good, Jason?"

"Yeah!" Jason piped up.

"And would Paul like to come with us?" Lindsey's

tone indicated that he was going whether he liked it or not.

"Course I will. What time youse going, like?"

"Dunno. Late morning, probably. Maybe lunchtime. I've got a few things to get in Whitley then head down after that. What's your plans?"

"Nowt today, really. I'm going to the gym, but I could meet you down there about one after you've done your shopping and that. I'll meet youse in Pantrini's for dinner. How about that, Jason? You fancy fish fingers and chips later?"

Jason nodded. "Yeah!" He was taking more notice of his cornflakes and the cartoon on TV than of what Paul was saying.

"OK, sounds good," said Lindsey. "Not fancy coming shopping with us, then?"

"Poundstretchers and Woollies? Nah, the gym sounds better. Can't be letting myself go just cos I've got a new bird, you know." he teased.

"Bird? Don't ever call me a bloody bird." She flicked him with her tea towel.

He laughed and moved over to her. He swung her backwards and kissed her before pretending to drop her as the toast popped up out of the machine. "Is my gym gear clean?"

"Course it is, lover boy. My life wouldn't be worth living if I forgot to do that,"

"So where is it?"

"All folded nicely and put away in the wardrobe, just where it always is."

"Thanks." He made his way to the bedroom, where he

packed his gear into his gym bag before returning to the kitchen to give them each a kiss goodbye before heading towards the door.

"You not having any breakfast?" Lindsey shouted down the passage.

"Nah!" he shouted back. "Burns more calories if you train on an empty stomach!"

On the short walk to the gym, he was on Cloud Nine. He realized that he felt happier than he'd ever felt in his whole life. He was waking up with the girl of his dreams and, so far, it had been amazing. No arguments and not even any bickering. The three of them being a family felt natural to him and was something that he was getting used to. He'd told Craig and Mark that he wouldn't be selling hash for them anymore and he'd given up the flat in Cullercoats two days after he first slept with Lindsey.

She'd suggested that he move in, and he didn't need to be asked twice. The landlord was agreeable and gave him his full deposit back without him having to serve the notice period. He knew who Paul hung around with and Paul supposed he'd be wary of any possible hassle of having Mark or George on the phone demanding it back. Even though the flat was cramped with his stuff as well as Lindsey's she was happy with the upgrade of electricals and furniture that came with him. But the thing she seemed happiest about was having him there, cuddling in with him on the cold nights, feeling the warmth of his skin in the morning and having him there for Jason.

As he jogged across Park View and up towards the gym, his mind turned to the job interview he had in two days' time and to the questions he'd be asked. At the grand old age of twenty-two, this was to be his first interview and he was more than a bit nervous. He could hold his own in a world of criminals and drug dealers, but he'd been in that life for so long he wasn't sure how to act in a straight environment. He also wasn't sure how he'd cope with being told what to do. In his world, if someone tried to order you about you had to stand your ground, even if it meant taking an occasional kicking. Showing weakness was the worst thing a man could do because the next time the liberty taken would only get worse.

He'd discussed it with Lindsey, who'd told him that the strongest thing a man could do was provide for his family, even if that meant that sometimes he just had to suck it up from someone he'd like to give a good hiding to. He knew she was right, and he was determined to go straight this time. Everyone had to grow up some day and this day was his. After the first night, he decided that his wild and foolhardy days were over and it was time to start being a real man.

His workout was good – he was really in the mood that day, thirty sweaty minutes into his time on the treadmill as he looked out onto the street below thinking positive thoughts about his future. He felt that the downward spiral of events over the last few months was finished. There was only one way his life was headed, and that way was up. Wiping the sweat from his forehead as he took a long drink from the fountain, he noticed that the gym was quiet, just the way he liked it – no idiot doormen talking nonsense and no drug or steroid deals being done on the side. Not in Ivy Court. This was for respectable people and for some who wanted to pretend they were respectable. He stared at himself in the full-length mirror and thought he looked much more grown up than he'd looked a few months earlier, before all the trouble and the drama started. If only, all that time ago, he'd left Lindsey's place five minutes earlier or later, he wouldn't have seen the blag on the newsagents and wouldn't have got to know Carl. But, then again there were a million other things that could have happened differently, things that would or could have made life turn out another way. But none of that carried any weight now. The important part was that he was together with Lindsey and, no matter who'd been hurt along the way, the end result was the perfect one for him, and hopefully for her.

He lay on his back and started counting off the sit ups. It was one of his favourite exercises and one that made sure he kept his six-pack intact. An older gym-goer once told him that if you let it get away you'd never get it back, so he normally finished off his work out with at least fifty to stave off an early beer gut.

A pair of lycra-clad young ladies flounced into the room and checked him out with a sideways glance. He did the same, but he looked away without giving them a smile like he usually would. *It must be love.* Feeling guilty over looking at another woman? He gave a little laugh to himself and shook his head. He couldn't quite believe it himself. He *was* in love, and he knew it.

Squat thrusts and his dreaded burpees followed before he collapsed to his knees, panting for breath and sweating like the proverbial hostage. He glanced at the clock; it showed just before eleven, and the only thing he could hear apart from its ticking was his own heartbeat, which sounded like it would explode through his chest. A shiver ran through him as a picture flashed into his mind of Kenny being shot, more specifically of his heart that had literally exploded. He pushed the offending image from his mind and made his way to the locker room. He'd have a quick shower, nip home and then take a walk down to the Spanish City to meet up for lunch Lyndsey

The warm water cascaded over his flexing muscles as he washed the soap suds from his hair while his thoughts again turned to Lindsey and how happy she made him feel. Once clean and feeling fresh, he made his way back to the changing room with its mirrored wall and dual sinks. He had a little dance to himself while he blow dried his hair. There was no need to feel self-conscious; he was the only one there. *"Call him Mr Raider, call him Mr Wrong, call him Mr Vain . . ."* he sang, while admired himself once more in the mirror.

As he dressed, he heard another patron enter, but he paid no mind as he looked forward to chilling out in the house for an hour. He took his comb out of his gym bag and laid it on the wooden bench seat while he packed up his training gear, then stood with his legs slightly apart and admired his pumped-up torso again. His fingers rubbed gel into his hair, and he combed it forward and glanced at the reflection of the other patron, who was undressing with his back towards him. There was a quick second glance, and Paul did the best he could to stop himself from shouting out and pointing at the stranger.

Before his eyes was the tattoo he'd seen on the night that Kenny was killed. The tattoo of a murderer. He averted his gaze as his heart rate quickened and he freaked out inside. Was he here for him – to finish off the only witness? How would he know he'd seen him and how had he tracked him down?

Thoughts flashed through Paul's mind in quick time, and he reasoned that the shooter couldn't be there for him. You needed a membership to get in and no hitman would come in under his own name or would be likely to kill someone in Ivy Court's changing room. But one thing was for certain: the tattoo and the man who stood behind him was the same one he'd seen in the Boy's Club car park on that dark and misty night.

Paul turned and dropped the comb and gel into his bag, which he zipped up and swung over his shoulder. As he walked towards the door, the unknown figure turned and their eyes met. Paul tried to keep as calm as he could as he lifted his chin and said, "Alright mate?"

For the seconds it took for him to pass, he made a note of the man's face and the clothes on the bench beside him. He looked like a man who could handle himself: ripped and muscular and body that looked like it could dish out some punishment. He guessed the man was around ten or more years older than he was, with a head of mousy hair that was prematurely thinning and a face that looked like it had seen a bit of action. Paul put him anywhere between thirty-five and forty, but with the weathered features it was hard to tell. He glanced down at the jeans and the new and expensive-looking leather jacket that lay beside him. At least he'd recognise the fucker outside.

"Alright?" The shooter nodded back towards Paul.

Paul tried to keep it natural. Just two strangers being polite to each other as they passed in the gym. He reached out and pulled the door open, hoping that his actions hadn't made the man suspicious.

He left the building and crossed Park View towards home. He knew he shouldn't do what he was about to, but he couldn't let an opportunity like this pass. He considered phoning Mark or George, but they'd just wade in, fists flying like always. He wanted to find out who the guy was and, if need be, he could call them in later. Or maybe he would break the taboo of the streets and call the police himself – anonymously, of course – let them know where he lived or where he worked and they could do the rest. One murder would mean twenty-five years, and if it turned out to be two then he would probably never be released. No chance of revenge attacks, then.

He was in and out the house and, thankfully for him, Lindsey had already left. He threw his gym bag into the passage and grabbed the car keys off the table before heading straight back out. Looking up at the sky, he gave his head a short shake. He knew this was a bad idea, but he was going to do it anyway. He was risking losing Lindsey and his relationship, the two things the meant the most to him, but he had to know who this man was. If he didn't, it would torment him forever.

The car started first time and he drove up the back lane and onto the main road where he turned back towards the gym. He parked up in the Masonic Lodge car park so he could get a good clear view of Ivy Court's main entrance.

Half an hour later, he saw the man leave and he slid down in his seat as he crossed the road and walked towards him. Fuck! Paul hoped the man would pass by and not see him. He couldn't afford to give the game away. If he'd killed once he'd easily kill again to cover his tracks.

Luckily the man turned right and walked up Norham Road, where he entered a dark red car and drove off towards Monkseaton. Paul started up and then hesitated. He'd been followed a few times by the police when he'd been with Carl, but this was the first time he'd been the hound and not the hare. He gave the red car what he considered to be a decent head start and pulled out with a hundred metres or so between them. Once on the road, he thought that was too much and sped up, only to drop back as he lost his nerve. He approached Monkseaton Metro Station and panicked when the car stopped at the junction and he prayed that it moved away before he pulled up directly behind it, and luckily for him it did. He followed on as it dropped down into Monkseaton and turned right and over the high hump of the Metro bridge that took him to the Valley Gardens Estate.

Paul indicated left and he pulled in before the car disappeared over the crest and then he parked up. There was only one way in and out of the estate and he considered that it could be a trap. Was this guy onto him? If he was, it would be the perfect place for him to pull in and watch Paul pass as he drove over the blind bridge. He waited. Ten minutes later, bravery got the better of him and he drove into the estate. He knew it was risky, but he also knew that he might never get another chance like this again. Driving the parallel streets in search of his prey, he scanned the houses and the driveways, hoping that he wouldn't be spotted. As he drove down the final street, he saw the red car parked up on the driveway of a house backing onto the Metro lines. He resisted the urge to stare into the front window as he passed. The clock on the dashboard showed 12.30 as he drove off to meet Jason and Lindsey.

* * *

Later that night Paul was back, all in black with a ski mask pulled down over his face and gloved hands. He crouched in the undergrowth and watched the rear of the house from the bottom of its garden as the Metro trains thundered past closely behind. One eye observed the unknown man through a crack in the fence. He sat at the dinner table with his child while his presumably unknowing wife served them all dinner. It was a scene being played out in thousands of homes across Tyneside at that very moment. But this one was different: in this one sat a murderer, and possibly a double one. The man was no more than fifteen metres from him. There was no mistake: it was him.

A tear ran down his cheek as he surveyed the scene. He pictured himself as the child and the parents as his own and contemplated that his dad would still be alive if this were so. If only they hadn't split up, then maybe he would have taken a different route through life, one that was free from the violence and the drugs, the police and the gangsters. He looked into the future with the roles reversed: this time he was the father and Lindsey was the mother and he realised what he was risking. She would leave him in a heartbeat if she knew. He'd be back living at his mam's, alone, single and kicking himself for not leaving it be. But he couldn't. He had to know who the stranger was so he could get Carl out of jail.

The roar of another passing train shook him back to the present and he knew it was time to leave. He moved slowly back, checked the tracks and exfiltrated himself from the bushes and away into the night.

Chapter 12: Danger, Danger

For the next three days, Paul pretended to Lindsey that he was job hunting so she wouldn't get suspicious, then he embarked on the next part of his mission. He needed information before planning his next move. He drove around the unknown man's estate and found a vantage spot to observe his car without being seen and parked up, hoping to see him leave so he could follow him.

It was third time lucky.

He was about to call it a day and head home when the red car passed in front of him. He started up and pulled out a safe distance behind. The traffic was light and he was unsure if that was a good thing or not; there was a fine balance between getting too close and being seen or hanging back too much and losing him. They turned right and up through Monkseaton, past the pubs and the shops and the unsuspecting public and out of the town towards Earsdon. Paul followed him onto the A19 and left a hundred yards between them. He tried to keep the target car in sight, pulling into the left-hand lane where possible to reduce the chance of him being spotted in his quarry's rear-view mirror. He presumed he wasn't onto him or looking for anyone behind: there was no anti-surveillance, no speeding up then slowing down, no doubling back at the end of a long straight road or going around the roundabouts twice. This put Paul more at ease, but he still had to be careful. This guy killed people, and Paul was risking his own life now.

The man drove below the speed limit, like any law-abiding citizen would, unaware that Paul was playing detective behind. If he'd known, he could have lost him in minutes in his more powerful car. It pulled off the roundabout and drove along the Great Lime Road before pulling off towards the garden centre. Had he spotted him?

Paul wiped his sweaty palms on his jeans and slowed down as the red car pulled over. Paul parked around seventy metres behind. By stretching his head to the top of the windscreen he could just see the vehicle over the brow of the road as it stopped. He watched the man get out, cross the road and stride through the gate into Gosforth Wood. He didn't look back, which gave Paul the confidence that he wasn't onto him.

Once he was out of sight, Paul climbed out of his car and jogged over to the six-foot stone wall that surrounded the wood and the racecourse. After a quick glance about, he threw himself upon it. It was high and an effort to climb, but his athletic frame made short work of it. Dropping down onto the other side, he ducked and looked around.

The wood was a mixture of oak and birch trees planted closely together, with bracken and small trees between. Their canopies interlinked and overlapped, broken in patches where the bare evergreens met the deciduous branches. Daylight cast varying shadows, and it took a minute for Paul's eyes to get used to the contrast. The smell of wet, rotting wood and decaying leaf litter filled his nose. The leafless trees reduced visibility to around twenty metres. He had to be careful in case he turned a corner and bumped into the guy. He had no idea what he was walking into. A small hedge lined the footpath to his right and, from the way the boundary wall was constructed, he reasoned that his prey would be over to his left. But he had to be careful; it could still be an ambush. His gut told him no; there was no indication that the guy was onto him and if he moved slowly and quietly then he should be alright.

He paused, moving low and with deliberate steps, struggling to stop himself slipping on the muddy ground as he crept from bush to bush, from tree to tree. He looked and listened but the only sound he heard was of the leaves rustling gently in the shallow breeze. He was being careful not to make sudden movements that would startle the wildlife and give the game away. Roe deer lived in these woods, and it wouldn't take much for one to take flight and alert his target. He came across a pathway and looked both ways, but he could see no signs of life.

The path or the woods? Which was safer? He weighed it all up and carried on through the woods and wet bracken. Further and deeper he went. He stopped and ducked when he heard what sounded like a whisper. As he crouched and inched closer, he heard two faint male voices, but he couldn't make out their words. Then he saw them standing in a clearing by the lake; one with his back to him, which shielded the other's face from view.

Peering through the bushes, Paul could tell they weren't arguing but they weren't in full agreement either. He wanted to move closer but that was too risky. So he hunkered down and observed. They were both well-built individuals and he didn't fancy being grabbed by either one of them in the middle of some woodland where nobody would hear him scream. Shifting his weight from one numbing foot to the other caused a branch to snap beneath his feet. The break in the silence was enough to make them turn.

They looked in his direction, but he was camouflaged enough as he crouched in the damp foliage. The mystery man turned and revealed the face of the other stranger. It was the face of Regan Southern. They looked for a few seconds more and called time on their meeting. Then the unknown man patted Regan on the shoulder and they left in opposite directions. Paul hunkered down for the next ten minutes until he considered it safe to move, then he slowly retraced has steps back to his car, taking care to pause and listen as he went.

He pulled himself up and peeked over the high stone wall. The stranger's car was gone.

* * *

Paul almost crashed his car twice on the drive to the coast as thoughts raced through his mind. He was looking in the rear view mirror almost constantly to see if he was being followed. His mind was elsewhere, trying to work out what Regan was doing with the stranger and where he fitted into all of this. Was Regan a part of this or was he doing a bit of business and an innocent party to it all? Was he back to help get Carl out of jail and onto the same thing that Paul was? Or could he be an upcoming target, the next one with a bullet in his back?

He discounted Regan being in with the guy because of how close he was to Carl. They were like brothers, and Paul couldn't believe that he would ever do him harm. There was always a doubt in their dog-eat-dog world and nothing was for certain, but to Paul it seemed a long shot.
The others were dangerous, for Regan at least.

He decided his best course of action was to call him up and sound him out. Then if all felt right, he could meet up with him and see if he'd returned to help. Paul hoped he'd be onto something so he could stop playing detective, tell him everything and let him take the lead. Then he could return to his own life and be done with it all.

The next morning, once Lyndsey had left for work, he opened his phone and called the Dutch mobile number.

"Hello?" came the usual deep voice.

"Hello, mate. It's your pal from the Dam's friend. Are you back in town?"

"Why's that?"

"Nowt, really. I passed you yesterday – well, I think it was you anyway. Just thought I'd call and say hello."

"Well . . . aye I am. But keep it to yourself. Don't go telling any fucker. It's on a need-to-know basis only. How's things with you?"

"Not bad, mate. Not bad at all. Been few things going on lately but thankfully it's all calmed down a bit."

"So I hear. You heard from our friend in the big house?"

"Not for a couple of weeks to be honest. Listen, that's why I rang. I could do with seeing you if you're around. I need to have a chat about him – but not over the phone."

"OK. But nowhere visible. I'm still on me toes and I don't want to be seen down the coast. Do you know Leazes Park in the town?"

"Aye," said Paul.

"Right. I'll meet you by the bandstand in an hour. Is that OK?"

"Aye, that's doable. See you there."

The phone went silent.

A fucking hour . . . he'd better get a wriggle on. He hung up the phone, jumped out of bed, showered and then dressed. Before he left, he took his flick knife from the top of the wardrobe and slid it into his jacket pocket.

*   *   *

The wind blew ripples across the lake, causing the water to lap over and spill gently onto the pavement, where it formed puddles that Paul hopped around to keep his feet dry. The park was quiet, which was to be expected on a cold wet afternoon like this. The reflection of the clouds gave the water a steel grey appearance, cold and uninviting. Two small children, three or four years old, played at its edge under the watchful eye of their ageing grandfather, ready to provide guidance and rescue if needed.

Paul scanned around the lakeside for Regan and his formidable bulk, a bulk that would be hard to miss. Not much chance of mistaking his well-built frame and bull-like head for anyone else out for a mid-morning stroll. Glancing at his watch, he saw that he was five minutes early and decided to get an ice cream from the bored-looking lad in the van to kill a few minutes.

"What can I get you?" bored lad asked, after sliding the window open.

"Ninety-nine please, mate. With monkey's blood."

He took the ice cream and scanned the park again, trying to look natural as he strolled around paths. He started to feel paranoid, wondering if he was being set up, picturing an unknown hitman emerging from the bushes or from the myriad of pathways to finish him off, leaving him to take his last breath on earth lying on a cold wet pavement in a Newcastle park.

As he reached the bandstand, he glanced at his watch again as he finished off his snack and admired the craftsmanship of the wrought iron structure and thought it a shame that that level of detail would never be reproduced again. Another sad sign of skills now lost. He wondered who the workman was who made it all those years ago and his mind turned to his maternal grandad Arthur Upton, who'd been a plater at Swan Hunter's yard in Wallsend. He stared into the middle distance, reminiscing how he'd taken him to the park to feed the ducks when he was a child like the bairns around the lake were doing now with their grandfather. How he'd play on the swings and hid behind the playground animals hoping for a chase, the lion was always his favourite. Now Regan was ten minutes late, and Paul was contemplating ringing him when he heard a low burglar's whistle. He turned to his right and saw Regan's big smile beaming at him through a gap in the bushes. He beckoned Paul over.

Looking to make sure there was nobody around, he squeezed between the stone balustrade and the bushes as Regan led him further into the trees. He was relieved to see that Regan was on his own and there was no one waiting to ambush him. They couldn't have been more than ten meters from the pathway but if his life was to end here then nobody would witness a thing. He took another nervous look behind him and then upwards to the giant plant pot that adorned the stone balustrade and he prayed that he wasn't going to end the day buried in a shallow grave in Leazes Park.

"How you doing?" Regan removed the glove from his right hand and held it out for Paul to shake. "Good to see you again."

"Spot on, how's you?" Paul shook Regan's sturdy hand. "Good to see you again as well. Just a pity it's here and not in the Dam. How long you been back?"

"A few days. I've got some shit to sort out here and I need to see if I can get to the bottom of a few things for Carl as well."

"Is it not a bit risky being around here?"

"Aye, but not so much up here. Me face isn't as well-known as it is down the coast so I'm only going down there when it's dark. And I fly in down south in case I bump into any bizzies at the airport."

"Makes sense, I suppose." Paul glanced around, still not fully comfortable in his surroundings.

"What's been going on down the coast? I hear George and Mark are pals again."

"I don't know about pals, but they're not trying to kill

each other anymore anyway. They managed to work out that it wasn't each other that killed Liam and Kenny."

"How's that like?"

For the next five minutes, Paul confided in Regan and told him the full story: how he'd seen the killer in the Boys Club car park and that he'd blurted it out to them all just as George was about to shoot Mark. They kept their voices to a whisper as they scanned the area for interlopers. Regan let Paul do the talking and said very little, nodding his head while Paul rambled on.

"Fucking hell," said Regan, as Paul reached the end of his tale. "Owt else?"

Paul paused for a second and looked him in the eye, unsure of whether to tell all to a man he hardly knew. But, knowing how close he was to Carl he decided to take the chance. "I think you're next."

"Next? What do you mean by that?"

"That tattoo on the back of Kenny's killer . . . I saw the same one on the back of some bloke in the gym a few days ago. I followed him home and then followed him yesterday to meet you in Gossy Park. That's how I knew you were back. That fella you met yesterday is the same one who shot Kenny, and maybe the same one that shot Liam."

This was the risky part and he knew it. If Regan was in on it then this could be the end for him. His fingers tightened around the flick knife. He readied his thumb on the button and mentally prepared himself to stick it into Regan's ribs if he lunged for him.

"I know," said Regan, calm as day and looking Paul straight in the eye. "I'm onto him as well."

"Eh? What do you mean you're onto him?"

"I heard some rumours a couple of weeks ago and that's why I came back. I'm trying to get into him to see what I can find out."

"Into him? So, who the fuck is he then?"

"He works for Les Cunningham. One of his right-hand men. They're wanting to move in down the coast and they need a few people out the way before they do. And, unfortunately, Carl was one of them. From what I can gather, it's his lot that broke into Carl's car, shot Liam and planted the key, and by the sound of it shot Kenny as well."

"Why's that? Cos he's been fucking his wife

Regan looked at Paul with widened eyes. "Well, I never knew that bit." He chuckled. "Dirty old dog! How long's that been going on for?"

"Aw fuck. I thought you would have known. He told us to say fuck all to anybody. And quite a while, I think."

"Don't worry about it. I don't think it had any bearing on what's going on... but you never know."

"So, what you going to do?" asked Paul.

"I have a plan. Sort of. And I'm going to need some help from you if you're up for it. If it works out, there's a good chance we can get Carl out of the clink and back on the streets, but I'm still working out a few of the details."

"What's the plan?"

"I won't go into it now 'cos it might change a bit. But keep your phone on and I'll be in touch in the next day or two. You OK with that?"

"Aye, course I am. But look . . . I've just got out of one drug war by the skin of my teeth and I really don't fancy getting stuck in the middle of another one – especially if Les Cunningham and his maniac fucking family are involved. I don't want to end up as plant food somewhere in Kielder Forest. My lass will bin us an' all,"

"Look, don't worry. You won't have to do much, just help us with a few bits of running around and that so I can sort a few things out. Trust me, you won't be anywhere near anything when it happens."

Paul nodded his head apprehensively, knowing that he was going to be an active participant in something that was way over his head.

Again.

*   *   *

"Thank God that's finished," Paul said to Lindsey, as the theme tune to *Coronation Street* played out.

"What you on about? It's the best thing on TV," she joked, before picking up her sleeping child and carrying him off to bed.

Paul took advantage and stretched his legs out along the full length of the settee. He picked up the remote control to find something worth watching that was more to his taste. A few minutes later she was back, lifted his legs and returned to her warm spot. She looked across and smiled while running her hand up his trouser leg and well past his knees, then gave him a look that said he was in for some action later on. He smiled as he looked at her face and then back to her hand, which was inching its way further up his thigh.

His phone rang. Ordinarily, he would have silenced it, but it was Regan's Dutch number and one that he couldn't ignore. He picked up and Lindsey must have caught sight of the dodgy-looking foreign number illuminated on the green display because her face turned to stone. Her hand retracted from his jeans and they looked at each other in silence. He was up to no good and she knew it. He'd broken the promise he'd made, and he didn't need to speak to confirm it. Hesitating, with the phone in his hand, he was in two minds whether to answer it or not. He knew he'd been sussed out as much as she knew he'd been lying and, without a saying a word, he went into the kitchen to take the call. He closed the front room door behind him. In the dark kitchen, illuminated only by the moonlight interspersed by passing clouds, he took a deep breath and then answered the phone.

"Alright?" asked Regan.

"Aye."

"I've sorted out that thing. Are you free tonight?"

"Aye, I can be. What's the crack?"

"Not over the phone. Meet us in the car park at Churchill Playing Fields in half an hour. And come on foot. I'll explain then. But it's on for tonight."

"OK." agreed Paul.

The line went dead and then the kitchen lit up as Lindsey opened the sitting room door.

"What is it, Paul?" she asked over folded arms.

"Look, I've got to nip out. I'll not be long."

"I don't care how long you'll be. I want to know what's going on. You said you were finished with all this shit. You promised me." A tear rolled slowly down her cheek. "Who the fuck was that on the phone?"

"It's about Carl."

"What about Carl? You said you were done with all that."

"I know. But this will be the last time, I promise." He didn't know if he meant it or not.

"You promised me last time as well. Remember? I can't do this. We can't have secrets and have you lie to me. We just can't. Not knowing if you'll be here tomorrow or not."

He moved over and wrapped both arms around her. She sobbed into his shoulder as he pulled her into his chest and rested his chin on top of her head. But she didn't return his hug. He stared into nothing and weighed up staying and letting Carl down or leaving and destroying his relationship forever. "I love you so much," he said.

"I love you too," she sobbed. "And I don't want to lose you, but I can't live like this."

"I have to go. I have to see this through. Please understand. It will be the last time, I promise. After tonight, it will be over. Then you, me and Jas–"

"Stop! Just go. But I can't guarantee I'll be waiting for you when you get back."

"I'm sorry. I didn't mean to let you down, it's just–"

"Go! Just go!" She wiped the tears from her eyes, broke free from his embrace, turned and went back into the sitting room without looking back. When she closed the door she left him standing in the passageway in darkness.

He looked at his watch. Twenty-five minutes to meet

Regan. No problem.

He went into the bedroom, stood on the drawers and reached to the back of the wardrobe top, behind the boxes to a place he knew Lindsey couldn't reach. Regan hadn't told him the plan, but he thought he'd better go prepared. He grabbed a bag that contained what he needed: gloves, ski mask and a flick knife. He rolled the mask up into a hat, pulled it over his head and put on his gloves. He checked the flick knife by opening and shutting it twice before he slid it into his jacket pocket.

On the way out of the door he caught his reflection in the wardrobe mirror. He knew that the events of the next few hours could change the course of his life. Fear ran through him and he almost changed his mind and stayed. He'd been swept along on this journey of criminality and no matter how strong the forces were that told him to stop and say no, to play safe and get out, the forces telling him to see it through were much stronger. The path was about to walk was a dangerous one, and he knew it.

* * *

He stood in the darkness, waiting for Regan to pick him up, loitering in the shadows to avoid the passing gaze of the evening's dog walkers. Regan hadn't told him what car he would be driving but he was sure he would recognise it when he came. The evening wasn't too cold and he could have dispensed with gloves, but whatever car Regan rocked up in he didn't want his fingerprints left on it.

He'd left the flat without saying goodbye and was

starting to regret it, unsure if he would ever be on speaking terms with Lyndsey again, never mind their being lovers. He knew that this could be his last night on the streets for a very long time and he wasn't even sure if he would live through it. He regretted not saying goodbye and telling her that he loved her.

He fiddled with the flick knife in his pocket, rolling it around and running his fingers over the contours of its sides before slipping it down the back of his jeans. Could he do it? What would it feel like when the blade was pushed in? He hadn't stabbed anyone before and hopefully he wouldn't have to tonight, but it was best to be on the safe side and come tooled up. Regan was there for the violence, and it would be preferable if it was him and not Paul that dished it out. Besides, he'd seen the fella they were onto undressing in the gym and, even though he himself was in shape, he was doubtful that he could take him on one on one and win.

Hopefully, it wouldn't come to that, but due to the situation and Regan's reputation he was sure that blood would be shed at some point that night. Ten minutes later, he glanced at his watch. It was almost twenty to nine and Regan was late.

"Don't fucking move," a voice spoke quietly behind him. He felt warm breath on his neck as something prodded into his rib cage. He froze and tensed up. "It's only me, you silly fucker," the voice behind him said.

He turned around to see Regan, smiling and dressed in head-to-toe black.

"For fucks sake!" gasped Paul. "I nearly shit mesel'.

How long you been there for?"

"Not long. Just a few minutes. I was making sure we weren't being followed that's all. Can't be too careful, now, can we?"

"Aye, suppose not, like."

"Howay, then. Let's go. Car's over here." Regan stepped out from the trees and made his way towards the darkened car park.

Paul walked behind him to a green Austin Montego parked up in the corner of the car park. Regan unlocked it with a key, which surprised Paul, who'd expected it to be stolen. But, in their world, having keys to a motor didn't necessarily mean you were the legal owner. They climbed in, Regan behind the wheel.

Paul stared out through the dew-covered window and into the deserted car park. "So, what's the plan then?"

"We're going to have a meet with the guy. It's all arranged. I've got the keys for a warehouse down the fish quay. It's perfect for what we're up to."

"And what's that?"

"We grab him, tie him up, smash him up a bit and find out exactly what he's been up to and why. We need to find out who set Carl up and then work out a way to prove it."

"Like what? He's hardly going to walk into the nick and admit to two murders, is he?"

"No, but we won't give him a choice but to help us. I can be pretty persuasive when I need to be."

"So I've heard."

"Look, we've got to start somewhere, and at the

moment this arsehole's the only lead we have. If it wasn't him that broke into the car, we can find out who it was by smashing him up. Then we can lean on them and make them confess to the bizzies that it was a set up. They don't have to say who they gave the keys to and grass up the shooter, but it'll put enough doubt into a jury's mind to convince them that Carl didn't do it. They can just tell them the part about breaking into the car, say they dropped the key and don't know how it got to Jesmond – or that they were paid to nick stuff out of the car and didn't know what it was for. If it was him that shot Liam then we can find out more about who he's involved with and who's paid him, then work out the next bit from there. And once I've fucked him up, he's gonna be in no fit state to make me his next target either."

"Owt else?" asked Paul.

"Aye. When Carl finds out it's his mate Les that's behind it all he won't be shy about admitting being balls deep with his wife on the night of Liam's murder will he? Look, we don't need a confession to the murders, we just need to make it look beyond a reasonable doubt to a jury that Carl did it."

"And what about Les and his maniac family?"

"Fuck them. The coast belongs to us. They're not coming down here from the town and starting their shit and taking over. No way, that's never happening. And they'll be getting a nice little message later on about what happens if they send people down here to try. Because, after we've finished with this cunt, he's getting dumped outside the front door of Les's fucking casino."

"And how do you know he's gonna to turn up? And if he does, he's probably going to come with one of *them*." asked Paul, who made a gun shape with his fingers, which he pretend-fired with his thumb.

"Let me worry about the rough stuff." Regan, pulled a revolver from inside his coat and showed it to Paul.

"I see," was all Paul could think of to say.

"And anyways, he thinks I've got a kilo of coke and he's getting it on tick, so he'll definitely turn up. You tooled up?"

"Nah. Not my thing. Not sure I could use a gun or stick a knife in someone. I'll help you out where I can, but that shit's not me."

"Look, Paul . . . if you're not up for this you don't have to come, you know. Me and Carl won't think any less of you. I can get somebody else, I just thought that because you and him are tight and he says you're trustworthy, then you'd be in."

Paul knew what Regan was doing by insinuating that he wasn't man enough to go through with it, playing with his pride and manliness. He hesitated for a second before answering. He didn't want to let Carl down and his pride meant he didn't want Regan to think he was scared. He looked straight into Regan's deep set brown eyes. "Nah, I'm in all the way. Let's get Carl out of jail tonight."

"Good man," Regan said, smiling.

"So, what's the rest of the plan? How are we going to get a hold of him?"

"I've got everything ready . . . chair . . . rope . . . gag – and a few power tools an' all."

"What the fuck do we need power tools for?"

"In case he needs some information coaxed out of him. I tend to find that when you drill a hole in sombody's knee while they're tied to a chair and watching you do it they'll pretty much tell you whatever the fuck it is you want to know."

"For fuck's sake." Paul, shook his head in disbelief. He wasn't sure if Regan was joking or not.

Regan looked at him and laughed. For him this was another day at the office, Paul doubted he tortured people every day, but he was willing to bet this wouldn't be the first time he'd done it either.

Regan started up the engine. "Right then, belt up. We don't want a tug from the filth on our way to the job now do we?"

The radio came to life playing *Ordinary World* by Duran Duran. *No, it's fucking not*, thought Paul, *it's far from it*. Regan dropped both electric windows to wipe off the moisture and lifted them back up to the top.

They barely said a word on the drive through to Shields. Regan took the quiet roads through the estates, all the while watching in the mirrors and looking out at each junction for police cars. He considered it less likely that they'd be spotted on the back streets. As they stopped at an intersection, Paul put his hand on the door handle while he considered bailing out and running home to the loving arms of Lindsey, but his sense of loyalty and the need to see it through made him stay.

A Metro thundered across the overhead bridge as

they turned down Tanners Bank, and Paul had a feeling that had become commonplace lately. It swept right over him, but he swept it back away. It was fear, something he realised was getting easier and easier to beat down when he needed to.

They turned right into the old, abandoned fish factories and Regan pulled the car over and parked it around the back between some bushes, hidden enough so that unless someone was right next to it, they wouldn't know it was there. "Right then, let's go," he said.

Without answering Paul stepped from the car and looked around. The place was deserted except for marauding seagulls circling above and a couple of fish quay rats that scurried off as they approached. They were no more than two hundred yards from civilization, but the near silence and the eerie surroundings from the overhanging trees made Paul imagine he was in an alien world. The isolation made him feel vulnerable and scared as he looked onto the towering brick structure.

A dilapidated, and once prosperous building now stood abandoned in front of him, a remnant of a thriving industry in a long and slow decline. His nose filled with the damp odour of wet undergrowth mixed with seagull droppings as he watched a lone pigeon escape the old brick structure through a hole in a half-broken window. He watched it fly away into the night sky, hoping that he too would be leaving in one piece – though not exiting through a window like the pigeon just had.

Regan gave a sideways nod for Paul to follow him. He unlocked a single door that was part of a larger sliding one.

It had once given access to the forklift drivers and their pallets of fresh produce destined for the local markets. Stepping inside the building, Paul half expected to be ambushed and was relieved when it looked deserted inside. Regan motioned silently for him to follow on with a sweep of his hand.

The long ground floor of the empty, cavernous warehouse lay uninviting in front of them. A doorway to the right led to a set of stairs that in turn led to the old office area. The wide-open factory floor was bare, apart from a few wooden fish crates scattered around in various states of decay. It was lighter than Paul expected; the walls were filled with floor to ceiling windows, each made with smaller glass panes that let in enough moonlight for them to navigate their way.

"Over here." Regan strode over to the doorway and began climbing the old wooden stairway. The creaking of the wood below their feet mixed with the constant sound of dripping water echoing from an unknown location somewhere above them.

"What's up here?" asked Paul.

"I've got the stuff up here," said Regan. "It's the old offices and storerooms. Watch your feet cos the floors a bit dodgy in places." He swept away a cobweb from his face.

Paul looked through the doorways and into the warren of corridors as he climbed the staircase that led to the disused offices, imagining what the place would have been like when it was thriving, but the reality of his situation soon brought his thoughts back to the present. The taste of mildew and dilapidated woodwork settled on his lips. He licked them then wiped them clean with the back of his sleeve.

Regan turned off the staircase on the second floor and Paul followed him to a room halfway down the grimy, deserted corridor. It was large and empty apart from a chair, a large dusty table and an old filing cabinet that Regan was busy opening. Paul guessed that this had once been a meeting room or a small canteen, as it was too big to be an office for one person. There were two doors, one at each end, which both led to the same corridor they'd entered from and a third that led to the room next door. The ceiling was interspersed with holes in the rotten boards and the sound of flapping wings spoke high from the rafters above. Green and black stains ran down the bare brick walls from where the broken roof tiles let in the rain that fell plentifully at this time of year. It smelled of mustiness and the air was heavy.

"Right, here's the gear." Regan opened the bag containing the equipment he'd told Paul about earlier.

"How long will he be?"

Before Regan answered, they heard a car approach, its tyres crunching over the stoney ground outside. The place brightened momentarily as its headlights swung across the ramshackle building.

"Right," said Regan. "You stand in the corner so he doesn't see you or the chair when he comes in. Once he's in, I'll pull the shooter out and you close the door behind him so he can't run away. OK?"

"Aye, sound." The familiar wave of anxiety pulsed through Paul's chest. He took in a deep breath, anticipating the coming events as he looked to the floor – and noticed for the first time a dark brow stain beneath the chair. He wondered if Regan had used the room for torture before.

"Then," said Regan, "you grab the stuff out the bag and we'll wrap him up."

Paul answered with a thumbs up and did as he was told. Standing in the darkness, he pulled his ski mask over his face and Regan chuckled.

The stillness gave them a warning as the approaching footsteps ascended the creaking staircase and slowly made their way along the corridor towards them. The first thing Paul saw was the man's shadow as he stood across the doorway; the second was the pistol that had entered before him. Paul looked across to Regan, wondering why he hadn't shot the new arrival down. Regan looked back as he and the newcomer stood in silence and pointed their guns towards Paul. It was a set up, and he'd walked straight into it.

"Take the mask off!" Regan ordered.

Paul reached up and peeled it back from his face before dropping it to the floor at his feet. Regan walked over with his pistol in his left hand and without breaking eye contact. Paul knew what was coming, and he braced himself before his head snapped back as the blow from Regan's fist knocked him stumbling into the corner. A sharp pain shot up the left side of his face. They were both surprised that he was still conscious. He was, but only just. Regan grabbed him and pulled him from the corner while the tattooed shooter lowered his gun and looked on.

"Get in that fucking chair, you!" barked Regan, as he

shoved a terrified Paul down onto it with one powerful arm.

"Regan, please . . . what the fuck you doing?" pleaded Paul. He'd partly expected it if he was honest.

"Get the rope, Cookie." Regan pointed towards the table. "It's in the bag over there."

"Regan, I've done nothing wrong. I just want to get Carl out of the nick and–"

"Shut the fuck up, you little prick! Do you not realise what's going on here? We're behind the shootings, you fucking mug. And you're going to tell us what you've said and who you've said it to. Get it?"

Paul tried to stand but was pushed back down. He wouldn't have been able to overpower the much bigger man anyway and he didn't fancy the odds of outrunning two loaded guns. He complied and sat back into the rickety wooden seat, which creaked under his weight. "No, Regan, please. I just want to help Carl and that's it."

Regan gave him another right to the jaw that reminded him not to move again. "So you keep saying. Right, Cookie, tie him up."

The man called Cookie pocketed his gun, pulled Paul's arms behind the chair and tied them to it. He felt the bite of the rough manila rope digging into his skin as he smelled the alcohol on Cookie's breath.

"What next?" Cookie asked Regan.

"I'm going to torture the little cunt and find out what knows."

"He's just a fucking kid," said Cookie.

"So fucking what. And he's not a kid, is he? If he's big

enough to run about with us lot then he's big enough to suffer the consequences, isn't he?" Regan made his way back to Paul and tucked his gun into his waistband on the way. He grabbed Paul by the hair and punched him twice in the face, causing his nose to pour with blood. Then forced Paul's head back and punched him as hard as he could in the solar plexus. Paul doubled over as the air rushed from his lungs and he started to spit and cough a mixture of blood and mucus from his mouth and nose together. Cookie turned to stare out through a hole in the filthy windows. Paul noticed that a tic had started up in his eye.

Regan looked at Paul without pity. "So . . . who else have you told about my mate, here?"

"Nobody," gasped Paul. "I swear."

Regan landed a left hook to the right side of Paul's face.

"Honestly," said Paul. "I only told wor lass about seeing the shooter. But she doesn't know anything about him."

"You sure?" Regan, raised Paul's jaw up with his left hand before aiming a massive blow at him with his right. The pain from that blow was the last thing Paul registered.

* * *

When Paul came to, he squinted through teary and half-closed eyes. The blurry face of Regan was front of him and he heard the whirr of the electric drill that he was firing on and off with his trigger finger.

"Back in the land of the living, are we?" he said. "See, the thing is, Paul, I don't believe you. I don't believe that you haven't told anyone else about our friend here. Remember what I told you in the car about how to get the truth out of someone? Well now it's your turn. We'll see if you're telling the truth." He wrapped his oversized hand around Paul's left knee.

Paul was scared and he started to struggle, but it was futile. The cord that held his arms to the chair was too tight and he felt the drill bit rotate against his knee. Regan held it horizontally as he spun it over his jeans, making him anticipate the coming pain.

"No, Regan, no!" he pleaded, as he started to shake.

Regan's eyes met his and he smirked a little as he tightened his grip on Paul's leg. He lifted the drill up vertically and Paul felt its tip brush his knee. He tensed up and prepared for the pain as the bit pierced flesh and bone.

Then Regan sniggered. He took his finger from the trigger and loosened his grip from Paul's leg. "Guess you didn't tell anyone else then, did you?"

"No, I fucking didn't," Paul sobbed. "I told you." His body relaxed and he slumped further down into the chair. His fingers touched the flick knife that was tucked into the back of his jeans. In the panic and the pain, he'd forgotten it was there, and he couldn't believe they hadn't frisked him before tying him up.

Regan walked over to Cookie, and from the corner of one swollen eye, Paul could just make them out in conversation, paying no attention to him. He looked straight ahead as he slipped his fingers down the small his back and took hold of the weapon. Managing to slide it up with his numbing fingers, he pressed the unlock button while it was still inside his jeans to stop its opening click alerting his captors. He withdrew it slowly, turning it cautiously in his hands, praying not to drop it as he cut through the rope while keeping his arms still. He was about to make a bolt for the door when Regan turned back towards him, gun in hand.

"So, what happens now?" Paul asked Regan.

"Now? Now Cookie's going to kill you."

"Am I fuck," Cookie said casually. "I'm not killing no fucking kid."

"Eh?" Regan sounded genuinely surprised.

"He's just a kid, for fuck's sake. He's got nowt to do with the other shit."

"What? You'll fucking do it alright. I mean, why not? You killed the other two, didn't you? And his fucking dad, come to think of it."

"What do you mean I killed his dad?" Cookie had a puzzled look on his face.

"Remember the Spring Gardens? The old man you topped? Well, this is his son."

"You're fucking joking?" snarled Paul. "You? You killed me fucking dad?" The blood continued to drip from his mouth and nose as a searing rage built up inside him.

"Aye, he killed your fucking dad," said Regan. "To be fair, it was an accident. It was me and him that robbed him." Like the true sociopath he was, he was clearly getting a kick out of the anguish he was inflicting on Paul before his death.

"What you telling him that for?" Cookie said.

"Well, it doesn't make any difference now does it?"

"No. I won't do it. I'm not killing for you anymore and definitely not a fucking kid." Cookie pulled his gun out and pointed it at Regan.

Regan saw it coming and drew his own gun. The two men faced each other. The difference was that Cookie's hand was shaking and Regan's wasn't.

"Shoot him or I'll shoot the fucking both of you!" hollered Regan.

"I can't. I won't. He's only a kid. I can't do this anymore." Cookie started to break down and cry. From his own experiences of the preceding weeks, Paul knew he was looking at a broken man. He wondered what Cookie had been through and for how long to bring him to this point. He shook as his gun hand lowered and he sobbed into the other which wiped a mixture of tears and drool from his face.

"Shoot him!" screamed Regan, at the top of his voice.

The loudness of the shout seemed to switch something inside Cookie's brain. As if it confirmed that he'd had enough and wouldn't take any more. He looked up quickly and raised his gun. But he only managed to get it half way before the reactions of the quicker man kicked in. Regan fired off two shots in quick succession before Cookie could aim true. The first one missed and ricocheted off the old brick wall causing a puff of dust to erupt from its surface. The second hit Cookie in the chest. He took two steps and collapsed onto the dirty, dusty floor and gasped for breath as he looked up at Regan. A pool of blood flowed out from under him.

"Fucking idiot!" Reagan shouted as he bent over Cookie. "What the fuck did you do that for?" He moved over and kicked the gun from Cookie's hand.

Paul saw his opportunity and darted for the door, expecting a bullet in his back at any moment. He heard a loud crunch and Regan's curse behind him just as he made it to the door. Then the gun went off again. The shot flew past Paul and exited the building through the partition wall, breaking a glass pane as it went and causing birds to call out and take off in flight throughout the old factory. When Paul glanced back, he saw Regan on one knee, his right leg trapped to the thigh in a hole in the rotten floor.

He didn't wait around for Regan's next shot. He ran right, not left to the staircase and safety. He wasn't thinking about an exit strategy, just how to get away from the maniac with the gun before he became cadaver Number Five. He caught hold of the door as he ran and pulled it shut, but the force of the closure made it swing back open and he heard the glass in the upper half shatter behind him on the recoil.

"Where you going?" shouted Regan. "You can't get away!"

From the crunches and curses behind him, Paul could tell that Regan was still struggling to free his heavy set frame from the floorboards. It gave him a head start, but not by much. Paul was now lost in the labyrinth of stairs, offices and storerooms that made up this part of the building.

At the end of the corridor lay a stairway that went up and not down as he hoped. He ran up it, taking the stairs two at a time and stepping on the outside of the treads, partly because he wasn't sure if they would give way and partly to avoid the creaking steps. Just like his dad had done in the Spring Gardens all those years before.

He stopped and listened for Regan behind him, and he faintly heard his feet crunch across the broken glass as his pursuit began. Paul kept going, looking for a way out or a place to hide. He looked down at the cars parked in the bushes outside and he considered jumping to his freedom. But he was on the third floor now, at best he would break his legs and Regan would be on him; at worst the fall would kill him. He had to keep going.

The stairs creaked under Regan's weight as Paul scrambled around for a place to hide in the maze of rooms and corridors. He crept up a small flight of six stairs into a store room and slid between a rusting filing cabinet and a small dividing wall, keeping the knife in his hand as he did so. A brown rat scurried between his feet and off into the night as he held his nose to prevent himself sneezing from the decade old dust he'd just disturbed. He looked up and saw a pigeon sitting on a rafter looking straight back at him less than five metres away. He prayed it didn't take off and alert Regan to his presence.

The sound of slowly closing footsteps was all he could hear.

"Where are you, Paul?" Regan was now sounding conciliatory. "If you come out, we can talk about this. There's only you and me now. We can sort it out."

Yeah, right. Having just admitted to killing three people, shooting Cookie and already trying to murder him, there was no way he was going to step out. He knew the consequences would be fatal if he did.

Regan had to be at the base of the small staircase. Paul heard his footsteps as he started to climb. Eventually, Paul could see his shadow as he neared the top. He held his breath and tightened his grip on the knife. Regan reached the top step and looked both ways into the small dark space. The pigeon took off and flew past his head, which caused him to wave his hands in front of his face. Slightly shaken, he took a step back and waved the dust from his head before continuing back down the stairs and on with his hunt. Paul listened as the footsteps grew fainter and he breathed out slowly and deliberately. He needed to make a quick decision: fight, flee or hide.

He chose the second.

Creeping cautiously down the small stairway, he looked to his left but there was no sign of his hunter. As he turned right to make his escape, a floorboard creaked loudly and he froze momentarily. He turned to see Regan's head appear from a doorway and he ducked as the shot from the handgun erupted behind him. The bullet missed, but not by much, and splinters from the beam above rained down upon him.

He dived into an office and ran across a corridor, then into another office and through another doorway. He became disorientated and now he was lost. It was cat and mouse, and Paul was the mouse. He ran for his life with the confidence that he was more agile than Regan so he shouldn't have a problem outrunning him. Then he crept around corners and through rooms, searching for the stairway to the lower floor and the freedom that he desperately sought. He stopped and listened, but all he heard was the sound of silence.

Eventually he found the stairway and inched down it using the same technique he'd used on the way up, holding his knife in his right hand as he gripped the rough wooden bannister with his left. And for the third time that week he prepared himself mentally to stick a blade into Regan. He walked slowly and purposefully along the second-floor corridor and he passed the room in which they'd all met.

Looking in, Paul saw Cookie lying static in a pool of red blood. He looked inside for his gun, but he couldn't see it and decided not to waste time searching. He needed to get out and get out fast. He crept on further, all the while listening for the sound of Regan's approach before glancing over his shoulder and making his way through the doorway and down the stairs to freedom. That was all he had left to do, away and forever, and away to the Police station. Not grassing was a code he'd always lived by but this was different. This was multiple murders, which included his dad and hopefully wouldn't include him by the end of the night. Psychos like Regan needed to be taken off the streets permanently, and it would also get Carl out of jail. Nobody would shed a tear for Regan. Fuck him.

He turned back towards the doorway and as he did so Regan appeared two feet in front of his face. They were just as surprised as each other and Paul's hand instinctively shot out at the same time as Regan lifted his gun. The razor-sharp tip of the flick knife drove into Regan's right hand, causing him to shout in pain and drop his revolver.

Paul thought he had him and he reached back to plunge the knife in again, this time with the intention of sticking it into Regan's stomach. But the bigger man was quicker and he hit Paul with a left cross that made him stumble back and crash through the flimsy partition wall, which threw up a cloud of dust. As Regan came at him with murderous intent, Paul jumped up and backed away. He ran around a large wooden desk and Regan pursued him. Paul knew he had to keep distance between them; if Regan grabbed him then there would be no getting away. Paul would be done for and he knew it.

Regan chased him around the desk and made a lunge, just managing to grab him by his jacket. Paul used all his available strength to stop himself from being dragged over the table as he hung onto it for dear life. He reached out to the girder that ran floor to ceiling, but his hand felt something else: a metal bar, which he swung around and clattered across the side of Regan's head. It clearly stunned him, but the big man didn't let go and he couldn't be stopped. It was more like a red rag to a bull. He screamed with rage and, with an almighty pull, he dragged Paul back over the table. The bar went flying and the clank of it settling in the corner was the last thing that Paul expected to hear.

Regan had him. He used his strength and bulk to pin Paul down and he straddled his chest. Their blood mixed together as Regan's dripped down from the cut on his head and onto Paul's face. He punched Paul alternatively with each fist until he was out of breath and Paul was semi-conscious. Then he paused to get his breath back before standing and looking down at Paul as he sobbed and whimpered in pain.

Walking back through the hole in the partition wall, he picked up the revolver from the doorway, flicked it open and checked to see how many rounds he had left. Paul tried vainly to crawl away and avoid the inevitable but Regan booted him in the ribs. There was no more screaming or crying in Paul; he accepted his fate as the blow from the kick flipped him over and onto his back. He stared up at Regan as he pointed the gun down towards him, and he watched the cylinder turn slowly as Regan clicked back the hammer – the penultimate step in the execution of Paul Docherty. He closed his eyes and prepared to meet his dad in heaven.

Bang! Bang! Two shots rang out and Paul opened his eyes as the pungent smell of cordite filled the room. Was he dead? His hands instinctively checked his chest.

There was a dull thud as Regan's body hit the floor, closely followed by the crash of splintering timber as the boards beneath him gave way and he fell through to the floor below.

Paul sat bolt upright and looked at Cookie, who was pointing his handgun straight at him, and for the second time that night Paul prepared to meet his maker.

But there was no shot, and the gun fell from Cookie's fingers as he blacked out again.

As Paul got unsteadily to his feet, he heard sirens, and then he saw blue lights as the first of the police cars swung off Tanners Bank and up to the building. He looked down at Regan through the hole in the floor and then across to

Cookie. He felt no remorse.

They'd both killed his dad. and the world wouldn't cry for either of them.

The first he saw of the armed police were the torch beams that cut through the murky dimness as they refracted off the dust particles in the filthy air. An armed cop approached Regan's body, then looked up and saw Paul looking down. He pointed his Heckler & Koch sub machine gun at him and the light from the torch blinded Paul's eyes.

"Stay where you are. Don't move and show me your hands," the rozzer commanded, calmly but firmly.

"I'm not armed," Paul said, "Don't shoot."

"Is there anyone else in the building?"

"Aye. There's someone else up here. He's been shot and I think he's dead."

Paul looked down and saw a plain clothes female cop check the pulse on Regan's neck. She shook her head to another officer which told Paul that Regan was dead.

Seconds later, two more armed bizzies appeared in the room, the red dots from their laser sights pointed at his chest. "Keep your hands on your head."

Paul complied.

"Get on your knees."

He complied again. He felt relieved as the adrenaline subsided. The moment he was arrested, he felt safer than he'd felt in a long time. And as the armed officer pulled his hands down and cuffed them behind his back, he pictured his father and he began to cry, relieved that it was all finally over. Now he knew the truth.

One of the police radios crackled into life. *"Get a paramedic up here! He's alive!"*

Chapter 13: My Heart and My Soul

It was the knock on the door that Paul had been waiting for, and he winced as he stood up from to the pain on his left side where Regan had booted his ribs. The hospital had x-rayed them and told him they were badly bruised and not broken, but they would be sore for a few weeks yet. His face was swollen on the right side and the yellow and purple bruises from the beating he'd received were still visible below his bloodshot eyes. His face would heal, but he'd carry the mental scars forever. But at least he was alive – last man standing.

"Good morning, Paul," said DI Manstone. "Can we come in?"

"Yeah, course," he said. "And you can leave your shoes on."

DI Manstone and her female colleague entered, and Paul directed them to the front room where they each took a seat on the settee. The colleague was tall and slim with short brown hair and the sweet smell of her perfume filled his nose as she passed. He offered them a cup of tea, which they accepted, and he returned a few minutes later, carefully placing a tray with three cups on the coffee table before taking a seat in the armchair.

"Paul, this is my colleague, DS Robson. DS Robson, this is Paul Docherty."

"Nice to meet you, Paul. You can call me Michelle if

you like." She extended her hand for Paul to shake.

"How are you feeling?" Sharon Manstone asked.

"Not bad, I suppose. Still a bit sore here and there but at least I'm still alive."

"Yeah, you were the lucky one I suppose." Michelle offered a sympathetic smile.

They all looked at each other for a second before Sharon broke the ice.

"OK then, let's do the good news first. In light of current events, we've discussed everything with the CPS and I'm delighted to tell you there won't be any charges coming your way, not for the drugs nor for the attempted burglary at the MOT place either."

He was relieved about that. Following his arrest after the incident at the warehouse, they'd searched Lindsey's flat and only found a small bit of hash, which Paul had said was his. "And what about him?" He couldn't bring himself to utter his name.

"We've extensively interviewed former Detective Constable Cook and I doubt that he'll ever be released. He's admitted to the killings of Liam Taylor and Kenny Reid, and to that of your dad. He's been charged with three counts of murder, but your dad's may get commuted to manslaughter later. On top of that, there's the kidnaping and torture of you along with the gun and drugs charges for him to contend with. So I think it's fair to say that he'll never get out. It'll all come out at the trial and be plastered all over the newspapers, I'd expect. He's been stealing from drug dealers and been involved in the supply of them for a while now."

"And did he say why he did it? He's a copper for fuck's sake."

"Are you ready for this, Paul?" said Michelle. "And if it all gets a bit much and you need us to stop then just say so." She smiled her sympathetic smile again.

"Yeah, I'm ready." He needed to hear the truth.

"Regan Southern and DC Cook were friends in their younger years, and they robbed the Spring Gardens together. The killing of your dad was an accident, a robbery gone wrong. They'd only meant to grab the money, but things got out of hand. Cookie hit him a bit too hard and, unfortunately, he killed him. He dropped the cosh he used to hit your dad with and Regan went back for it. And, apparently, he'd found Cookie's membership card for Sands Nightclub in the blood and held onto it without telling him."

"Some friend," said Paul.

Sharon replied with a raised eyebrow and a slight sideways nod.

"After the robbery, they agreed never to see each other again for obvious reasons. And they didn't until Regan found out that Cookie had gone straight and became a copper. His fucked-up logic told him that if he joined the Police Force then nobody would suspect him of anything."

"Well, it looks like it worked," Paul said, drily. There was nothing either of them could say or do that would excuse the fact that the Police had failed to solve his dad's murder then let his killer join the force.

"Regan found out he'd joined up," Michelle said. "He started to blackmail him with the murder charge a few years later. He'd kept the card, so he'd always have something over him – evidence soaked in blood, so to speak."

"Where's he now?"

"Locked up," said Sharon. "He's a right mess. He's been addicted to alcohol and pills for years, but he did a good job of hiding it from us. The sad part is that on top of all this he's got a dying daughter. He said he the needed the money he was making on the side to pay for her treatment. He'd been at it for years. And I shouldn't say this, but his wife's enough to drive anyone to drink on her own."

Michelle gave Sharon a sideways glance.

Paul shuffled uncomfortably in his armchair. "So, were did Regan fit into this?

"Regan is some distant relative of Kenny Reid and George Bolton," said Michelle. "Apparently, they borrowed the proceeds of a robbery from him a long time ago to get them started in the drugs business. But Regan didn't get his money back or the recognition that he thought he deserved, so he hatched a plan to get them out of the way and take over things using Cookie. He faked being on the run and went to live in Amsterdam to bide his time. When he heard George and Kenny had fallen out with the Taylors, he saw his chance and used Cookie to prod the cage. He had Cookie plant the idea in Mark's head to take over George and Kenny's business because he knew it would start a war. Then he had Cookie shoot Liam and set up Carl to get him out of the way."

"Why Carl? Him and Regan are supposed to be friends – or were."

"One less person in the way, I suppose," said Sharon. "We believe that he banked on Mark or one of his lot shooting one of the Bolton's in revenge for Liam, but when that didn't happen he had Cookie shoot Kenny as well to keep things going and to start a war between them."

"So why did he come back from Holland now?"

"Timing apparently. It was nothing to do with you. If you hadn't played detective and contacted him, you wouldn't have got yourself in the situation you did the other night. He thought George was weak without Kenny and that Mark and his mob didn't have the contacts or the brains to run things. When you confided in him about seeing the shooter, he realised that he needed you out of the way – and quickly,"

"I guess I was the lucky one."

"If you can call it that." Sharon smiled. "And good detective work, by the way."

"And what about Carl?"

"The murder charge will be dropped, and I would expect he'll be released in the next few days and back out to his normal antics."

"Stay away from him, Paul," advised Michelle. "He won't do your life any good."

He didn't reply and stood up with the two detectives as they made to leave. He shook hands with them both and showed them to the door.

"Bye, Paul," Michelle said.

"Thanks, Paul," Sharon said. "I'll be seeing you."

"No offence, DI Manstone, but I hope not."

The front door closed onto the two coppers and onto a

chapter of Paul's life that he'd rather forget but knew he never would. He turned and faced up the passageway and saw a sight that made him the happiest man in the world: Lindsey smiling and holding Jason. He walked over and threw his arms around them both, holding them tight in an embrace that he never wanted to break.

"Is it over, Paul?" Lindsey asked.

"Yes, it's over." He stared over her shoulder and out through the kitchen window, relieved that he hadn't lost them.

"Swear?"

"I swear."

Chapter 14: And the Big Wheel Keeps On Turning.

It was early afternoon, and Paul stood across the road from the big old walls of Durham Jail as he waited for Carl to be released. He shivered a little from the cold, clear day; there was hardly a cloud in the sky. A white box van passed with blacked out slit windows and stopped outside the entrance gate. He wondered whether Cookie was behind one or was already inside the stately institution on protection with the pedophiles and the informants, starting out on a long and uncomfortable journey through the prison system. Paul hoped he would never see the streets again, but knew that one day he probably would, even if it was just to be released to die. He'd destroyed the lives of the people he'd killed and destroyed his own, along with the lives of the family he'd left behind.

The high blue vehicle gate opened and he looked inside for a glimpse of Carl but saw none. He wondered how much longer he had to wait – an hour had passed already. For such a large prison, and with its proximity to the city centre, it surprised him how quiet it was. He turned to look out over the cricket pitches and across the River Wear and he counted his blessings that he was still alive. He had a life to live now and that was what he intended to do, live it to its fullest.

He'd run through his head a hundred times the

scenario for when he saw Carl. He'd give him a hug and congratulate him on his freedom and then tell him he was out. Tell him that they would always be friends, but he couldn't see him anymore; Lindsey wouldn't allow it. There were no more chances. It was him or her, and he'd chosen her.

Looking up he saw three men emerge from the doorway, the last of whom was Carl. The big striking mass with his freshly shaved head walked towards him with a smile that was almost as big as he was. He held a clear plastic bag of belongings in one of his outstretched hands.

"Come here, you!" he said. "I'll never be able to thank you enough." He wrapped his arms around Paul and squeezed him so tight that he thought his ribs would be crushed. He hugged Paul back and then their embrace loosened. Carl took Paul's face in both hands and he kissed him on his forehead. He smiled, and a tear rolled down the hard man's cheek.

"I'm glad you're out," said Paul.

"I'm fucking glad I'm out too."

"Look, Carl, I've got something I need to tell–"

"Never mind that, mate. That can wait for later." He wrapped a muscular arm around Paul's shoulder and led him off down Old Elvet Road. "I've got something to tell you first. I've got big plans for you and me. Listen to this . . ."

THE AUTHOR

Austin Burke is a fresh face in the world of North East crime writing. He grew up in Whitley Bay and has lived by the North East coast all of his life. His debut novel, Crazy on the Waltzer was inspired by his experiences around the now long-gone bars and clubs of Whitley Bay. He works as an oil rig Engineer and decided to try his hand as an author after watching some series on TV and deciding that he could write a better and more believable story than most of them. He likes to write in a gritty and realistic way and true to the time period they're set in. When he's not working or writing crime thrillers, he can be found on the ski slopes and beaches of Europe.

The book is titled after the Dire Straits song Tunnel of Love which is set in the also long gone, Spanish City fairground in Whitley Bay and the chapters are named after couplets in the song.

"Rock away and rock away, from Cullercoats to Whitley Bay"

Printed in Great Britain
by Amazon

56083491R00202